Sleeping with Strangers

Also by Eric Jerome Dickey

Waking with Enemies (August 2007)
Chasing Destiny
Genevieve
Drive Me Crazy
Naughty or Nice
The Other Woman
Thieves' Paradise
Between Lovers
Liar's Game
Cheaters
Milk in My Coffee
Friends and Lovers
Sister, Sister

Anthologies

Voices from the Other Side: Dark Dreams II
Got to Be Real
Mothers and Sons
River Crossings: Voices of the Diaspora
Griots Beneath the Baobob
Black Silk: A Collection of African American Erotica
Gumbo: A Celebration of African American Writing

Cappuccino (movie)—original story

Comic Books

Storm (Six-issue miniseries, Marvel Entertainment)

ERIC JEROME DICKEY

Sleeping with Strangers

DUTTON

BRIDGEVIEW PUBLIC LIBRARY

DUTTON
Published by Penguin Group (USA) Inc.
375 Hudson Street, New York, New York 10014, U.S.A.
Penguin Group (Canada), 90 Eglinton Avenue East, Suite 700, Toronto,
Ontario M4P 2Y3, Canada (a division of Pearson Penguin Canada Inc.);
Penguin Books Ltd, 80 Strand, London WC2R 0RL, England;
Penguin Ireland, 25 St Stephen's Green, Dublin 2, Ireland
(a division of Penguin Books Ltd);
Penguin Group (Australia), 250 Camberwell Road, Camberwell,
Victoria 3124, Australia (a division of Pearson Australia Group Pty Ltd);
Penguin Books India Pvt Ltd, 11 Community Centre, Panchsheel Park,
New Delhi – 110 017, India;
Penguin Group (NZ), 67 Apollo Drive, Mairangi Bay, Auckland 1311,
New Zealand (a division of Pearson New Zealand Ltd.);
Penguin Books (South Africa) (Pty) Ltd, 24 Sturdee Avenue,
Rosebank, Johannesburg 2196, South Africa

Penguin Books Ltd, Registered Offices:
80 Strand, London WC2R 0RL, England

Published by Dutton, a member of Penguin Group (USA) Inc.

First printing, April 2007

1   3   5   7   9   10   8   6   4   2

Copyright © 2007 by Eric Jerome Dickey
All rights reserved

 REGISTERED TRADEMARK—MARCA REGISTRADA

LIBRARY OF CONGRESS CATALOGING-IN-PUBLICATION DATA
HAS BEEN APPLIED FOR.

ISBN 978-0-525-94999-2

Printed in the United States of America
Set in Janson Text
Designed by Spring Hoteling

PUBLISHER'S NOTE
This book is a work of fiction. Names, characters, places, and incidents either are
the product of the author's imagination or are used fictitiously, and any resem-
blance to actual persons, living or dead, business establishments, events, or locales
is entirely coincidental.

Without limiting the rights under copyright reserved above, no part of this pub-
lication may be reproduced, stored in or introduced into a retrieval system, or
transmitted, in any form, or by any means (electronic, mechanical, photocopying,
recording, or otherwise), without the prior written permission of both the copyright owner and the above publisher of this book.

The scanning, uploading, and distribution of this book via the Internet or via any
other means without the permission of the publisher is illegal and punishable by
law. Please purchase only authorized electronic editions, and do not participate
in or encourage electronic piracy of copyrighted materials. Your support of the
author's rights is appreciated.

BRIDGEVIEW PUBLIC LIBRARY

for Dominique

Sleeping with Strangers

One

way of the transgressor

"What's your goddamn name?"

I stared at the huge man who wore the preacher's collar. He'd been crippled by paid-for violence, dragged down stairs, and tossed on the marble floor. His arrogant face and body bruised by the brass knuckles that were at my side. He was a big man, much bigger than I. He looked like John Coffey, from *Green Mile*, in a $3,000 suit and gators.

"Who are you? Why are you doing this? What's your goddamn name?"

I yawned, exhausted from traveling. I told him, "I don't have a name."

"What do you mean you don't have a name?"

I had rented a hotel room near Oakland University. Oakland University was in Rochester, Michigan. Not Oakland, California. This Oakland wasn't black. The winters in Michigan were not to be played with. I had on a serious coat, one big enough to shelter my weapons.

From the hotel, I had traveled a few miles away, was creating terror at midnight in the Bloomfield Villas subdivision. On Oak Avenue in Birmingham, Michigan. A sweet $2 million home.

Four-sided brick. Four bedrooms. Three full baths. A half bath on the main floor.

We were in the basement. A finished basement that was laid to the bone. Marble. Golden fixtures. Game room. Full gym. Bar. Bathroom. Jacuzzi. Kid's playroom. Wine room.

I had disabled his alarm system in less than ten seconds. People bought million-dollar homes and never had the phone company move the D-Mark box inside their cribs. If they didn't have backup power, all it took was a pair of dime-store wire cutters to slice the phone lines and shut down the alarm system. I already knew what kind of system had been installed before I crept around back and cut a single wire. I had information on the floor plans for the house, had studied its layout before I compromised his mansion. I had sat in the dark, just another shadow, waiting for the reverend to come home. Church had run longer than I had expected.

He shouted, *"What political organization are you representing?"*

"It's freezing down here. I hate the cold."

"In God's name *who are you?*"

"Is this marble floor heated? Has to be. Marble gets damn cold."

"Who. Are. You?"

His voice echoed, but no one could hear him scream.

Pictures of the reverend and his family were on the walls. Photos of people who could be his parents and in-laws, political figures and church members, were in every nook and cranny. High-end art from Europe, sculptures from many parts of Africa, Ralph Lauren paint on every wall, the place was decorated to the bone. On the back wall was the largest high-def television I had ever seen. Had to be one hundred inches wide. Had to have been imported straight from Japan. Picture so clear it seemed like I should be able to get up and walk right into the screen.

It was so clear I should've been able to leave this world and leap into a better life.

There were gold-trimmed stairs. He had spent the congregation's money well.

I tugged at my leather gloves, said, "I'm watching the news. Do you mind?"

My cellular was in my hand. I took a picture of the injured man, sent it to the person who was responsible for this job. The phone on this end was a clone, stolen and untraceable, just like the one on the other end, both to be disposed of when the evening came to its premeditated conclusion. I looked out the window again, stared at the freezing tundra. The weather was in the low twenties, was going to hit zero before long. My breath fogged in front of me.

Reverend raised his pain-filled voice and asked, "How much are they paying you?"

I looked at him.

"I'll pay you one hundred thousand to reverse this shit and . . . and . . ."

"Do unto others."

He growled. "An eye for an eye."

"In the name of the Lord."

"I'm offering you one hundred thousand dollars."

Religion had vacated his tone, replaced by vulgarity and desperation.

I said, "Let me think about it."

I went back to watching *Local 4 News.*

There were accidents on Stephenson Highway, Thirteen Mile Road, and on the connector ramp to the Lodge Freeway. Weather was getting so bad that all of the public schools were being closed. New Haven Marquette Elementary, Monnier Elementary, many more.

I said, "I didn't know there was a Beverly Hills, Birmingham, and Berkley in Michigan."

After talking about layoffs at the Big 3 automotive businesses that dominated the Detroit economy, they talked about more layoffs at Lear and Johnson Controls.

I shook my head. "Economy is fucked up here. Didn't know it was that bad."

Then they reported on a rap war. Two rappers had gone at it Tupac and Biggie style. One called himself Sledgehammer. The other called himself the Big Bad Wolf. They both made cuts dissing each other. And fighting each other. Fights between their crews had just broken out at a radio station up in New York. A few people were shot, more than a few had been hurt.

The reverend struggled to breath. "Are you . . . planning . . . to kill me?"

"Will you please shut up?"

He shouted, "*If this is a robbery, get to robbing and get the hell out of my home.*"

"What part of shut up don't you understand?"

"I have a family." He was crying. "A beautiful wife. A daughter. A little boy."

I forgot about the news and looked at him. His right eye was swollen, the size of a baseball. His left eye wasn't too much smaller.

"There isn't any money here at the house, I swear, but let me ring my wife. She will pay whatever you ask, without question, without reporting the incident. Let me talk to my children. I want you to hear their voices. Hear the love. You have a heart, don't you? You have children?"

He spat on the floor. Blood and saliva. Marked the floor with his DNA.

I looked at my watch.

Reverend sounded like he was in the pulpit, fire and brimstone in his voice, as if he were in charge. "I have two. Two wonderful children. Both attend Christian schools."

Confirmation was due five minutes ago.

Palms sweating. Listening for sirens. That had left me more than nervous.

"Greater Life Academy. A *Christian* school. Children must attend schools that are not afraid to acknowledge Jesus and give praise to the Lord. Do you believe in the Lord? My daughter is six. My son is four. Straight-A students."

"Hallelujah, Reverend. Now shut the fuck up."

He closed his eyes, prayed.

Back to the news. The mayor's recent State of the City address was being talked about, debated, said the mayor was forthright when he said Detroit was in serious trouble, refused to let Motown die on his watch, pundits saying the city was already dead and needed to be funeralized.

"Reverend . . . is that you and a group of protestors standing behind the mayor?"

"Is that what this is about?"

"With the religious power you have, you could get a political stronghold on Detroit."

"Is that what this is about? My announcement that I was considering running for mayor?"

"Wow. Look at that close-up of you as the mayor is speaking. Man, you look pissed off."

"Because we disagree with all the mayor has done. Under his rule, Detroit has been run into the ground. I'd rather live in Ninth Ward of New Orleans than watch my Detroit fall apart."

"Ninth Ward. Cutthroat City. Where you were born."

"I was born . . . in the Mighty 9. Came to Detroit when I was a boy."

"Now you're going up against the mayor of Motown."

"Did he send you to do this?"

"You sure publicly disagreeing with the sitting mayor was the right thing to do?"

"That overrated, pimp-suit-wearing son of a . . . does he have something to do with this?"

"He sort of reminds me of Suge Knight. Whatever happened to Suge?"

"Is the mayor behind this? Is this about the church protesting and demanding the mayor to step down so we can once again make Detroit the great city it once was? Watch us. We will put the motor back in the Motor City. We will be mo' better than when we were Motown."

"Running for mayor. Didn't know you were that famous."

"I am a man of God. I have been a pillar of the community for three decades."

"Big church?"

"Twenty thousand members and growing. My message is broadcast around the world."

"I don't know you."

"They know me from Seattle to South Africa. So you may want to reconsider."

"Hot damn. You're famous. International. Maybe I should get your autograph."

"Please, let me go."

There were enough pictures of him and politicians to display his lust for power. His photos told me he was a man who had to be in control. Now he had no control.

His joy was in controlling the sheep of this city.

One sheep had stepped away from his flock, refused to bow down to his power.

My eyes wandered the room again. The reverend had a lot. Seeing his wordly possessions reminded me that I'd been robbed of all I owned. Robbed by Thelma. I thought about Thelma. Thought about the last time I saw her. I thought about all she had taken from me. I should've put a bullet in her heart and killed my anger.

My eyes went to the pictures of the reverend's family. Images of his children and his wife all over the place. So much love in the picture between him and his wife. That forever love.

Sometimes I wanted that. What I saw in those pictures, I wanted that shit for myself.

I said, "I caught feelings for this woman a long time ago."

The reverend grunted. "What you say?"

"Was talking, telling you about this girl. Met her at a pool hall in California. I was about an hour outside of Los Angeles, in North Hollywood. The old man they called Big Slim ran this hot spot. A bona fide thieves' paradise. A simple girl, she was. At least she was back then. Beautiful, exotic girl dressed in Salvation Army clothes. But the part of her I found so beautiful, nobody could see. She didn't see it herself. I saw beyond her daddy issues, the issues she had with her mother, saw beyond the sibling rivalry she had, saw beyond all of that shit in her life."

"What's your problem, son?" Reverend coughed, spat up blood. "Speak your mind."

"Arizona."

"It happened in Arizona."

"No. That's her name. Arizona."

"Speak your mind, son."

"Sure you want to hear this?"

He grunted, struggled to breathe. "Speak your mind."

"She was seeing somebody else. Flimflam man. A high roller. But I put my bid in. She laughed in my face, told me that if I wanted to be with her, I needed a million dollars in the bank."

He released more pain.

I whispered, "A million dollars."

"So that is what motivates you. Your love for a woman."

"My hate for one woman fuels my anger while my love for another fuels my purpose."

"Hate is cancer of the soul. Tell me about the one you hate."

"I don't want to talk about that whore."

"A man should not speak of a woman with such venom."

"No, Reverend. *Whore* is accurate. She's a woman of the night. She's a whore."

"Like Mary Magdalene."

"The one I like, I've been trying to get a million dollars in the bank ever since I met her."

"The one you hate is a whore."

"Yeah."

"The one you love, she hung out on a den of thieves and wrongdoers."

"She's a thief." I nodded. "Runs scams. An artful dodger. Bona fide flimflam woman."

"A thief and a whore. Criminals and the unrighteous. Transgressors. Like you."

"I don't scam or steal. I've been stolen from. But I never steal. Never been a righteous man, not like you. Guess you could say criminals always end up being drawn together."

His pain was getting the best of him. Sweat dripping from his skin like rain.

Then my cellular phone vibrated. It was a text message. I flipped the phone open and finally saw a three-word message. *Funds transferred, proceed.* Followed by a smiley face.

I told him, "Time for us to raise up out of here."

"Where are you taking me?"

"Cold as hell outside."

"Can I please get my coat?"

"Afraid not."

"I need to take my Bible. A man of God must always travel with His word near his heart."

"Sure." I took a deep breath, both tired and irritated. "Get your Bible."

He loosened his collar and limped his gigantic frame across the room, went to the wall filled with leatherbound books, and with his injured hands struggled to pull out a worn Bible.

It was a beautiful red Bible with golden letters across the front.

He said, "This was my first Bible. My *first*. It was Father's *first* Bible. He was a minister. He owned it before me. And this Bible, it is to be my son's first Bible. *Hallelujah*, glory to *Gawd*."

He held his Bible to his chest like it was his salvation. Or his bulletproof vest.

Again, in a shaky voice, he said, "Who are you?"

"I don't have a name."

"You have to have a name."

"Why?"

"So people know who to be afraid of." He laughed a pained laugh. "How are people going to know who to be afraid of? You can't be afraid of someone who doesn't have a name."

"I don't need a name."

"What if Jesus didn't have a name? What if Satan didn't have a name? Good or evil, everyone must have a name. We name what we praise, we name what we fear."

The Bible he held, his hands were wounded, at least two fingers were broken.

He said, "The wrong you're doing . . . stop doing evil while you can. Stop because one day somebody will come for you. One day what you do to other people, that will be done to you."

His righteous words slowed me down, sent a chill through my frame.

I said, "Hopefully you and my employer can work this out for the best."

"Two hundred thousand. I'll get you two hundred thousand in thirty minutes."

"Both of you care about the future of Detroit."

"The mayor. It's that self-righteous, arrogant motherfucka. I knew it."

"Let's go."

"I'll get you three hundred thousand to kill that son of a bitch."

"You have that kinda cash on hand?"

"Not here. At my church. In the safe. No one has access to the safe."

"No one?"

"There is only one person I trust."

"Don't tell me God has the combo to your safe?"

"I mean here on earth. Only one person on earth I trust."

"Who?"

"Do we have a deal?"

I almost smiled. Three hundred thousand would put me much closer to my goal.

I shook my head. "Sorry. I never double-cross my clients."

He asked, "And you're going to kill me?"

"Yes."

"Why?"

"Because some people deserve to die."

A rush of fear and desperation bloomed in the reverend's face. He began praying. With those damaged fingers he fumbled with the Bible. Struggled to open the damn thing.

The pain in his hands was too great. But he never stopped praying.

He dropped the Bible and it popped open. God's words had been hollowed out and replaced with a snub-nose .38. That four-inch barrel leapt out, hit the marble floor hard, slid ten inches in my favor. His swollen eyes met mine, panic came out of his body on the winds of the loudest scream I'd ever heard. I raced for his .38 like I was racing to stop my own death.

He tackled me like he was a Pro Bowler, lifted me up quick and fast, ran with me, knocked over North African sculptures; the sheep became a raging bull as he slammed me into the one-hundred-inch television against the wall. I swung at his head, connected a few times, but it did no damage, not enough to take him down. He slammed me into the wall again and again.

I gritted my teeth, grunted with each blow. One final slam and I screamed.

Pain consumed me like fire and I went limp, almost blacked out.

He was winded, out of shape, and had to let me go.

I went down fast and hard. So did he.

He collapsed and lay there praying and breathing hard. I lay there rolling in pain.

Reverend made it to his feet first, staggered away from me, limped toward the .38.

"Satan will not defeat me. Not in my home. Not in the Lord's house."

He picked the gun up, frantic, grunting, his swollen fingers getting the best of him.

"Son of a bitch. The mayor . . . I'll kill every motherfucking devil he sends my way."

He wasn't the reverend anymore. He was a pissed-off gangster born in New Orleans.

He grunted and with his aching fingers raised the .38, pointed it at my head.

I was staring at the long barrel of death.

Time slowed down.

By sunrise, the reverend would be a hero. Attacked in his home by an assassin. Then killing the assassin. God was on his side. He'd be a statewide hero by noon. His congregation would be with him on the evening news. CNN would call. Larry King would want to chat with him. *USA Today* would cover this, a picture of the reverend on the cover, followed by a photo of the reverend and his family on page two. He would become the next mayor of Detroit.

All from my death.

There were three explosions.

The first bullet whizzed by my head and hit the wall.

The second bullet would've been in my left eye, had I still been there.

I scampered across the frozen marble, rolled, and yelled out my own fear, came up one knee, crouched, now a smaller target. Sweat in my eyes, pain in my lower back, I had come up facing my enemy, my hand reaching underneath my coat, pulling my .22 from its holster.

I was trapped against the wall, broken television behind me, death in front of me.

It was .38 against a .22.

The third explosion came from my gun.

I had aimed at his chest, but my pain lowered my gun and my shot was way off, the bullet hitting his right leg. He screamed, staggered, went down on one knee.

He wasn't running. They always ran. He was coming after me. Minister by trade, soldier at heart. He'd become the wounded animal going after his hunter.

His next shot hit the marble floor near my feet. The next hit the shattered television behind me.

If I hadn't beaten him down, if his hands weren't broken, I'd be dead right now.

There were two more explosions. Both came from the .22 I was holding.

One tore into his left arm, that brand-new pain slowing him down.

The second ripped opened a tiny hole in the front of the reverend's head.

There was another explosion, one last echo. The final sound from the battle. His gun fired at the ground, the bullet ricocheting off the marble and shattering glass.

The gun fell from his swollen hand; the reverend slumped into his death. He lay there like a big rag doll, his body in a pool of blood, part of his brain decorating the wall behind him.

I swallowed. Trembled. Looked down at the gun in my hand.

For a moment I was seven years old. There was no joy in killing, not for me. The nauseous feeling that came after I did a job told me there was no joy at all.

I used the camera phone, took a photo, sent that image to the other side of the country.

I was still trembling.

First I was as cold as a Siberian wasteland. Cold and detached, like a whore with her john. It was as if I were watching someone else do horrible things. Then I realized I was drenched, face damp. Sweat glands were pumping hard. Chest rising and falling.

My cellular rang.

Sweat in my eye, I pulled myself together and answered, "Talk to me."

"Is he . . . the reverend . . . did you . . ."

I panted. "You get the picture I sent you?"

"Yes."

I got my breath and firmed my tone. "Then don't ask stupid questions."

Another chill hit me. Like Death was in the room collecting souls, passing through me, its icy fingers grabbing at my insides, knowing it wasn't my time, but warning me nevertheless.

I asked, "Where are you?"

"My suite. Mayflower Hotel. Downtown Seattle."

"Why are you in Seattle?"

"I'm . . . I'm . . . uh . . . T. D. Jakes conference."

"Pull yourself together. You're at a conference. Doing what?"

"Hosting events for the preachers' wives, giving seminars on family values."

"Lots of people have seen you."

"Thousands. Was onstage at the convention center all day."

"Washington State Convention and Trade Center."

Her voice trembled. "Yes."

"Good. You have your alibi."

"My husband . . . the reverend . . . he's due here tomorrow."

"He won't make it."

"So it's . . . it's really . . . it's done."

"Where are your kids?"

"Sleeping. Different part of the suite."

"You're alone."

"I've sequestered myself from the others in anticipation of this moment."

"You sound drunk."

"Had to . . . yes, I've had a few drinks."

"Sober up. Go take care of your kids. This time tomorrow they'll know they don't have a daddy. Get yourself some rest. And you'll have to face the media and plan a funeral."

"Detroit can bury that cheating bastard in a cardboard box for all I care."

"Either way you have to tell your kids their daddy is gone."

"He was fucking the babysitter. Cliché, but true. The babysitter was a live-in. That black bitch was living under my roof. I went to Puerto Rico to visit my family. She took me to the airport. Was all up in my face smiling. I was gone for two weeks. Had taken the kids with me, but had forgotten to turn off the hidden camera. It recorded two weeks of . . . of . . . them fornicating."

She sobbed smooth and easy, made anguish sound beautiful. Soft music was playing in the background. Yolanda Adams. Hadn't heard her spiritual ambiance until that moment.

"In my own house. They did it in my house. Disrespected me right under my nose."

I held the phone, staring at their wonderful photos. He was dressed in an expensive suit, like he was the Donald Trump of Christianity. She was his stunning wife. Power and Beauty.

Then I looked down at that hollowed Bible, looked at the reverend's smoking gun.

Anger rose up inside me.

I said, "He said there is three hundred thousand in the safe at church."

She paused. "What else did he tell you?"

"That you have the combination."

"I see."

"There's probably more undeclared tithe money sitting around."

"Okay. So there is a little money in the safe. Big deal."

"I want twenty percent of the three hundred thousand."

"What? Twenty percent of . . . you've already been paid."

"The loaded gun tucked inside the red Bible, you failed to get me that information."

She didn't say anything. Her breathing betrayed her true knowledge.

I said, "Think of it as a sixty-thousand-dollar penalty. Or think of it as sixty thousand reasons for me to not catch a red-eye to Seattle. Think what you want. Just wire it to me."

"If I refuse to wire it to you?"

I paused, then whispered, "Marriott."

That one word halted her.

I said, "You're not staying at the Mayflower. You're at the Marriott Waterfront."

That deflated her arrogance.

I said, "Who do you think sent that basket of fruit to the presidential suite?"

She made a sound that radiated her fear.

"Send my money. Or I will find you, Mrs. Reverend."

I closed the phone, stepped over the reverend, went inside a small room hidden off to the side, one that housed the central vacuum system. It also housed systems for DSL, the phone lines, the DVR, the system for the home surveillance. I took the brains of the system, took the recording of me walking up to this property, and got ready to head out into the freezing night air.

Again I trembled, battled another wave of nausea, then pulled it together.

If I had listened closer, I might've heard the sound of a terrified vixen making calls, then the sound of $60,000 being transferred to a numbered account in a faraway land.

I opened all the windows. The frigid air would throw off his time of death.

At the basement door, breath fogging out of my mouth, I wrapped my scarf around my neck, pulled my beanie down over my head, and prepared to ride through an area that reminded me of South Park and the Dilworth District; big-money areas in North Carolina that had plantation homes situated at least a quarter mile from the streets. North Carolina. Where I was born.

I looked back.

Over the years I'd learned that the most common reason for murder for hire was in relation to the dissolution of an intimate relationship. Especially when a lot of money was involved. If he had three hundred thousand in a safe, I'd love to see his bank account.

Now Mrs. Reverend would be doing the breaststroke in a pool filled with Benjamins.

The red Bible rested at her deceased husband's side. My eyes went to the cover.

In golden letters, a name stared up me.

Through my pain I whispered, "Gideon."

I killed the lights, limped across the garden, each uneven step crunching frozen grass.

The reverend was right. Every man needed a name.

People needed to know who to praise.

Or who to fear.

Gideon.

My name would be Gideon.

Strangers

Two

the damned don't cry

She wore black.

The hue of grief and mourning.

The color of a new death.

Tears ran from behind her dark shades. She'd taken them off right after she got into her seat, while the rest of the plane was trying to get settled. She sobbed as the plane took off, the expression on her face revealing her anxiety. College Park and the Dirty South faded behind us. Tissue to her face, she shook her head like it was too late to change her mind, wiped away so many tears. More appeared. The redness of her eyes was as strong as the heat of the sun.

The woman dressed in Prada and Rolex was dying one tear at a time.

The black dress she wore. Reminded me of Audrey Hepburn. *Breakfast at Tiffany's.* She didn't remind me of Audrey Hepburn. Just the dress. It had class.

I'd seen her crying at the gate, looking like she was about to have a breakdown, then as we boarded the British Airways aircraft with the rest of the world travelers. I hoped she wouldn't bounce her leg and cry the entire eight hours we would be on this flight, hoped she wouldn't sob and blow her nose all the way to London. She put her shades back on, hiding from the world.

I had my own problems. I'd made a bad move in Tampa and almost lost my life. Hadn't been that careless since the reverend in Detroit. That Detroit contract had been years ago.

My face ached. Would ache for a while. I had taken a BC Powder, the only thing that ever seemed to work for my pains. The swell above my left eye didn't hurt as much, but my bottom lip still throbbed. My wounds were less than a week old.

She wept. The woman dressed in death cried like she was at her mother's funeral.

She felt my energy, might have caught me peeping at her, and shifted away from me.

Thick book resting in her lap, she ran her hands through her big Afro, hair with old-school flair and contemporary highlights, hair with two personalities, two moods, and glanced at me. No words, just a quick, almost embarrassed glimpse as she raised her dark shades and dabbed her bloodshot eyes. She took a deep breath, shook her head, took off her high-priced sunglasses, eased them into the seat pocket, made her leg bounce, and she fastened her seat belt. She straightened out her clothes, continued manufacturing more tears than she could wipe away.

My face. My hand. Both hurt bad. I opened and closed my fingers, felt pain in my hand.

I was glad to be leaving the U.S. Needed to get far away from what I'd done.

I grunted with my suffering, ached, and the woman dressed in mourning cried.

As soon as I began to drift and land in a peaceful place, my agony grabbed me, woke me up with a start. My hands became swollen fists, my teeth clenched, until I realized where I was.

She was looking at me, her mouth wide-open, almost terrified.

The unknown woman smelled nice, her aisle seat one empty

seat away from my window seat, and she was dressed in a black dress that hit right below her knees, her black heels now off, seat reclined, overhead light on. Her toes were pretty. Sexy. She reached into her purse and took out two miniature bottles of pinot, a small plastic cup, filled her cup, and began sipping.

Bouncing her leg. Sobbing. Shaking her head. Drinking.

She wiped her eyes again and again, got her crying under control, and picked up her book. I saw the cover. *Skin in Darkness*, a collection of erotic novellas by Maxim Jakubowski.

I broke the silence, asked, "Good book?"

She shrugged. "Better than reading wretched legal documents."

"What do you do?"

"I was an attorney." She hesitated. "Used to work in law. Not anymore."

I repeated, "Not anymore?"

More tears fell from her eyes and she turned away.

Our conversation ended.

I had all the information I wanted.

I thought she was British, had assumed that because of her proper demeanor, but she was American. She said *attorney*, not *barrister*. She was born outside of the U.S. Her accent told me that. But her accent wasn't primary, didn't subdue the few words she had given me. She was born somewhere else and moved to the States. She was married. She was rich.

Didn't take much information to create a package.

She blew her nose. Dried her eyes. Went back to her book, her body angled away from mine. That shapely leg was bouncing, drawing my attention to her flesh. Forcing me to notice.

Had been a while since I'd been inside a woman. Had been too long.

She was beautiful. Intelligent voice with a hint of accent, just enough to make her words ring as exotic. Like Arizona. But not like Arizona. The lady next to me cried. Arizona would never shed a tear. Had known Arizona for a criminal's lifetime and never saw her shed a single tear, not even when she had been slapped in the face by the man she was with when I met her, not when she was betrayed by the man she was seeing, not even when she was betrayed by her own family. We had that in common. The part about being betrayed by people we cared about.

I put on my headphones, popped in a DVD.

The crying woman never said a word. She wore a silver cross, one that hung to the swell of her breasts. Her wedding ring was the size of a weapon, large enough to kill any man or slay any conversation of a particular kind. She wiped her eyes, went to the bathroom, came back, her red-rimmed eyes taking her right back to her erotica, her black dress clinging to her like unseen hands made of high-end fabric.

Drink service came by. I went for the hard stuff. Whiskey. The good stuff. I took my liquor straight up, no chaser. She ordered two more bottles of white wine, sipped on her first glass as soon as it was handed to her, wiping away her tears and falling back into a world that Maxim had fabricated, that strange woman not wanting to be disturbed until her liquor was gone.

She shifted, moved her leg in an easy, stimulated way. I cleared my throat, my peripheral catching her peeping around, checking to see if anyone was watching her in her literary voyeurism. I was right there with her. As she read, with every page, she was being read.

I wondered if she was wet. If the folds of her secrets were moist.

A while later a sensual noise rose in her throat. A sinful and naughty sound. Again she shifted. Another noise. More shifting. She licked her lips. Then, another sex-inspired noise.

She returned to the real world, looked around, took her headset off, closed her book, disturbed, no doubt stimulated by what she had read, or by the cups of wine, maybe both.

She finished her second glass of wine, asked, "What movie are you watching?"

"Sci-fi." I hit the pause button. *"Battlestar Galactica."*

She swallowed, a deep frown set in her face. "My husband . . . his favorite show."

I didn't know if her abrupt disdain was because of her husband or sci-fi. My bet was the husband. Even the people who disliked sci-fi never rendered a stare of contempt for the genre.

Still frowning, she went back to her book, returned to sex and fantasy, her silver cross taking refuge in the sweet mystery of her bosom, her wedding ring glittering in the faint overhead light.

She began working on her third glass of wine. Not as many tears right now. Even in the middle of sorrow she was esculent, in the sensual sense of the word. Nice brown skin. Her voice had been strong, professional, accented with a mild erotic tone. She was streamlined, everything in its place, as if she had gone shopping for T&A and other accessories, shopped all over the world until she'd found the perfect match for everything, then draped it all in the color of death.

I looked at my hands and expected to see streaks of crimson, but there was no blood, just swollen hands. For a moment I saw the dead bodies scattered in the parking lot. My flesh turned hot. Had to focus to keep from feeling nauseous. Stomach hadn't felt weak in years.

My subconscious was playing itself out, fucking with me.

Mild turbulence shook me away from that memory. As soon as the turbulence eased up, that nauseous feeling ceased. The FASTEN SEAT BELTS sign went off, and one of the flight attendants came down the aisle, looking at passengers, then stopped at my row.

No way would they send a fight attendant to look for me on a plane.

But then again, there wouldn't be a way for me to get off a plane.

The flight attendant held the seats to stay balanced.

He said, "We have a bit of a situation."

I tensed. But I smiled too.

The woman in black put her book down, dried her eyes, tensed as well. No smile.

Flustered, the flight attendant stood over me, his British accent so thick and cockney that I had a hard time understanding what he was trying to explain to me and the woman in black.

"The flight is full and unfortunately we have to do a tad bit of rearranging."

I stared at the attendant, anger and dread in my injured expression.

He asked, "Is that middle seat taken?"

The woman in black looked at the vacant seat, we glanced at each other, the first moment we connected, if there was a connection, and we bonded like soldiers in a war, like strangers who had a common enemy, and that enemy wore a blue uniform, white shirt, red tie.

I said, "Harvey is sitting there."

"Harvey?"

"My rabbit. Don't tell me you can't see Harvey."

The woman in black didn't miss a beat, said, "I see him. Hard to miss a six-foot rabbit."

The flight attendant was confused, then made a face that said he wasn't amused.

"So that seat is available." The flight attendant shrugged as if our tribulations were no one's but our own. "Tell your rabbit we have a full flight. We have to make a few adjustments."

The male flight attendant hand-signaled, then halfway down the aisle another, female flight attendant acknowledged the gesture; then she waved toward the front of the plane.

The woman in black cursed. Called the flight attendant a *bloody blood clot*.

She was from the islands. Married. Crying. I wondered if she was crying, reading erotica, and on her way to attend a funeral, or if she had just buried someone she loved.

A moment later another woman was being ushered down the narrow aisle, her supersized and overstuffed backpack and coat being held in front of her.

"Oh, God." The woman in black groaned. "Not her."

The young woman heading our way. Her easy brown complexion the same hue as sugar in the raw. Dressed in tight jeans. T-shirt cut to expose her stomach, a stomach that had done hundreds of sit-ups. The swell of her breasts made it hard for any man to maintain eye contact. Her T-shirt read MAKE POVERTY HISTORY. But the jeans sent another type of message.

The girl snapped at the flight attendant, "I don't see why I have to change seats."

She was black American.

The way those dungarees fit her small waist and rocked her thick thighs was obscene. Tight, low-rise pants that were well below her belly button. Built for both speed and comfort.

The flight attendant remained proper. "Please, ma'am. The other couple, they have a baby and they were supposed to have those seats assigned to them. They need the seats designated for babies. It's policy."

"Show me that policy in writing."

"We apologize for the inconvenience."

"Well, you're going to be apologizing to the NAACP as soon as I land. Wait, is there a NAACP in England? Has to be a NAACP office in Brixton. That's where the black people at."

"You can check, ma'am, upon your arrival. Somehow I doubt if there is one of those."

"Well, could you stick me in first class as compensation?"

"Afraid not, ma'am."

"At least hook a sister up with a free drink or something."

The flight attendant walked away, left in a hurry, left the angry girl and her pissed-off attitude standing in the aisle. She cursed and flipped the bird. Her headset was around her neck, her iPod on her hip, her music loud, spilling into the aisle, Prince singing about Lolita.

The angry girl looked at us. "Sorry, but they put me on the back of the bus. No wonder their asses are being investigated for price-fixing. Need to investigate them for seat-fixing too. And they need Jesus. They sent an employee home because she wore a crucifix. Heathens."

The woman in black raised her head, did that with reluctance, got up with a sigh.

The angry girl looked the woman in black in her face, smiled, said, "Hey, it's you again."

The woman in black dabbed her eyes with a napkin, created a smile. "Surprise."

"Sorry about this. But they moved three of us because of a baby. You're stuck with me, I guess. Better me than the three-hundred-pound woman wearing floral spandex. They sent her wobbling the other way. Bet those people are mad as hell right about now. All because of a damn baby."

They shuffled around a bit, tried to get by each other.

"Can you believe what they did to me? First they *asked* me to move. I said no. Actually, I told his ass *hell* no. That's why I booked online and checked the box for a *window seat*. So I could put my head against the window and sleep. So I wouldn't have to move to let people out every time they want to get up. Then they kick me to the back of the plane like it's the back of the damn bus. This is a long flight and people will want to get up. I bought a ticket from Orbitz and I checked the box for a *window seat* and I had a damn *window seat* and now I'm being forced to get stuck in a *middle* seat? Why didn't they ask some of those *white* people to move? Why me?"

The woman in black sighed. Shifted.

The angry girl went on, "Then that anorexic-looking, pale-ass bitch got all the flight attendants, all of them in my face, trying to encourage me to move back here. Had everybody watching the black girl, trying to see what I was going to do. I wanted to knock that bitch the fuck out."

The woman in black sighed again.

The angry girl asked the woman in black, "How are you feeling now?"

"Better. Can't believe I'm on a plane to London."

"You're still crying?"

"Off and on."

The woman in black hurried by our new seatmate and headed toward the long line of people waiting to get into the claustrophobic-size bathroom. Our reluctant seatmate opened and slammed the overhead bins; each time she tiptoed, her tight jeans slipped down below decency. She marched up and down the aisle, complaining, hunting for some place to put her backpack and coat. She stuffed her coat in a bin about ten rows up, struggled to get her backpack in a bin in the same area, not enough room, went down five rows, found another bin, same result, gave up, and dragged her gear back to the seat, bent over, and squeezed her backpack in the little space we had, that move making her low-rise jeans fall even lower, low enough to see she was wearing a blue thong, a lacy number that contradicted the rest of her urban gear, and struggled to stuff her backpack underneath her seat, gave up, let it rest at her feet, her legs on either side of her luggage. Her left leg would be touching mine for the entire flight. She tried to shift, but there was nowhere to shift, no room left, would be even less when the woman in black came back.

"*Hate* damn middle seats. Can you believe that shit?"

The girl sucked her teeth, shook her head, enraged.

"This *sucks*. This really *sucks*. Can't wait to find the NAACP."

She saw me looking at her, saw me shifting, watching her struggle.

She gave up a stiff smile, her headset still dangling, music loud, Prince still wailing.

She asked, "Mrs. Jones hanging in there or what?"

"What?"

"The lady who is sitting next to you. Mrs. Jones. She was going through it at the airport."

"Mrs. Jones . . . a friend of yours?"

"Nah. Met her when we were in line getting tickets. Had a problem with mine and had to go to the counter. Had an e-ticket but they couldn't find my damn info. Nothing but drama."

"What's up with her?"

"Heartbroken. Running away from home."

"She's too old to run away from home."

"I'm just repeating what she told me. Heartbroken and running away from home."

"That explains all the crying."

She took a deep breath. "She told me she hopped on a damn plane and decided she was going to London. She's *never* been to England. She just passed by LAX, went inside, broke out her American Express, and bought a ticket. Being traumatized will make you do that. Just snap, break out a platinum card, slap down your passport, hop on a plane, and go as far away from your problems as you can afford to go. Or being in love. Being in love will make you spend your last dime. Will make you borrow money against your future. Love is an investment, you know?"

"I heard it could be traumatic."

"Watch what you say. I'm in love, which is different than being traumatized. Or crazy. I decided this morning to just get up and go see my boyfriend. Well, I didn't just decide. We were talking and he told me he wished I were there, in London. He's an actor. I'm an actor too."

"Are you?"

"Or an actress. Some call us actors, some say actress. I don't care as long as they spell my name right on my check. But things are slow, not working right now. My agent sucks. I do massages on the side. No happy endings. People always ask. Men. And women too. Would you believe women ask other women for happy endings? I guess all the touching, you know, the dark room with candles, the soft music, I guess, you know, people are bound to get aroused."

"I guess. Touching does create arousal."

"My boyfriend is in London. He's starring in a play. *Rent*. You heard of *Rent*?"

I shook my head.

"You haven't heard of *Rent*?" She beamed. "It's a play and a movie."

"What's it about? People struggling . . . to pay their rent?"

"Nah. It's like . . . like . . . like *Brokeback Mountain* and *Queer as Folk* meets *The L Word* with the crackhead from *Jungle Fever* and it's set in the eighties. I have it on DVD if you want to—"

"I'll pass on that one."

"Sure? It's really good. It's about love and loving unconditionally."

"I'll pass. I'm sure. But if you have something with Clint Eastwood or Wesley Snipes . . ."

"My boyfriend, he's so good. From Boston. Never thought I'd fall in love with a black man from Boston. Hell, didn't know there were any black men in Boston. Besides Bobby Brown. Maybe that's why he left. Got tired of being the only black man in Boston. Just kidding. Lots of black people in Boston. My honey is straight gangsta. Public-housing baby. From Mattapan aka *Murderpan*. Aka *Ratattattattapan*. You know Boston? I looked it up. Used to be Jewish area but when black people showed up, white flight like a mofo. He grew up around Blue Hill Avenue. Blue Hill Ave., like the movie. My boo is six-four. Two hundred plus. Bona fide soldier."

I shifted, hoped she was done.

She said, "My boo plays the part of the landlord. A *straight* part. He's not a homophobe, but he wouldn't audition to play a gay role to save his life, not at this point in his career. He said you didn't see Denzel and Sidney Poitier or James Earl Jones playing no fag, and I'm not talking about a cigarette. No, sir. They played straight men all the way down the line. He wants to be famous and not get typecast, like, like, you know, like other famous actors. Wesley Snipes almost made it, but he played a transvestite and *BAM*, career went downhill from there. Wonder if he's going to pay the IRS that twelve million or be on the run like he was in that movie with Tommy Lee Jones."

I put my things to the side, let my tray table up, told her to let me out.

I had to get out of that corner. Was starting to feel claustrophobic like an American soldier during Vietnam, held captive in a small cage, being tortured by the enemy in Vietcong.

As soon as I was free, she put her headset on, bobbed to Prince.

The lady in black was hanging out in the back of the airbus, near the bathroom.

I headed that way.

Still anxious.

Still looking for trouble.

Still swimming in Lake Panic.

Something told me I was being watched.

I looked behind me.

He was wearing a dark gray suit.

Had bandages on his face.

And he was coming toward me.

Three

the man with the broken nose

A man in a dark gray suit was coming down the aisle.

Dressed like he was a high-end preacher. Yellow book in hand, like it was his Bible. He was halfway down the airbus before he stopped walking. Came to an abrupt stop.

Midfifties I'd guess. Seasoned.

Pretty unremarkable except for the huge Band-Aids over his broken nose. The Band-Aids were bloodied, large enough to obscure the top part of his face. He'd suffered a good blow.

We paused.

He regarded my injuries. I did the same with his.

Yellow book in hand, he turned around and went back toward business class.

I turned around, heading deeper into the poverty section of the plane.

My mind photographed what I had seen. Injured man in suit. I doubted if those were Fortune 500 injuries. Light-skinned man. Could've been black or white. Bald. Gray suit and red shirt. The shirt was the $200 kind and the suit had to cost ten times that.

I looked back again.

Book in hand, he made his way back through the curtains that separated the classes.

In the end, it wasn't his injury that made me notice him, I'd seen many injuries on people. It was his clothes and his deep-set eyes. His eyes had maintained an unblinking cold stare.

He could've been the air marshal.

For a moment I saw the dead bodies scattered in the parking lot. My flesh turned hot. Maybe they knew about Tampa. Maybe my fake passport had been compromised and they knew. Maybe they'd be waiting for me at the other end of this journey.

Mrs. Jones was in front of me, staring at me. Standing up, she was stunning, the way her black dress hung over her breasts and the swell of her modest ass was like two shots of Viagra.

That was the effect she was starting to have on me.

The lady in black wiped her eyes, smiled at me. "I'm impressed."

"How so?"

"You lasted a whole five minutes with Chatty Cathy."

"I was ten seconds from asking for a parachute."

"You were going to jump?"

"Was about to throw her out."

"And you'd waste a parachute?"

"Good point."

She laughed.

I said, "So you're Mrs. Jones."

She smiled. "What else she tell you?"

I smiled. "Nothing. Was she supposed to tell me something?"

Her smile faded. She let go of her illusion. "Sorry for crying. Trying to stop, I really am."

"What's wrong?"

"Guess I'm just mentally and emotionally tired of being mentally and emotionally tired."

"When you're done crying, you'll be good as new."

She smiled again, this one real.

We stood back there, moving around that tight space, a line of people going in and out of the toilets. I realized why she was there. She was avoiding going back to her seat. Me too.

She asked, "Can you . . . uh . . . can you recommend any hotels in London?"

"Which part? In the city, outside the city? What area did you have in mind?"

"Anywhere. First timer. Never been to London."

"Maybe Central London. Try Bloomsbury. Nice hotels in that area. Try Myhotel."

"You own a hotel?"

"No, it's called Myhotel. Nice place. Sushi bar. Great lounge."

"Sounds . . . sounds . . ."

"Sexy?"

"Well, wasn't going to say that."

"It's trendy and hip and sexy."

She shifted. "Is that where you're staying? At the trendy and hip and sexy hotel?"

"Depends."

"Depends on what?"

Point-blank I asked, "Your husband's not meeting you across the pond?"

"No." She hesitated. That simple question changed the temperature. "No, he's not."

"So you're alone?"

She looked down at her wedding ring, took in a slow breath. I had been too obvious.

But the man part of me had to go there. Always had to try, even if it was in vain.

Hunters. We were all hunters.

I asked, "Your marriage . . . your husband . . . everything okay?"

"All I can say is . . . we make promises we know we can't keep. Promises that start with *always* and end with *forever*. We take on the impossible and fail miserably. Or stick it out and pretend that there was some great reward for enduring a life lived in depression and torture."

Again, we paused.

I said, "A cynic."

"You noticed."

"Of course."

She motioned toward the Chatty Cathy who had invaded our space.

Mrs. Jones said, "I used to be just like her."

"Talkative?"

"No. Idealistic. Happy. Ignorance is truly bliss."

She wiped her eyes with the back of her hands. Crying again.

I asked, "Would you like to do dinner?"

"Dinner? On the plane?"

"In London."

"You're asking me out to dinner?"

"Yes."

We stared a bit. Her eyes went down. Maybe she was appraising my crotch. Or admiring her wedding ring. Maybe she was just looking at the floor. Wasn't sure.

I said, "You're a beautiful woman."

"Makeup running. Eyes swollen. I don't feel beautiful."

"Well, you are."

She bit her top lip, disturbed, thinking.

I said, "What's on your mind?"

"This."

"What about this?"

"This . . . this . . . you're flirting with me. I haven't been flirted with in . . . forever."

"Then your husband should be charged with neglect."

"Or should I charge you with criminal trespass?"

"Can't jail a man for thinking about doing something."

Mild turbulence. More staring between us. I held her gaze

the way her dress held her slender frame, with both respect and disrespect, tight and loose all at once.

Her brown eyes narrowed.

She waved her wedding ring. "Testing the waters?"

"I'm a good swimmer."

We stood there, saying nothing as people went in and out of the bathroom.

She touched her wild hair and walked away. She looked back. We stared at each other for a moment, maybe five long seconds. Then she went inside one of the vacant bathrooms.

I headed down the aisle, passed my seat, kept going until I got to the blue curtain, stopped like I was at the rim of a foreign country, flight attendants guarding that area like border patrol. I looked for the man with the broken nose. That $6,000-a-seat section had reclining chairs, half facing forward, half facing backward, the seats in sets of two, side-by-side recliners with red partitions in between. Two rows up. I saw his dark gray suit pants, his shoes.

He was in a rear-facing seat, one row in. I crept across the border.

The yellow book was in his lap. He held it like it was his Bible. Two empty whiskey bottles were on his tray. He was horizontal. Might've been sleeping. His monitor was on a movie. The thick covers they gave the privileged were pulled up to his injured nose.

On the way back I looked at other passengers. No one was interested in me.

There was a overweight women in floral spandex squeezed between two people. There was a crying baby in the section of the plane the happy actress had come from. So the happy actress wasn't a setup, so far as I could tell. The woman in black seemed legit too. Nobody could cry that long without being in emotional strife. There were no dots to connect. There was no conspiracy, none that I could find. And there weren't any vindictive rappers on the plane.

I looked at my swollen hands. There was a mild tremble.

I grabbed a few newspapers, headed back to my third-world section of this flying world.

The front page of *The New York Times* had an article on THE DAY HIP-HOP DIED. Three days ago rapper Big Bad Wolf, aka Big Bad, had been slaughtered in a dark alley down in Tampa.

The paper said the scene was gruesome, looked like a gang war had broken out.

That was how it was supposed to look. Like the battlefield at the end of a war.

I was almost done with this business.

In a few hours, outside of the three properties I owned, I'd have a million dollars in cash tucked away. I remembered being homeless, on the run, living on the streets of Montreal.

I tossed *The New York Times* into an empty seat, kept the British papers in hand.

On the way back, with guilt swirling inside me, everybody looked suspicious.

At this rate, by the time the plane landed, the small children would be suspects.

But no one was after me.

Not on a plane.

An airplane was the safest place to be.

It would be a different story when I was on the ground.

When I was close to my seat, I saw something else.

Something that made me clench my teeth.

I had been robbed.

Four

between tears and laughter

The happy actress had jacked me for my window seat.

My newspapers had been moved to the middle. Her stuffed backpack was crammed at her feet, the tray table down. Not only had she stolen my seat, she had her elbows spread out and she'd gotten too comfortable; most of the space and the shared armrest was now hers.

Without complaining I took the middle seat.

The girl slid her headset off. "I wasn't finished talking about my boo."

"There's more?"

"We've been together for three years now. We met doing this play in L.A. A musical, actually. He was the lead. He was so good. I was the understudy for the female lead. She got sick. So I got to kiss him every night. I mean we kissed for real. Well, nobody told me I wasn't supposed to tongue-kiss him. But I did. He was holding my butt and everything. You know, got into the part. We got a standing ovation. Actors have to get into the role, you know?"

She laughed.

Down the way, food service for the second-class fliers had

begun. Flight attendants were coming down both aisles of the airbus, feeding the two rows on both sides, doing the same for the five seats in the middle, throwing us food in cardboard boxes the way zookeepers feed monkeys.

She went on, "We started kicking it after that. The first year was re-mark-able. We were shacking. Well, he was staying at my apartment in West Hollywood, splitting the rent. He's been on the road with *Rent* for two years, so we haven't had a chance to be together too much, only when he came home on break. But we send e-mails and text-message.and don't really talk because he's always either distracted or in theater mode, always jibber-jabbering and going on and on about the play and the people in his cast when I want to talk about us or have some sexy conversation. Don't think we've had any real sexy conversation in at least two months. At least. Maybe three. Hard being the patient girl-friend, you know? Not one of my stronger points. Because, I mean actors and actresses, we need attention, need to be in the spotlight, you know?"

"In other words you're self-centered and narcissistic, you know?"

"That was mean."

"You talk a lot, you know?"

"I'm wound up." She laughed. "And I'm tired. I ramble when I'm exhausted."

She put her headphones back on. She searched, found a magazine in her seat. *Pride.* London's version of *Ebony*, a red-haired Toni Braxton gracing the cover. I glimpsed the cover and saw it had articles on great sex saving Samuel Jackson's marriage; lesbian love; black men and oral sex being the last taboo. She went straight to the article on black men and oral sex.

When I thought she was comfortable, she took off her headset.

She tapped my leg and said, "One more thing, then I'll let you get back to your movie. Mrs. Jones, she's married but she said she was about to get divorced, that her marriage was *irre-*

trievably broken. *Irretrievably.* That's why she's crying like somebody cut off her foot."

"Okay. Her marriage is *irretrievably* broken. Your point?"

"Check it out; she's not the one who wants the divorce, if you get my drift."

"So she's scorned and rejected."

"Did she tell you that she hopped on a plane with no goddamn luggage? She told me she was going to London, no luggage, no clothes, no nothing. All she has is what she has on. Would you believe that? Not even a clean pair of drawers. Crazy, huh?"

"I wouldn't call that crazy."

"C'mon, man. What woman in her right mind leaves without shoes? Without drawers?"

"A rich woman who doesn't want to be found."

"Hmmm. Hadn't thought about it from that angle."

"You done trying to play Nancy Drew?"

"I'm done." She yawned. "She's all screwed up and here I am going to hook up with my boyfriend, about to have the time of my life in London, and she's . . . I feel sorry for her. God, hope she doesn't start bawling again. Can you imagine being on the plane for hours sitting next to somebody going to work your nerves from the U.S. to the UK?"

"I think I can."

"That was mean."

"I thought you were done talking."

"Winding down." She yawned again. "What's your name?"

I stared at her, stunned and irritated by her rambling.

I said, "Gideon."

"Gideon. The hero of Israel who saved his people from the Midianites."

"Somebody knows the Bible."

"Top to bottom. Book of Judges."

"Yeah."

"I'm Lola. In case you were wondering. Lola McVeigh."

"Nice to meet you, Lola McVeigh."

"Lola McVeigh but I use the stage name Lola Mack. Sexy and cool, huh? Lola, like Lola Falana. Mack like the movie *The Mack*. And like that Mark Morrison song 'Return of the Mack.'"

I rubbed my temples, really did wish a door blew off and sucked Lola out of the plane.

Lola shifted, hummed a bit, put on a huge smile. "Can't wait to see my boyfriend."

"Lola. Please. Give it a rest."

She said, "You're sexy, got this rugged way about you that's hot, you know that?"

"Uh . . . Lola . . ."

"Not hitting on you. Just saying. I got a man. My man is so damn fine it's ridiculous. Was just pointing out you got this mad aphrodisiac thing working, but you probably know that."

"You finished?"

"Nnnnope. Even with your face beat up like that, you look good. Man, either you got it bad, or somebody got it worse. Serious, what happened to your face? All red and swollen around the eyes. Hands scratched up. Looks like somebody just kicked your ass or vice versa."

"Fell down."

"Did you fall down on somebody else's wife?"

I opened my eyes, actually laughed. "What did you say you did for a living?"

"Actress. Singer. Masseuse with no happy endings. Oh, 'happy endings' are orgasms."

"I know what a happy ending is."

She laughed. "I know this guy at the Ritz who does that for his clients, men or women."

"Men or women?"

"He services both. Men and women ask me to give them a happy ending all the time."

I asked, "Women want happy endings from women?"

"Devil talk has your ears burning now, huh? I'll be quiet now."

"No, tell me about this women and happy ending thing."

"See, talk about sex and a man is all ears."

"Go to sleep, Lola."

The woman in black returned, tipsy, two bottles of wine in her hands, moving at a slow pace. She eased into her seat, found her seat belt, adjusted it, found her sex-filled novel again.

In the softest, kindest voice I'd ever heard, Lola asked her, "Sure you're gonna be okay?"

The woman in black nodded, went to her wine and her book, shutting us out.

Lola said, "This is Gideon. Gideon, like the Bible."

Mrs. Jones said, "Gideon."

"Gideon, this is Mrs. Jones. Like the love song 'Me and Mrs. Jones' or the movie called *Devil in Miss Jones*, only this isn't that Mrs. Jones, not the one in the song or the woman in the nasty movie. You met Gideon, Mrs. Jones?"

Mrs. Jones said, "We chatted. He recommended a hotel in Bloomsbury."

"Which hotel?"

"Myhotel."

"You own a friggin' hotel? You rolling like that?"

"No, that's the name of it. Myhotel. Right, Gideon?"

I nodded.

Lola frowned. "That's a *stupid* name for a hotel."

Food service finally made it back to us.

We all let out our tray tables, ate the bland food without talking. When we were done, Lola took our trash, stacked it all up on her tray. She let her seat back, popped in her earphones, cranked up Prince, and fell into that purple world.

Mrs. Jones picked up the *Pride* magazine, went straight to the article about great sex saving Samuel L. Jackson's marriage. I asked Mrs. Jones to let me out. Needed to stretch my legs. I wandered the aisle, went to the back, did some stretches, then made a bathroom run.

When I came back, Mrs. Jones had moved to the middle seat, *Pride* magazine in her lap. The armrest between her and Lola was up. Lola was giving Mrs. Jones a shoulder massage. Mrs. Jones's eyes were tight, face looking ethereal.

Lola said, "Turn a little bit so I can work on your neck."

Soft moans from Mrs. Jones. *"Oh God, Lola, oh God, oh God."*

"No wonder you can't stop crying. All these knots and rocks in your shoulders and back."

"Lola, Lola, oh God, Lola." Mrs. Jones shivered and sighed and moaned. *"Oh, God."*

"If I had my table and oils, I could really hook you up."

I let the armrest between the aisle and middle seat up, Mrs. Jones's warm leg rubbing up against mine. First she twitched. Then her leg started to shake. Lola asked her if she was okay. Mrs. Jones bit her bottom up and let out soft moans, held on to the armrest like somebody was licking figure eights on her fleshy folds. Her hand ended up on my hand, felt her quivering from deep inside, felt her riding the waves of pleasure. Lola was humming, singing low, sounding like an angel, doing that without thought as she finished her work. Mrs. Jones let my hand go, stopped moving. Lola whispered her name. No answer. The woman in black was sleeping. Light snores, like she hadn't slept in years.

I was aroused. Very aroused.

Lola looked over at me, winked, then whispered, "Told you I was the bomb."

"Never doubted you."

"Soon as I get to London, I'm going to give my boyfriend one. With a very happy ending."

A while later Lola put her headset back on.

I looked at my hands again. I could've been dead.

I'd stop at a million dollars.

The flight attendants came back down the aisle, collecting trays and trash.

Mrs. Jones shifted, leaned up against me, still in a deep sleep.

Mrs. Jones. The heartbroken runaway. Her marriage *irretrievably* broken.

Lola wiggled, still in my stolen seat, her head against the window, snoring a little.

Lola McVeigh. Stage name Lola Mack. The hopeless romantic.

And me, the man with the gentle smile that hid so much anger.

Thelma. The source of my anger.

Hadn't thought about her for a few hours.

Anger rose so high it choked me. Couldn't get her out of my mind.

It had been years.

I'd be in England soon. Close to Amsterdam once again.

Thelma.

Some people deserved to die. Thelma was at the top of that list.

Amsterdam. Window 120. All of a sudden those images flashed in my mind.

I handed the trays and trash to the flight attendant without waking Mrs. Jones or Lola, opened another BC Powder, washed it down with the last of my hard liquor, then let my seat back. I had hoped the caffeine in the BC Powder would keep me awake. But I leaned against Mrs. Jones's softness, her bushy hair like a pillow, her warmth and easy breathing soothing me.

Her energy soothed me the same way Lola's touch had soothed her.

I slipped into a dreamless slumber. But my sleep never stayed dreamless for long. Just like every flight had some turbulence. Tampa remained on my mind, found its way through the darkness and into my dreams. So did my last trip to the Netherlands.

Memories of Amsterdam rose up and created a thick shadow that darkened all thoughts of Tampa. Holland was personal, a promise I needed to keep before I finished this career.

I had eliminated many, but there was one person I had to destroy to find my own peace.

Five

you can't escape forever

Four summers ago.

Amsterdam Centraal was hot and humid, packed with tourists, most loaded down with huge backpacks. Signs were everywhere warning neophytes to beware of pickpockets. Summertime. The season of tourists, when the thieves came out of hibernation.

I had flown into Schiphol Airport, then caught the train into Amsterdam Centraal. Wearing worn jeans and a tank top, backpack and sandals on, I put on my shades and followed the crowd, took a number and waited my turn, then exchanged dollars for euros at the train station, tried to use some of the Dutch I remembered, told the old, stout attendant *bedankt* for her help, not sure if that was the right word, but she smiled and in stiff English told me that I was welcome in return.

We smiled after butchering each other's language.

She looked at me with endearing eyes, no idea of what was going on inside me.

I'd come here on business. Business from me always put grief in the hearts of others.

My whole life had been one big business trip. I'd never played. Never had fun.

Business was wearing me down.

She said, "American, no?"

I nodded. "Yes. American."

"If you taxi, use the TCA taxi. The others will give you a higher rate, overcharge you."

"*Bedankt.*"

"Make sure you stop at the Sex Museum. It is by McDonald's. Look for McDonald's. The museum has the biggest penis. Maybe three hundred centimeters tall."

"A nine-foot-tall penis?"

"And maybe one hundred eighty centimeters around."

"Did Shaq donate his organ?"

She didn't understand my American NBA humor. "Take picture. Then go take picture of the marble penis fountain at Casa Rosso. The penis gushes all day and night."

"*Bedankt.*"

"And McDonald's has a urinal shaped like a woman's mouth with big red lips. It was in the newspaper. Crazy people angry, so it might not be there for long. Photograph as well."

"*Bedankt.*"

"The *Opstapper.* The weather is very nice so ride the *Opstapper* to sightsee everything."

"*Bedankt.*"

"But the best way to see Amsterdam is from the canals. Look for St. Nicholas Boat Club."

I became patient, let the old woman finish telling me where to find the best shopping and where to buy Mark Raven art, let her tell all she wanted to tell me before I left her window.

I headed out into the heart of Amsterdam, a liberal city that had more weed-selling coffeehouses than Seattle had Starbucks. A place that sold international pussy the way IHOP sold Rooty Tootys. Air was so damn clear here, skies so damn blue, more beautiful than the godly blue that hovered over North Carolina. The area around the train station was buzzing with languages I couldn't comprehend. Coffee in hand, I was almost run down by an old woman on her bicycle. She was yapping on her cellular phone as she sped by. Others were pedaling and smoking. One was pedaling and putting on makeup. I looked to my left, saw the Amstel Brewery, a Heineken sign on top of that brick structure, the Museum of Sex straight ahead.

In the land of wooden shoes and bicycles, my target was less than a mile away.

For a few moments I stood on the sidewalk, part of me wanting to turn around.

But I mumbled, "Some people deserve to die."

Anger checkmated reason.

I bypassed the cabs, headed by the bicycle parking lot, a lot that was at least three levels high, passing at least a thousand parked bicycles along the way. Most of the population was on bicycles. Maybe that's why, relative to the overeaters in America, everybody looked so goddamn slim and sexy. Even the ugly had sex appeal, bad teeth and all. There was something different about the European women. There was something about America, maybe that racial divide that existed from coast to coast, that beast that created fear based on ignorance, maybe that made American people unlikable. Between racism and classism, not many people liked anybody.

Maybe it was that every other building here was a coffee shop and every coffee shop sold weed, that and the open sex market, that made the Dutch people more congenial. Getting high kept you mellow. Sex killed stress. America had laws and taboos about both. Amsterdam didn't have the racial divide, no hyphenated citizens. There were no black-Dutch, at least on job applications there wasn't a box to check. Race belonged to America, for the most part.

But hate belonged to the world.

Hate ruled the world.

Hate ruled my heart.

Hate was making me a rich man.

I moved deeper into the dark and seedy part of the city, if only in reputation and not in appearance, and stopped at Lunchroom 52, a coffee shop that faced the Oude Kerk, a Gothic, old church that cast its shadows over all the windows in this red-light district. As if God were looking down on, maybe looking over, all the whores, taking care of all the children of Mary Magdalene.

Most of the glass windows that housed the whores were in sets of threes, un-air-conditioned rooms smaller than a jail cell, fans blowing on high, recirculating odors that had permeated sheets and walls, the edge of their worn mattresses no more than two feet from the alley, the room barely big enough to house a sink and a bed with come-stained sheets. She'd been easy to find because all the windows had numbers the way homes had addresses. She worked out of window 120. A sign in the window said that all major credit cards were accepted.

I didn't bring any weapons, no way to transport deadly hardware on a plane. From canal to canal, warning signs were posted, letting everybody know that it was illegal to possess any kind of weapon. The second part of that warning was that, in a country where the world's oldest profession was legal, where people could buy hash or marijuana at any coffee shop, hard drugs weren't allowed. The warning ending with a notice that there was a regular police patrol.

I was more concerned with the warning about the weapons.

No weapon was needed. I knew at least twenty-two ways to kill with my bare hands.

I contributed to the local economy and bought three packs of weed. Purple haze. The pure stuff. The pre-rolled dope was cut with tobacco. I rolled a joint. Smoked it as I sipped a Heineken. Even when it was legal, it felt like the police should rush in and handcuff everybody in the place. But all over, in every seat facing the canals, people were firing up their medicinal cigarettes like they were Kool Menthol, that secondhand smoke giving the city a contact high.

I studied the roads and canals, mapped my exit. Her information was already memorized, already knew in which section of Raamverhuur I would be able to find her working her window. I knew she was renting a one-bedroom flat near Wijde Kerksteeg and Warmoesstraat. I knew she was renting because even though selling pussy was legal, it was hard for a whore to own a home, the lenders didn't want to gamble and lend the whores money.

The business was legit, but the whores weren't trusted.

Never trust a whore.

I took her pictures out of my pocket. I had several, all with different-colored hair.

She was a beautiful woman.

I checked window 120 again, her red light still dark, the red velvet curtains closed. As I walked the narrow alleys, some whores had their doors open, sat on the edges of their beds smoking, fans on high, faces made up and damp with sweat, looking like mannequins in a Victoria's Secret window who would come to life for a price. Some were on cellular phones, a few jumped out in bondage gear, whips in hand, playfully swatting the asses of young men as they walked by. One grabbed a man and tried to entice him and his wallet into her tiny room. Other working women were tapping on their windows and smiling that insincere whore's smile.

Nothing they did shocked or amused me.

The lack of sleep and heat was getting to me. Amsterdam rarely had hot days. That day heat was rising as if the devil was passing through town. I walked around looking at the whores, looked at all the girls in all of the windows. Unimpressed until a girl working in a window near Brouwersgracht and Palmstraat caught my eye. She was working window 693. I paused and stared. At first I thought she was someone I knew, someone I wanted to be with. The girl in window 693 was exotic and dark. Her beauty was disturbing. Scared me that she reminded me of someone I desired.

I stared at her awhile.

I fell into a trance.

I stood in front of her window.

Filipino music played from the boom box sitting at her feet.

She wore six-inch clear-heeled shoes. Red lingerie. Arched eyebrows. Long black hair.

Same type of outfit that was in a thousand red-lit windows within a square mile.

She eased off her barstool, adjusted her tits, came to her window.

As crowds passed and evaluated her, she stared at me.

Her eyes were glazed over.

She opened her door.

I didn't move.

She extended her hand.

Almost touched me.

I backed away from her, left taking steps backward, and watched her as long as I could.

I only went a few feet, then I turned and looked at her again.

My breathing had become ragged and uneven.

I turned around, went to go back to her.

Just that quick another man was at her window, being led inside.

I shook it off.

Shook away that desire.

Desire for a woman who she reminded me of.

I regained my focus.

Reminded myself why I was here.

I was here for the woman who worked window 120.

She wasn't in the window.

I had her home address.

So I walked the canals toward where my target lived. To the apartment she rented.

Too many people were out. I didn't go to her door. Stood a block away.

I waited.

Thirty minutes passed.

Then an hour.

She came out wearing a long dress. Her hair in long, blond

braids. Had seen her hair in many colors, but had never seen her mane braided before. She was bringing a bicycle down the stairs. I walked toward her. Tourist season. People were all over the *rue*. Too many eyes to take her right now. If I had known she was home, I could've broken in and had this over with.

I could do this right now and be gone, could blend with the crowd.

I walked toward her, my steps quick.

I was almost close enough to grab her braids when she started pedaling. Her legs were strong and she took to the bicycle lane fast, made her horn *ching-ching* and mixed in with the cars and bicyclists and pedestrians that shared the same narrow roads without complaint.

There wasn't any need to run after her. I knew where she was going.

She was going to work her window.

I had time.

I went back toward Brouwersgracht and Palmstraat, went back to window 693. The exotic girl was there, her curtain open, her red light on. I stood in front of the window.

I stared at the doppelgänger of someone I desired. Her doppelgänger stared at me. Her disturbing beauty anchored me.

I put my hand on her window, my palm resting right above the VISA AMERICAN EXPRESS MASTERCARD ACCEPTED sign. She took everything but food stamps.

I could have her. By cash or credit, I could buy an illusion. I could finance fantasy.

She slid off her barstool; put her hand up to mine, the scratchy glass separating us.

I nodded.

She opened the door to her world.

Thirty minutes later I was back near window 120.

Another thirty minutes passed before those red velvet curtains opened.

I froze where I was. Waited for her to appear. And within a minute, she did.

There she stood in white lingerie. Her face was made up. Her blond braids had been covered with a dark wig. A wig with a Cleopatra cut that hung down over her shoulders. Presentation of her wares in full effect. I stood off to the side. Men slowed at her window, most in groups, some alone, all of them in awe. Group after group paused and stared at her as she stood in that window, gave her more attention than the other whores received.

People hired me to exact death for different reasons, but most contracts, if not all, had one thing in common: freedom. The death of one person always freed another from some prison.

I wanted to get out of my prison. I wanted my own freedom.

My target pulled up a barstool, sat, waited for work to come her way. Men and women stared at her, but she made eye contact with no one, her eyes on the ground most of the time.

It seemed dehumanizing, sitting on display while people passed by on the cobblestones, sitting for hours, almost naked, with people staring like they were watching animals at the zoo.

I approached her from the side, was standing against the wall in front of her window, listening to the Bob Marley tunes coming from the beat box on the floor of her tiny space, looking inside her world, seeing a small bed and a sink that housed a few toiletries, looked at her as droves of people passed between us, had been frowning at her for five minutes before she looked up.

I said, "*Suces moi*, Thelma?"

She heard her birth name and almost fell off her barstool.

Her hand went up to her mouth, then her eye, before she crossed her arms over her breasts. I walked to her window, a few inches of glass separating, my reflection lying on top of her face, our bodies lining up, most of our features lining up in a surreal way.

She asked, "How did you find me?"

"I found you."

She shivered. "What do you want from me?"

"Some people deserve to die."

Terror took over her eyes. Her jittery body language showed her fear.

I tried her door. Despite the heat, most of the girls had their windows open. Window 120 was locked. Inside this peaceful country that bred pickpockets, she'd been living in fear.

Teeth clenched, I whispered, *"Open the goddamn door."*

The curtains closed. Her red light darkened.

I tapped on her window. I said, "Open the door. *Pute.*"

She heard me. I know she heard me.

Three men showed up a few minutes later. I had expected at least one more.

They walked up on me, gangster intentions in their eyes.

I turned around and walked away. Took to the narrow alleys, kept my pace normal, headed down a strip that was empty, no surveillance cameras overhead.

They were on my heels the entire stroll.

I was nervous. Nervousness was a mainstay I'd learned to live with.

I turned fast, the biggest of the three had his arm cocked, his fist aimed at me, and I took a blow to my jaw, staggered into the brick wall. That blow had hurt me. Sobered me. I worked through the pain, traded blows in a filthy alley, bobbed and weaved his destruction, put my right knee in his gut, and when he bent, came up and landed a fist in the big man's throat.

He was good at giving but horrible at receiving pain.

One blow landed and he stumbled from me, was about to fold. My fear was on him unleashing a barrage of elbows that left his face a bloody mess. He went down gagging.

Then there were the two more, both looking surprised, scared, and angry.

I was all on the next one, had put a simple foot in his nuts, made him fold in agony, a blow that hurt my ankle as well. While the second one went down, the third one swung at me, missed, and I went after him, my ankle aching, and I tackled him, grappled with him, wrestled him to the ground, and slammed my fist into his face as many times as my hand could stand.

I delivered one final enraged blow that cracked his ribs.

I looked up at the one I had downed with a groin shot.

He was slowed by agony and frozen in fear.

I pounced and attacked him, left him in the same state as his coworkers.

Without thought, I picked up a brick. Raised it high, brought it down on the big man's hands, bones cracking with each blow. Then I did the same to his two friends.

Sweating, favoring my left ankle, I limped away, bruised and battered, damn near thirty broken fingers and more than a few broken ribs writhing in pain in the filthy alley behind me.

I was kind to them that day. I had smashed their hands. Smashed hands couldn't grab guns and shoot, couldn't pull out knives; smashed hands couldn't hit you with a sucker punch. I'd learned that early in my career. Take out the hands first. Take out their legs to keep them from running for help. They crawled away from me, made it to their feet, and stumbled down the canal, never looking back. I could've beat them senseless. But I walked away. Their hands were so mangled that they'd have to pop a Viagra and use their dicks to dial for an ambulance.

I limped back to window 120. The red light was off. The curtains open. The bed empty.

She was gone.

Insane and fuming, I rushed back toward her apartment, moved as fast as I could, limped down the canals, stopping when the pain in my ankle felt too great. I was going to break into her apartment, but didn't have to. Her door was ajar. She had run back, gathered her things, and left minutes before I had arrived. The place she had rented was tiny, outside of the paint she'd left on the wall, door to door, closet to closet, it was mostly empty, a few things left on the floor in haste.

The bicycle had been dropped and left in the kitchen.

I supposed she had taken too much to leave on a bicycle.

I imagined she was running with fear in her heart and suitcases in her hands.

I took that bicycle with me when I left.

Injured, I rode toward the train station.

Didn't find her at the station.

I rode from Amsterdam Centraal to the Anne Frank Museum, then back to Rembrandt Square. Sweating and searching every canal, looked in so many coffee shops I had a contact high, looked in every red-lit window until my eyes owned the same devilish hue.

Then I was too tired, was in too much pain to keep going.

I checked into Hotel de Gerstekorrel, a short walk from McDonald's and the Sex Museum. From my bed it was a two-minute stroll down the canal back to window 120.

I tended to my wounds and iced my ankle and, after very little sleep, checked out of the hotel the next morning, rode the canals again, began searching for the runaway at sunrise, riding while the party people were staggering back to their rented rooms, while the unshowered whores were bicycling home, was on the cobblestone roads before the street was crowded with bicycles.

I rode until the sun started to set again.

During peak business hours I checked window 120. A new Dutch girl was there. I asked for the woman who was there the day before. She said that that woman was gone, then offered me her services. I passed. I walked the canals, looked in every window, just in case she had changed. She could've moved two blocks away, could've leased a new window in one of the other two red-light areas in the city, could've started selling her worn hole out of someone's home.

Wherever she had gone, she was still a whore.

Whoring was all she knew.

Like killing was I all knew.

"Gideon?" Lola's soft voice. "Let your seat back up and put your seat belt on."

"We're here?"

"Can't wait to run through customs and get to my boo."

The plane was descending into London. The plane went down as my anxiety rose up.

I looked over at Mrs. Jones. She was reading *The New York Times.*

The picture of the Big Bad Wolf was staring at me as I came back to this world.

The Big Bad Wolf was everywhere.

I didn't know if Mrs. Jones had opened that paper to taunt me.

Didn't know if she was one of them.

The plane taxied into the airport.

"I am so pumped up." Lola yawned. "This time tomorrow, me and my boo will be riding the London Eye and drinking champagne while we're *way, way, way* up in the sky. By next week I'll be chilling and watching *EastEnders, Kumars at No. 42, Big Brother,* living on *Love Island* with my boo, riding the red buses, tubes, and trains, being knackered and happy."

We landed. The ding came that told us we could get up.

Mrs. Jones was still quiet.

Lola was still hyped.

I said, "So, your boyfriend is in *Rent.*"

"You have to come to the play. Both of you. You have to see my boo rock it."

"And you said you want to play the Mimi part."

"Hello? You hearing me? I want to get in *Rent* and play Mimi so fucking bad."

"Who is Mimi?"

"She's the stripper strung out on drugs. Awesome part. Her solo is off the chains."

"Then you'd get to be on tour with your boyfriend."

I helped Lola with her backpack, grabbed mine.

Lola said, "You know? When I get in *Rent*, it's going to be on and popping. We're going to be rocking and shacking up and doing the damn thing UK style. Shit, we're going to be like Ruby Dee and Ossie Davis. Just watch. You're gonna look up and see me onstage playing the hell out of Mimi, spotlight on this ass, people applauding, the whole friggin' nine."

I thought about how the flight attendant had brought Lola back here.

How they had strategically sat her next to me.

Didn't know if Lola Mack had been sent back here to keep an eye on me.

Lola went on, "Can't believe you haven't seen *Rent*. Mrs. Jones, did you see the play?"

Mrs. Jones shook her head, still no eye contact.

Lola asked, "The movie?"

Mrs. Jones offered the same distant and unkind response. She focused on moving with the crowd. There was some sort of holdup. We had landed but we weren't getting off the plane.

As if they were waiting on law enforcement.

I kept Lola talking, kept making everything look normal.

I asked, "Which is better, the play or the movie?"

"I like the play better. Theater person, you know? They used most of the original actors from the play in the movie, but ten years or more had gone by since it was on Broadway . . . or off-Broadway . . . wherever it was . . . and the actors . . . well, they looked old as shit. For that play, they were just too old, you know? I mean, like, Hollywood old, not real people old."

I answered Lola, "Is that right?"

We finally started moving.

I said, "So the actors in the movie were too old for your taste."

"The play was written for people in their later teens and twenties. Not pushing forty. Who wants to watch some over-the-hill, old-ass actors almost in their forties acting like they were fags and addicts in their late teens and early twenties? Oh, you know in London, a *fag* is a cigarette, so don't get offended if someone asks you for a fag or says they haven't had a fag all day, or say they can't stop because they've been fagging since they were a teenager."

"Thanks for the info on fags."

"Snap. My bad. You're not gay, are you? I mean, I don't want to offend you if you are."

"Not gay. Not offended."

Then we were leaving the plane. Making turn after turn, customs being at least a mile away from where we landed. Lots of walking. Lots of jet-lagged people on moving sidewalks.

Lola said, "I have gay friends, I mean real friends, not associates. A woman is supposed to have gay friends, you know? We all need men who dress well and won't try to screw us in our lives. And gay men are the best dancers. Gay clubs are the best clubs. Anyway, I live my life guided by love. I treat people the way I like to be treated. Serious. I don't hate anybody. Not the kind of person born to be a hater. What they do and how they do it ain't any of my business."

"That's the way people should live."

Mrs. Jones was behind me. Still silent. That newspaper still in her hands.

Big Bad Wolf's face refused to stop taunting me.

Then we were corralled at customs, standing in the long line for non-UK citizens.

Moving up one by one.

The agents were checking passports and asking questions, then stamping passports.

Police were all around.

As were the drug- and bomb-sniffing dogs.

I flipped open my bogus passport. Reminded myself what my name was this time.

Hoped this passport hadn't been flagged.

My nerves had me shifting and sweating.

Lola smiled at me. "You okay?"

"Jet lag."

"Me too."

I said to Lola, "You were saying about the play?"

"Oh, yeah. The play, those old-ass actors, even the chick that played Mimi . . . Rosario Dawson . . . she's *so* beautiful . . . but too damn old to play nineteen, you know? Why couldn't they hire age-appropriate, out-of-work überactors? It's better to act up than act down, you know? They needed to hire somebody who could act and sing and dance and pass for nineteen."

"In other words, instead of Rosario Dawson, they should've given you the part."

Lola laughed. "Yeah, I'm hating."

I said, "You're stuck on yourself, you know that?"

"Duh. I'm an actress."

"Right, right. Part of that narcissistic lot."

"Stop being mean to me."

Mrs. Jones was in front of me.

Lola was behind me.

Mrs. Jones was directed to an agent.

She handed him her blue passport.

She said a few things to the agent.

Then she glanced back at me.

From the newspaper she held, Big Bad Wolf's face was staring at me.

Mrs. Jones was let through without too many questions.

I thought she would walk on, keep going, and head into London.

But she stopped and waited.

No tears in her eyes.

No expression on her face. As if the tears had been a sham.

I'd grown up around treacherous women. Had worked with cons and killers all my life.

Mrs. Jones waited.

I felt trapped.

I was directed to the same customs agent. While Mrs. Jones stood there, the picture on the front page of her newspaper glaring at me, I took easy steps toward the agent.

Throat tight, palms damp, I handed him my passport.

The agent stared at me. Stared hard. Treachery lived in his blue eyes.

Mrs. Jones and her wretched newspaper remained in front of me.

One of the custom agents looked Mrs. Jones. He nodded at her. She nodded in return. A coconspirator to this treachery.

She touched her wild mane in a telling way, like she was signaling the authorities.

The customs agent in front of me swiped my passport.

Something went wrong.

He swiped my passport again.

He read the screen and stared at me with a stiff poker face.

Stared at my injuries.

He looked me over again. Stared at the passport, stared at me.

Not too far away more policemen appeared.

Sledgehammer.

I thought about Sledgehammer.

Going to meet him had been a big fucking mistake.

Six

big bad wolf

Sledgehammer aka Sledge.

Überrapper of the year.

He hated being called Hammer. Said he was better than that old-school rapper. Did a record and spent a million on a hard-core video with him screaming about how he hated being called Hammer. A sledgehammer was what John Henry used, not a small, pathetic hammer.

I had a package on him before we met. That meeting was just a few days ago.

His birth name was Ronald Chin. Asian with a black man's disposition. He'd grown up in Harlem on Eighth Ave. and changed his name. Now his legal name was Sledgehammer Jackson.

Married for six years. Two kids from that marriage. One kid out of wedlock. Child support current. Taxes paid. Had bought his parents a brand-new house. Gave to charities. Went to church off and on, but based on his tax write-off, he sent his tithes on time.

People claimed that he paid Karrine Steffans a grip to not mention him in her book.

Others claimed he was mentioned by the name Papa.

Had to know who I was dealing with. If he had a record.

If he had police ties. Or Mafia ties. Or gang affiliation.

If he was in debt.

Had to see how liquid the man was, know what he could afford.

Lot of rappers bragged about money and cars but still had to put their bling on layaway.

The rap game had been profitable for Sledge.

More than twenty times as profitable as my occupation of choice had been for me.

What he rapped about doing was what I did without rapping about it.

Sledge had done a series of concerts that week at HiFi Buys Amphitheatre in Lakewood, down off 166 in the heart of the hood, then had an after-party downtown at Club Vision, the club on Peachtree that would soon be closed down, destroyed, condos rising where party central once stood. The day after the last show he'd rode out to Cascade Heights and closed down J. R. Crickets, a hot-wing joint that doubled as a sports bar. That building was the dividing line between the megachurches that sat across from million-dollar homes and the start of low-income housing and crackhead row. When I pulled up, I saw that J. R. Crickets was on full blast. Looked like a dozen televisions were on the walls, most on sports channels, the eight or nine booths were packed, so were the bar tables and the seats lining the bar. The women outnumbered the men ten to one. The best peaches Georgia had to offer. Women with small waists and big butts, not many had more than C cups, hair to perfection, were all over the place.

At least eight men were there who could stunt-double for Michael Vick. Three of the eight came up when I walked to the door. They came up fast, like three moving walls.

The first bodyguard: " 'Sup, dawg?"

Big guy, huge shoulders. Reminded me of Michael Jai White. Had seen Michael Jai White on a flight to ATL the night before. Coach. AirTran. Him with a woman. Me solo.

I said, "Gideon. Here to talk to Sledge."

"Need to pat you down."

"Men don't touch me. Unless we're fighting."

"Then you ain't coming up in here."

"Tell your boss Gideon came through. And I won't be returning his call."

I walked away.

Behind me I heard one of them barking into the two-way.

I was passing Wachovia Bank when one of the bodyguards ran and caught up with me.

He said, "Didn't know that was you. *That* Gideon."

"What Gideon is that?"

"Uh . . . look . . . Sledge is waiting on you. You don't come back, I lose my job."

I went back. Now the bodyguards looked scared. All of them moved out of my way.

The music was blasting so loud the windows were shaking. *Killing 'em with a Sledgehammer*. That was his hit, his trademark song. The room was crowded. People were dancing in the aisles, hot wings and beers in hand. Music thumping, I passed under banners for Atlanta Hawks, Miami, Alabama, the bar-and-grill showing love for so many Southern teams.

I passed by the Michael Jai White look-alike.

He regarded me with his eyes; I offered him the same greetings and salutation.

I'd killed bigger and stronger men many times over.

I went inside without being searched. But three Michael Vicks followed me inside, led me beyond banners for Morehouse, Spelman, and Florida State, then two more added to that posse and walked me by the Pac-Man machine and booths, led me out on the covered patio facing Cascade Road. Coors banners swinging overhead, two hundred people were in the main part, an area that was made to hold about one hundred, but only thirty were on the patio. Twenty of the thirty were women. They were in the VIP section, drinking Patrón and playing dominoes.

When I walked out, Sledgehammer frowned up at me, that nervous look in his eyes.

Two of his boys pulled their jackets back, showed me they were strapped.

They did that to impress the girls.

I said, "You're expecting me."

Sledgehammer stood up. He was all of five foot six. All muscle, but that five foot six became five-eight with the added vertical help from his thick Air Jordans. His thick build and his photos made him look like he was six foot nine. His attitude added a few inches to his deficit.

He growled, "Yeah. I'm expecting you."

Sledge was an Asian rapper but he had a deep voice and sounded blacker than Isaac Hayes. He didn't look as Asian as the stereotypes because he wore his hair in stylish cornrows, he dressed hip-hop and swaggered like a felon. The only thing that was Asian about him was his eyes and size, but as soon as he started talking, you forgot about that. He sounded like Florence and Normandie, 125th Street in Harlem, East Oakland, he sounded like everything black.

Sledgehammer came over to me, extended his hand. A hand that was as soft as a newborn's backside. His palm was damp. His hand was shaking. At first I thought he was afraid of me. But his fear was larger than that of the moment. The number of bodyguards he had posted up spoke of his true fear. He was terrified. Had been scared stiff for a while. The number and size of the bodyguards around me told me that his paranoia was off the meter.

All of this security was because Sledge was afraid of the Big Bad Wolf.

I asked, "What name you want me to call you?"

"Sledge is cool. Or Sledgehammer. Never call me Hammer."

I nodded. Looked at all the eyes grimacing at me. A patio full of men who carried hardware for decoration, as accessories to the bling-bling gold fronts they wore, men who had never shot anyone and would run as soon as the first piece of hot lead whizzed through the air.

I nodded. "Let's get to business."

I followed Sledge past the scent of lemon pepper hot wings, past the sweet aroma of barbecue hot wings, past the Heineken and Budweiser ads, past the lemon and four-layer-chocolate and caramel cakes, followed him past the women up front doing karaoke like they were *Dreamgirls* wannabes.

Two of the guards went out the back door first. After they had checked out the parking lot, they signaled and I followed Sledge outside. I'd never seen this much paranoia in my life. Never been around this much fear. His stretch SUV limo was parked at the back door, facing the exit. All the windows were tinted midnight black. I'd bet the glass and side paneling were bulletproof.

Once we got inside his pimped-out ride, his guards stood by the stretch SUV, backs to us.

I sat at one end, near the door. He sat at the other. Godfather at the head of the table.

Sledge said, "You don't talk much, do you?"

"Get to the business."

"Yeah. Guess I better." He lost his hip-hop smile and shook off some of his nervousness. "Actually this beef between me and that motherfucker started four years ago, when our group split, had to leave them haters and do my own thing, made my CDs, did a few movies, but they never let it go, kept slandering me, and this craziness came to a head two months ago."

"Another bona fide war between the rappers."

"Call it what you want. We were at an award show and shit got crazy backstage. Then we ran into them again when I was about to do some shit at a radio station in New York."

I coughed, waited for him to get to the point.

"*New York Times* covered the melee between our bodyguards in Manhattan. Shit was crazy. Would you believe that motherfucker came at me like that? You didn't hear the CD that motherfucker dropped? YouTube, MySpace, shit all over the Internet and shit."

I sat still, not moving.

"Motherfucker jocked the beats from Ice Cube's 'No Vaseline.' Back in the day, after he left NWA, Ice Cube had slammed Eazy-E, Dr. Dre, had slammed his whole crew."

I stared at him, still silent.

"Me and Big Bad Wolf were in the same group too. I started that group. Motherfucker. I started the group that gave his punk ass a name. Shit, I gave him that name. Big Bad Wolf. I was reading that book back then and told the motherfucker he should call himself that shit."

Again, not a word from me as irritation rose up to my chest.

"Motherfucker coming at me like I'm some bitch."

I checked my watch.

"Yeah, we started out with the same crew. Motherfucker got mad when the spotlight hit me, and when I started blowing up, that hating bitch turned on me, dissed me the way Kool Moe Dee had slammed LL Cool J. Coming at me the same way everybody coming at 50 Cent."

"Sledge, either open the door or move the conversation forward to its conclusion."

He pulled it together, ran his jittery hand over his braids, took a few deep breaths, let his inner terror escape on a thin stream of air, nodded, then said, "Want you to listen to this shit."

He popped in a CD. It was a recorded interview.

On air, during a live discussion, Big Bad had gone too far and called my client's wife a whore, called his four-year-old child ugly, referred to him as a *gook*, a lo mein eater, then thumped his chest and said that he'd love to do an R. Kelly on Sledge's little girl.

He said, "That itself is a good enough reason to bust a cap in a fool's cranium."

On CD, Big Bad went on, said he wanted to skeet-skeet on the face of the Sledge's seed, kept saying he wanted to come and piss on the child's face. It was revolting and disgusting.

Threatening to abuse a kid. That got to me. But I didn't let it show.

He said, "Shit got my wife scared, man. Got my children scared."

"You scared?"

He trembled. "What you hearing, that bullshit went out live on the number one hip-hop station in the world. Millions heard that shit. You hear me? That shit went to millions. Millions."

In the song the Big Bad called Sledge a *faggot-ass chink*. Said he was going to come after Sledge's kids and *slant-eyed, whore wife*. Then, as the Mary J. wannabe sang, Big Bad threw down a hard-core rhyme claiming that him and his homies had run a train on my client's wife, said they were all hitting it hard, *fucking that slant-eyed ho' from the flo' to the do', fucked her so hard her eyes weren't slanted no mo*, claimed they had fucked my client's wife, *gave the bitch what she needed, fucked the bitch until her pussy bleeded*, while my client was onstage performing at a show at the Fox Theater in Oakland.

I wanted to ask him if that part was true, but decided against it.

Live on radio, after the song ended, the DJ interviewed Big Bad and he laughed it up and boasted that he had fucked my client's wife in her ass while one of his homies ejaculated all over the woman's face. Big Bad laughed along with the NYC DJ on the top-rated morning show, which broadcast on the Web at the same time, and dared my client to call the station. Dared Sledgehammer Jackson to meet him in the parking lot. Like he was the Big Bad Wolf. Actually, he was the Big Bad Wolf.

"And bring me some goddamn Chinese food, ya punk-ass wigger chink."

The broadcast ended with the Big Bad Wolf of rap going freestyle, then shouting out his trademark rap, *I'll huff and puff and blow down your weak lyrics. . . .*

The CD was shut off abruptly.

Forehead crinkled with anger, Sledge said, "Fifty large."

"He rolls at least six deep. With a team of felons. This would be a special case."

"One hundred."

I said, "Add twenty-five to that and we can talk."

Stress sweating and trembling, he added fifty to that. Then offered me an extra twenty-five for anyone else I had to kill to get to his enemy.

He said, "An extra twenty large if you can make it happen in the next fourteen days."

"Make it an extra fifty and we might have a deal."

"If it's done in the next two weeks, I'll make it an extra seventy-five."

I nodded. Anger and fear had him throwing a lot of money on the table.

Something bloomed inside me. Greed.

My overseas account would be right at a million dollars when all was said and done.

Arizona was on my mind.

Desire had followed greed.

Whenever Arizona came to mind, irrational feelings rose up inside me.

Didn't care about Sledge or Big Bad.

Just wanted a million in my account before I saw her again.

I said, "So you want this done in New York."

"Not in New York. I live in and love New York. New York has had enough problems."

"Where?"

"Make it go down in that motherfucker's hometown. Put blood on the streets of Tampa."

"How do I get him to Tampa?"

"He's in Tampa all next week. I got the word that motherfucker there recording his next CD and shit. I know where he hangs out. Strip club. He always goes to the same strip club."

I asked Sledge where he would be when it all went down, just in case.

He said, "For the next fourteen days I'll be out of the country. Taking my family with me."

I nodded.

"I want to send my own message. To him and every motherfucker like him. Motherfuckers like him been fucking with me since I grew up on Eighth Ave. Tired of this shit."

His bodyguards tapped on the window. Seconds later Sledge let the window down. His boys were checking to make sure he was all right. While we wrapped up our business, another one of the bodyguards came out back, one of the finest girls Atlanta had to offer at his side.

Sledge let the window down. I moved where I couldn't be seen.

He snapped, "What?"

The girl leaned her breasts toward the window. She said, "You forgot about me already?"

"Who you?"

"Last night at Body Tap. I danced for you for about an hour."

She turned around, showed him her ass and tits, made her body shake, smiling.

Sledge said, "Oh, yeah."

She slapped her backside. "Sure you remember me now?"

"The business major at Spelman, right?"

She smiled.

Sledge said, "Hold tight until I get out of this meeting."

The window rolled up on her enthusiasm.

I said, "When my deposit is verified, we'll take it to the next level."

We shook hands. His hand was still dank and trembling.

I asked, "What's the matter?"

"This is crazy. I'm actually going through with this shit. But he started it, you know? He used to be my homie. We came down here, hooked up with Dupri, went to New York, met Jay-Z . . . damn shame it came down to this. But it is what it is. He brought this on himself."

I got out. And the heavy-bottomed girl smiled at Sledge and crawled inside.

I headed out front, walked a block east, passed by Wachovia Bank, and went into the parking lot that housed Big Daddy's Soul Food and other businesses. I put on my helmet and gloves, got on my motorcycle, and headed up Cascade, breezed by John A. White Golf Course and sped toward Langhorn, then made a left and got on I-20 heading east, back toward Stone Mountain.

My phone buzzed in my pocket.

The deposit had been transferred.

The deal had been sealed.

I'd been homeless.

Abused.

A fugitive.

Now I was damn near a millionaire.

I should've been happy.

For the first time ever, I wished the money hadn't come.

London

Seven

strangers in a strange land

Gatwick Airport sparkled with European flair.

Marble and glass, everything contemporary from the rooter to the tooter.

With my fake passport, I had made it through customs, no alarms sounding.

When I took my jet-lagged stroll by the last of the police officers, I took a deep breath.

Lola was excited, eyes wide. "This is an airport? This joint looks like both the Grove and the Beverly Center in Los Angeles. Look at all these places to shop. They have so many stores in here . . . off the chains . . . this is like walking down Rodeo Drive."

Mrs. Jones was quiet and unimpressed, the opposite of Lola.

Lola went on, "Caffè Nero. They have a friggin' Burberry store up in here. Chez Gerard, whatever that is. HMV. Lacoste. Nike. Nine West. Starbucks. WHSmith. This is awesome."

Local time was eight thirty in the morning, my body still on eastern time, my every cell crying for a warm bed and few more hours of sleep. We'd been on the ground just long enough to battle our way through customs and make our way over to the

North Terminal; Mrs. Jones walked at my right side, her expensive heels clinking. My backpack was hanging from my right shoulder and I was pulling an overpacked suitcase that had bad wheels, Lola's cheap luggage. Lola had her backpack on and was pulling her second suitcase, that one having better wheels. Since she had so much to carry, I'd waited for her at baggage claim. Kept her talking, kept her laughing. Kept my eyes on the police.

"Aww, man." Lola cursed at her phone. "Cellular doesn't work here."

I shook my head. "Not unless you have tri-band."

"Damn Verizon. I have to find a Verizon store and handle this."

"No Verizon here. If you had T-Mobile, you could upgrade, make the phone international."

"They have Starbucks every ten feet but they don't have one Verizon store?"

"You need a phone with a SIM card."

"What's a SIM card?"

"SIM card. Subscriber Identity Module. Gets you international service. About the size of a postage stamp. Stores all kind of info. Like saved telephone numbers. Text messages."

Lola cursed. "How am I going to survive without a phone?"

"You can get a SIM card for about five bucks U.S. over in Chinatown."

"Yeah, but I need a freakin' T-Mobile phone. You okay with that bag, Gideon?"

I asked, "Did you have to pack your entire life in these bags, Lola?"

"I'm a girl, Gideon. I never know what kinda mood I'm going to be in, so I have to bring clothes to match my mood. Assholes made me pay extra. Said my bags were too heavy."

"How much did your bags weigh?"

"One was like ninety pounds. The other one weighed a little over a hundred."

"How long are you staying with your boyfriend?"

"The rest of my life. I'm going to be his Mimi, without the drug habit."

Mrs. Jones fell back behind us. I glanced and saw her break her cellular in half, then she dropped the remains in a trash can. She caught up with us, then once again she fell behind.

She had freed herself of her electronic leash.

Lola asked, "Gideon, think I could borrow a few dollars?"

"Pounds. Or quid. Same thing."

"Okay, pounds," Lola said. "Can I borrow a few pounds, quids, whatever they use?"

"For what?"

"Check it. Kinda broke. Spent all of my money on the plane ticket. Was gonna ask my boyfriend to come get me. No signal, no cellular. I don't have enough to make a phone call."

"How much you need?"

"How many pounds or quid do you get for a dollar anyway?"

I motioned to a huge screen right above a money exchange station.

EXCHANGE RATES	
US/CAD	1.1244
US/AUD	1.3237
US/ZAR	6.1190
US/Euro	0.7971
US/SF	1.2521
US/BP	0.5534
US/Yen	114.24
US/Rub	27.26
US/Yuan	8.0099
US/Rupee	45.01
US/Mexican	11.11

She said, "Eighty cents for a dollar? The Euro is kicking the dollar's butt."

"Not eighty cents. That means eight-tenths of a Euro for a buck. London is still on the pound system. Look at BP. British pound."

"Are you serious? Does that mean . . . I'm confused. Fifty-five cents for a damn dollar?"

"Means fifty-five percent of a pound for a dollar. Less than that once they take their commission."

"That's *robbery*. We need to be in Mexico. You can buy Mexican for like five dollars."

"How much British money you need?"

"Well, I'll need enough to get to Embankment. My boo is chilling down in that area. The theater is on St. Martin's Lane. He said his hotel was a two-minute walk from the theater."

"You have the address?"

"Got it right here."

"No problem. I'll get you to your man."

"Cool. My boo will have my back after that. I can get some money from him and kick you down what I owe you. Just holla at me down there and I'll bring you what I owe you."

"Don't worry about it."

"You sure?"

"I'll get you a day pass for all the zones. Just in case."

"And can you throw in enough for me to buy some condoms?"

"Condoms?"

"In case he doesn't have any. Lose your momentum, spoil the mood."

"How many condoms will you need, Lola?"

"A dozen should get me through the weekend. At least until Sunday."

"Today is Friday. And you want a dozen?"

"You're right. I should get more."

Tired and irritable, we ate upstairs at Brasserie Bar.

Lola had three scrambled eggs and smoked salmon. I had veggie sausages, grilled tomatoes, and fried eggs. Mrs. Jones sat across from me, away from Lola, without talking. Mrs. Jones hadn't said much to Lola since we'd left the plane and made it through customs.

She hadn't said anything to Lola since that massage.

At the table next to us were four Africans, all speaking French. Beyond them were Europeans speaking a language I couldn't make out, not at first. One of the Europeans, a young Slavic blond wearing a T-shirt with a picture of a Nigerian writer across the front, Folasade Coker, had put her backpack on her the floor near mine. It was a generic blue backpack, identical to mine.

The blonde smiled at me, then told her male friend, *"Is dit het echte leven?"*

He responded, *"Is dit enkel fantasie?"*

I looked down at their backpack.

Lola said, "These accents."

I asked, "What do you mean?"

"All kinds of African. German. Russian. Don't hear a lot of that gibberish in L.A. And I haven't seen a Mexican for hours. Not one Mexican in sight. This is straight-up weird. I mean, if there are no Mexicans, who keeps the city clean? Who cuts the grass? Who babysits?"

One of the Europeans next to us said, *"Open uw ogen."*

I turned to them, smiled, and said, *"Kijk tot de hemelen en zie."*

They laughed. The blonde looked at me again. She nodded.

Lola said, "What language is that?"

"Dutch."

"You speak Dutch?"

"Not really." I winked at her. "You were saying this feels like an alternate universe, huh?"

"People, especially the black people over here, they sound so smart. Speak all these languages. Their accents are the bomb. Even the stupid people sound like they have Ph.D.s."

Mrs. Jones drank her latte from Caffè Nero without acknowledging Lola, but her red eyes came to mine. She was in London, free to go, but she was still here with me.

Lola headed to the bathroom, left me and Mrs. Jones sitting at the table.

I asked the woman dressed in the color of sorrow if she was okay.

She asked me, "Why do you like *Battlestar*?"

"It's filled with Greek mythology and Christianity and atheism and zodiac references. . . . Caprica . . . that's their home planet . . . Caprica . . . as in Capricorn."

"The number twelve comes up a lot."

"As in twelve disciples and twelve signs of the zodiac and twelve colonies."

"The number twelve keeps coming up, implying earth was part of something larger."

"So you like the show."

"I despise it. Only way I used to spend time with my husband on Friday nights."

"Guess you won't be asking to borrow my DVDs."

She hesitated, looked a little embarrassed. "Seen enough. Felt like I was forced to. Had to pay attention just so we would have something to talk about. Just so we could . . . communicate. Just to get some conversation out of him. But I . . . I guess I don't have to watch that nonsense anymore."

We let that settle between us. That tension returned.

Her eyes were on her sparkling wedding ring. She spoke without moving her gaze.

"My husband . . . he doesn't touch me."

"I find that hard to believe."

"He hasn't touched me for years."

"As beautiful as you are? I'd never stop touching you."

I put my hand on hers. Her eyes came to mine.

She asked, "Are you testing the waters?"

I smiled. "Only if you're inviting me for a swim."

The Dutch-speaking Europeans finished their breakfast, grabbed their backpacks, and left. Again the blond girl looked at me. She was nervous. I saw it in her eyes.

She said, "*Scaramouche.*"

I nodded, said, "*Bismillah.*"

They left, talking first in Dutch, then changing to French. My focus went back to Mrs. Jones. I was looking in her eyes, holding her hand. She was holding my hand too.

She said, "You're a liar, Gideon."

"What have I lied about, Mrs. Jones?"

"No luggage."

"You don't have any luggage either."

"Are you on the run?"

"I have a backpack."

"A small backpack. And you didn't bring a coat."

"Neither did you."

"My trip wasn't planned."

I winked at her. "Maybe we have more in common than we realize."

"Your voice . . . your tone . . ."

"What about it?"

She said, "You're intelligent. Very. I'd guess you're an attorney or a thief of some sort."

"Is there a difference?"

"Not that it matters." She smiled. "I love the way your hand feels on mine. Love touching you."

"Are you flirting with me, Mrs. Jones?"

We sat there looking at each other, in provocative silence, until Lola came back.

The man with the broken nose passed by. Gray suit and red shirt looking wrinkled. He was on his cellular. He took a seat at a table near us and took out a London Underground map.

He was preoccupied, didn't notice us.

A second cellular phone rang.

He put down the first mobile and answered the second one, his face all business.

He juggled phone calls. Then hung up both and took out that yellow book again.

He had come through customs and wasn't carrying anything, not even a backpack. All he had was that yellow book.

I said, "Looks like he had a rough night."

"His eyes are black as hell." Lola rubbed her nose, as if seeing his made her conscious of her own. "Thought that was from plastic surgery or something."

"He's traveling light."

Lola said, "Not as light as Mrs. Jones. Not like you have much luggage yourself."

I regarded Mrs. Jones. Inside that moment, I was once again suspicious of her too.

She said, "Maybe he left an unhappy life. Maybe he had been cheated on, cuckold. Maybe his kid, or kids, became his worst nightmare. Maybe he had to leave or go insane."

Lola and I looked at Mrs. Jones.

Mrs. Jones said, "Maybe he's trying to start over without baggage."

I said, "What about his face?"

"We're all wounded in some way. Maybe he came here to heal."

Her mind was on something else, something more promising, something more urgent.

After the man looked at the menu, he sat back, rubbed his eyes, and opened that yellow book. He took out a pair of reading glasses, struggled to get them over his bandaged nose, gave up, and held the book close to his eyes. He bothered me. I kept him in my periphery. He never glanced my way, just read his book and checked his watch. He ordered breakfast and ate like he was in a rush, or starving, not at the easy pace of the Europeans. He ate like an American, and most Americans ate like they were convicts, fast and in a hurry, like men and women in prison.

We left before he did, left him eating and reading his book, the pages and words right up to his eyes. I looked back as we took the escalator, looked again as we left the airport.

He never spied my way.

We rode the Gatwick Express nonstop toward London Victoria Station.

It was going to be a thirty-minute ride.

Thirty minutes before I was alone with Mrs. Jones.

Thirty more minutes of Lola.

We sat in the red seats, two facing forward, two facing backward. Lola crashed across from me. Mrs. Jones sat next to me, again not talking to Lola, avoiding any contact with the animated woman, but every now and then gazing at Lola, a quick glance before looking away.

Mrs. Jones kept her eyes on the graffiti and countryside we were passing.

Lola bounced around, humming and smiling her ass off, then said, "This is crazy."

I asked, "What?"

"Gas is cheap as hell. We just passed a gas station and gas was a dollar a gallon."

"Wrong money. That was in pounds. One pound is about two dollars."

"My bad. Then two dollars a gallon. Still damn good."

"They measure in liters, not gallons. Four liters equal one gallon."

"That shit's too much like algebra for me. How much is gas over here, Brainiac?"

"Petrol is about eight dollars a gallon."

"*Get the fuck out.* No wonder they're in these itsy-bitsy-ass clown cars."

Lola closed her eyes and, at last, did the same with her mouth.

Then Mrs. Jones's eyes returned to mine. She licked her lips, sighed, shifted around, spoke to me in restless silence.

Her eyes went to my backpack. Then her eyes met mine head-on.

She remained expressionless, then turned her head away.

Again she wiped her eyes. Tears came and went.

I asked her, "How are you feeling?"

She set free one soft word. "Scared."

Victoria Station.

British accents dominated the international chatter; announcements from a woman who sounded like Miss Moneypenny reminded everyone to *Mind the gap* and to please tap in and tap out their Oyster cards. British culture met us head-on as we followed the WAY OUT signs from the trains up to the streets, blended in with the pace and pandemonium that was equal to being at Union Station in D.C. during rush hour. It was damn cold. Everyone had on gloves, scarves, hats, and coats. On the escalator we followed the rules and stood to the right so the impatient people could hurry by on the left. Lola was behind me, Mrs. Jones in front. Lola called to Mrs. Jones, offered to let Mrs. Jones use her Old Navy coat, said she had an extra one in her bag, but Mrs. Jones refused her offer without looking back, only gave Lola the somewhat detectable shake of her head. Still not a single word for Lola.

Something was wrong. Something bigger than the two women at my side.

Instinct told me to look back. Instinct told me to always look back. Instinct had me on edge, being on edge created paranoia. Paranoia was my alarm clock.

The man with the broken nose was back there, map of the tubes unfolded in his hands.

This time I put my luggage down and followed my paranoia.

I asked, "You okay? Need help?"

He looked up from his map. "Weren't you on my flight from Atlanta?"

"Yeah. Saw you on the plane too."

"You're American?"

"Yeah."

"Good. Maybe you can help me. I'm trying to figure out how to get to Tower Hill. The directions my friend gave me didn't make sense. I asked inside, but the accents are killing me."

His accent was soft and Southern. Genial. Like Billy Bob Thornton in a good mood.

I looked at his map.

He looked toward Mrs. Jones and Lola.

He said, "Beautiful women you're with."

"Yeah, they are."

"Saw the woman in the black dress crying at the airport."

"She's doing much better."

I saw the yellow book he was holding. *Divorce for Dummies.*

He was nobody.

Just another nobody.

"That's good to hear. Now, how do I find Tower Hill?"

I told him to go back inside, find out what zone he was going to, buy a travel card, down to the tubes, follow the yellow line on the map, and take the Circle Line to Tower Hill. It was morning rush hour in London, so he'd get there faster and cheaper if he took the tube.

He checked his watch and rushed back inside the station.

Then I watched him until he vanished. I looked around.

No police.

No trouble.

I let all my anxiety mix in with the voices from the city.

Mrs. Jones looked at me.

I smiled at the woman whose marriage was irretrievably broken.

Eight

body heat

We hustled by the nine-to-five crew.

We found the long line for the hackney carriages, what they called the black cabs. Ugly, bulky cabs that looked like they were from the seventeenth century. I gave Lola enough British currency to get to the theater district, then, even though we were all pretty much heading in the same direction, offered my cab to Mrs. Jones. Desire danced. She hesitated, didn't answer, just stood in the cold, still silent. Mrs. Jones was ready to get away from Lola. Lola was ready to get away from us so she could get to the man of her dreams. And I wanted Mrs. Jones to myself.

I told her, "I can show you my hotel room. Then you can decide."

There was a moment of indecision, a few breaths of contemplation.

Mrs. Jones climbed inside my cab. She sat facing forward, legs closed.

I pulled down a seat, sat across from her, facing backward, looking at her as we traveled.

I put my hand on her knee. My eyes searched hers for either rejection or approval.

There was no approval, but there was no rejection either.

Only tears. The tears returned.

I asked, "What that wedding ring set you back?"

"Guess."

My fingers traced her kneecaps, moved up her thigh, back to her knees. Her eyes were on my fingers, watching me, her breathing tight, almost asthmatic.

I said, "Ten, maybe fifteen."

"Try twenty."

"I hope taxes and a big rebate were included."

"I was talking years. It set me back twenty years of my life."

My fingers moved between her thighs, back to her knees, kept feeling her heat.

She looked at my hand, then slowly raised her watery eyes to mine.

She said, "My husband . . . he doesn't touch me."

"Is that right?"

"He has been with other women. He fell in love with someone else."

"Sorry to hear."

"So I've . . . I've . . . I've had to turn to other men."

"Desire is a beast that must be fed."

My hand moved up her leg, stopped right above her thigh. For a moment I was in North Carolina, not far from Pope and Fort Bragg military bases, at a strip club on Bragg Boulevard. Then I was in Tampa, on Martin Luther King Boulevard, on the front row of the midnight show at Crazy Horse, putting my money in the garters of naked women.

This was not a dancer at Déjà Vu. Not a whore in Brazil. This was a real woman.

"Do you think that's wrong, my turning to other men . . . to be made to feel like . . . a woman? . . . I mean . . . every woman needs to be made to feel like a woman . . . to feel special."

"When you're honest with yourself, oftentimes you betray someone else."

"This is true."

"Everyone needs to be touched. We all need contact, you know?"

She yielded a weak shrug. "I mean, is it really cheating when it comes to that?"

I repeated, "When you're honest with yourself, you betray someone else."

She wiped her eyes. "I broke my vows to God and the church."

"We're all sinners, Mrs. Jones. All of us."

"I wanted to be righteous."

"Even the righteous man is just a sinner living in between sins."

"I allowed other men to touch me, men who wanted to own me because I was unattainable. Men who knew my forever love was somewhere else, for someone else, they wanted me in the ways I wanted my husband to want me."

"It's a human thing, Mrs. Jones. To need to be touched is a human thing."

"It was just two men. Over ten years. Only two men."

"We all need to be touched."

"Three if you count . . . well, one experience was oral, wasn't really sex, you know?"

My hand moved up her leg, stopped short of her vagina, but I felt the heat. The heat from a woman could make a man's instincts go cold while his vision went bad. At the wrong time, the heat from a woman made it hard for a man to see beyond the end of his dick.

This was all I could see right now. This was all I wanted to see.

I whispered, "And you need to be touched."

"Desperately."

She closed her eyes. Bit her bottom lip.

I whispered, "You're vulnerable right now."

"I am. So very. So very. Vulnerable."

"I'd be taking advantage of you."

"Perhaps I'd be taking advantage of you. Using tears to get what I need."

There was a raging furnace between her legs. My finger grazed her panties. She jerked, tightened her thighs around my hand. Then she caught her breath and relaxed.

I asked, "Are you?"

"Am I what?"

"Using your tears?"

"Would it matter? The end result will be the same."

"You want me to touch you."

"At this moment, what I need supersedes what I want."

Her words remained the hymn of love gone bad. What had been sweet to the tongue now had a bitter taste. She was juggling love and hate, not knowing which one to drop.

She said, "On the train. The way it creaked and moaned. Like sex. The way it moved side to side. Like lovers. Like new lovers engaged in give-and-take. The train moved like sex."

"I didn't notice."

"I noticed. God, I noticed. It was . . . stimulating. I was imagining you. Us."

I moved to her side of the cab, put both arms around her, held her, pulled her breasts close to my chest, one hand moving across her body, her curves very nice.

She sighed, trembled.

She brought her hands up my back, gradually held on to me.

I whispered, my lips on her ear, told her how beautiful she was.

She said, "You don't have to say that."

"You are."

Again she cried, this time her tears came with a smile.

The taxi stopped. The area bustling. Signs said the British Museum wasn't far away. We were in Bloomsbury. Parked in front of Myhotel. Redness dominated Mrs. Jones's eyes. I doubt if mine looked any better. The skies made it seem as if it were an hour before sunrise.

Mrs. Jones shifted, more nervous than before, said, "My watch says two in the morning."

"It's ten. Set your watch to Greenwich mean time; get acclimated to the time change."

I paid the driver and we got out of the taxi on Bayley Street, the narrow avenue in front of Myhotel, stood on the double yellow lines that marked the no-parking zone, the equivalent of America's red curbs. Sky gray, cold, rain starting to fall. Since she wore no coat and I didn't have one to offer, Mrs. Jones shivered, her nipples were standing tall.

I asked, "Sure you want to come up to my room?"

Without hesitating she answered, "Carpe diem."

"What was that?"

"Carpe diem." She looked out at Bayley Street, evaluated Bedford Square. "It means the enjoyment of the pleasures of the moment without concern for the future."

"Would you like to engage in pleasure without concern for the future?"

Her breath caught inside her throat. She closed her eyes and nodded once.

Again, in the softest voice, she whispered, "I don't want to be alone."

We went inside a warm five-star hotel that owned a fabulous sushi bar.

Mrs. Jones took a seat right inside the glass doors, remained in a small seating area, fidgeting and facing the streets while I checked in. Her eyes and thoughts remained in the direction of all the red-and-white St. George's Cross flags hanging from the windows of almost every flat. She saw me watching her, pushed her prim and proper lips up into a loose smile.

She asked, "How much does a condo cost in this area?"

"At least a million pounds."

"How many square feet?"

"Doubt if those flats are much larger than this room."

"Remarkable."

"Read it was a good investment. With house cost rising something like thirty percent, those flats will be worth a lot more in a few months."

I turned my back and checked in. That took a few minutes. She waited in silence, back straight, legs crossed, right foot barely bouncing, proper and sophisticated.

Room key in hand, I headed for the elevator.

She followed, her wild hair down, eyes avoiding the hotel staff, not saying a word.

On the elevator I put my hand to her face.

We were alone. In a lift easing up. Easing up like I wanted to ease inside her. My warm hand on warmer flesh. Mrs. Jones let out a spiraling moan. Her tongue grazed my palm. Drove me insane. I held her close, put my hand between her legs. Felt her global warming.

The woman dressed in black moaned. The woman dressed in mourning shuddered.

She closed her eyes tight as the vertical carriage took us closer to a brand-new sin.

I wanted to rip that dress off her, wanted to fuck her right there, fuck her between floors.

Already I was caught up.

Caught up and unaware of the evil that was happening over four thousand miles away.

At that moment, at Turtle Beach, a resort in Trinidad, a family was yawning and piling inside a rental van for a family outing. A young Asian man who walked with a hip swagger, along with his beautiful African-American wife, his three interracial kids. His parents. His in-laws. At least ten people all together. One big family vacation. They were making a forty-five-minute drive from Port-of-Spain to Maracas Bay. Yesterday he had partied at Chacacabana, the day before at Macqueripe. Today was another day for tanning and parasailing while the children enjoyed their grand-parents and played in the warm waters. Maybe even a day for taking a trip to Tobago.

The Asian man looked at the front page of the *Trinidad Guardian*. It showed that the Big Bad Wolf had died in Tampa. As planned. The Asian man had thrown barbecues, spent money on exotic dancers and Cristal, been celebrating the death of his enemy like he'd won the lottery.

Now it was family time.

His beautiful wife finished loading their beautiful children inside the van, leaned over, and kissed him. She was happy too. She had been humiliated and ridiculed across the country.

Now it was over.

The Big Bad Wolf was dead. His enemy had been destroyed. Now they were free.

The Asian man turned the key to the start the van.

The van exploded.

On a peaceful morning in the islands, fire and screams filled the tropical air.

That Asian man was born with the name Ronald Chin.

Had changed his name to Sledgehammer Jackson.

The world knew him as Sledge.

His death was filled with fire and brimstone. On a piece of land surrounded by water.

I wouldn't hear about that revenge until later.

I wouldn't know I was a wanted man for a few hours.

Being hunted was the last thing on my mind.

Right now I was the hunter.

Hunting for carnal joy.

Underneath gray clouds, my mind was on a different prey.

Right now my mind was on the pursuit of a brand-new plea-sure.

My mind was on fucking Mrs. Jones.

Nine

wag

The man with the broken nose found Tower Hill.

Trains had been delayed due to service. He had been lost most of the morning.

He was still lost in Savage Gardens; one of the landmarks he had been given, a hotel called Novotel, was down the street. He couldn't find 1 Pepys Street. He walked the block, passed by Fenchurch Street Station, The English Club, Cheshire Cheese, Ladbrokes betting shop.

He made a frustrated sound, double-checked his instructions, then went back to Tower Hill tube station and started over. He was in EC3. EC3 was the postal code. And that postal code was posted on the corner of almost every building. Once again he passed the first landmark, looked up, and saw the blue heritage plaque on the wall of the flat where the Reverend P. T. B. "Tubby" Clayton had lived. Again he passed the Wine Library. And St. Olave's Church.

He didn't want to ask for directions. Not this close to his destination.

He didn't need to be remembered.

Again he circled the block, passed by all the pubs and betting shops. Then he found the apartment building. It had been right in front of him, it's address etched in glass and impossible to read. The building was on a narrow street barely wide enough for a taxi to negotiate, faced Novotel, was directly across from the hotel's main entrance.

He took a deep breath and almost smiled. He had found where the famous barrister lived.

He was running late. Very late. He hated to waste time. Time was unrecoverable.

As he walked to the glass door, he saw the beautiful barrister rushing off the lift, tension in her face. Without looking up she hurried across the marble floor in the pristine lobby.

She looked just like her photograph. Actually better. Not many did.

The woman was part of the elite group known as WAGS. Wives and Girlfriends of footballers. Stunning woman. Long yellow hair. Could pass for a Spice Girl. He had made it to her flat just in time to catch her leaving, dark sweats on, iPod on, heading out for her morning jog.

She came out of her flat, jogged right past him, never looked at him.

He hated the way he was invisible to women. Especially to beautiful women.

He turned around and watched her hair bouncing as she passed by buildings where historical figures had resided, crossed the narrow street, darting toward Trinity Square, arrogant enough to ignore Smart cars and mopeds. As if she owned the road. Her form was bad. Her back wasn't straight. She moved her arms too much. Ran flat-footed. Six miles. The package said she always ran six miles. His intel said that took her an hour. And she still had cellulite.

With better form she could knock a minute off each mile in no time.

He couldn't help her with the cellulite.

He had an hour. Plenty of time to read some more of his book. *Divorce for Dummies*.

The WAG always ran toward Embankment. Part of him wished he could've gone running with her. He touched his nose, yawned as he walked up to her flat, took keys out of his pocket.

One was a sensor key. He waved it in front of the sensor pad. The glass doors opened.

He took the elevator to the fourth floor. Went to her flat, stopped in front of her door.

He had almost put the key in the lock, then decided to ring the doorbell.

No one answered. Her new boyfriend stayed with her every other week.

The boyfriend she had started up with a few months after her marriage.

The man with the broken nose rang again. No one answered.

He used the key and with a simple turn the dead bolt was undone.

He walked into a well-lit flat, closed the door, engaged the dead bolt.

It was quiet.

Birds-of-paradise were on a glass table, along with a mushy card from her lover.

Red leather furniture. Granite counters and marble floors. Stainless-steel appliances.

From the window in her living room he had a view of Novotel.

He wondered how much a suite cost in that swank hotel.

He went and looked in both bedrooms. Her king-size bed was unmade. The second bedroom had been converted into an office. He wondered how much a tiny place like this cost. Compared to what real estate cost in Texas, the property prices were outrageous in London.

He was hungry. The rabbit food on the flight hadn't done a thing for him. He hated the food at the airport. He had stopped at Tesco, a grocery-store-type place, to get a muffin. But the English had all of their muffins and rolls in open containers. He watched people pick over the food before they chose the one they wanted. Hands that had touched unsanitary tube rails and doorknobs, hands that touched their penises and vaginas and wiped their asses and masturbated and picked noses, those filthy hands were picking over fresh muffins and rolls, not taking the first muffin or roll they contaminated, leaving the tainted one on the pile, that infected one rolling over on the fresh ones. Unsanitary. He thought that shit was plain old disgusting.

He looked inside the WAG's refrigerator. Saw a lot of ready-made food from Marks & Spencer, crisps on the counter, *fruit and fibre* cereal, and a few figs, nothing of interest.

He looked at the package of crisps. Had no idea what those were. Saw a picture of potato chips on the package. He realized the English called their potato chips *crisps*.

He went to the bathroom, put his book on divorce down, looked at his nose.

Broken. He got a little angry. Someone had gotten the best of him.

It had happened four days ago. Jacksonville, Florida. At the Modis Building. A $10,000 job, half his usual fee. He'd done the job, then gone back to his room at the Omni, iced up his nose, and waited for a bootleg doctor to show up and fix his face. He sat there in pain watching Angela Spears deliver the noon news. He fell into a trance, watching the news anchor on WTLV. Beautiful woman. Just like his wife. Or soon-to-be ex-wife. She had a smile that made a man want to relocate to Jacksonville. Angela Spears did, not his soon-to-be ex-wife.

He wanted to touch himself, his hand drifting, but they switched to a man doing weather.

He took some pain medication, sat on the bed, and read about Jacksonville.

He wanted to get out of Texas. Away from those memories.

He thought about Jacksonville, thought long and hard. Read that crime was up in that area, but crime was up all over the world. Might even marry a J'ville woman. Like Angela Spears.

He wondered if she was married. He had to get marriage out of his head. He had heard someone say not to let money ruin his marriage. That got a small laugh out of him.

He mumbled, "Shit. It's the other way around. Don't let marriage ruin your money."

He cared about his money. What was left of it. But he loved being married.

He read that J'ville was one of the most recession-proof cities in the country. No local or state income tax. Office space was cheaper than L.A., New York, and most spots in between. Five colleges, so he could to talk his daughter into going to college down there. She was only ten, but he was thinking ahead. Maybe his son, Skeeter, would like it down there.

Maybe he'd go back to school himself. Finally work on that Ph.D. His two brothers and three sisters all had Ph.D.s. He only had a master's. He was the dumb one.

He'd spent his youth being married. Then widowed. Then married again.

He wanted another wife. A new one. A beautiful one. Like his first wife.

Maybe have four more kids. He wanted a big family. He loved kids.

Even if he didn't luck up on a beautiful newscaster, the area was crawling with military, so there were plenty of hardworking women in uniform in search of civilian men. Hiking and biking, could do both of his favorite sports. Had to be plenty of marathons in the area. The same for triathlons. He could train year-round, like in Texas. Hard not to love a place that had 113 miles of pristine beaches. And had a professional football team. As far as he was concerned, Jacksonville had more perks than the first-class lounge in heaven. Spanish influence was everywhere. Spectacular archways and stained-glass windows.

He could start over in Jacksonville.

Maybe he'd meet a Spanish woman this time.

He'd think about that some more after he left London.

After he was done with the WAG.

His nose ached. He had a high threshold for pain, but still it ached.

He took bandages out, was starting to change them when the front door opened.

An hour hadn't passed. Only ten minutes had gone by.

Barely enough time for her to run a mile.

Her profile said that she *always* ran six, showered, then went to her office.

Sounded like she dropped her keys at the door, dropped them hard. She moved with an urgency, came running down the short hallway toward the bathroom, moving and moaning like she was in agony.

She bolted into the bathroom, iPod still on, her running pants already halfway down.

She had cut her run short because she had to pee.

Everything couldn't be factored in. Nothing ever went according to plan.

Not until then did she look up.

Then they were eye to eye.

The WAG stopped pissing, jumped up from the toilet.

Her iPod blasted a song by the Pussycat Dolls as she opened her mouth to scream.

The man with the broken nose charged and hit her in the nose. Right-handed punch. Like when he worked out on the bag. His punch had great form. She went down hard, just like that. Unconscious, just like that. Nose crushed, just like his. Bladder emptying itself.

If it were in a movie, it would've been funny, like *Scary Movie*.

He said, "Sorry about that, ma'am. Not polite for a man to hit a woman. Just business."

He tied her hands and feet. Pussycat Dolls singing for a man to loosen up their buttons.

Then he stood behind her, covered her head with a plastic bag.

Suffocation left no blood. Minimal amount of noise.

As the WAG twitched, he was thinking how the UK weather sucked. Thinking that he couldn't wait to get back to Gatwick and catch the next plane back to the States.

Long day. But he'd be back in time to pick the kids up from school tomorrow.

He looked down at the WAG. Pretty woman. As if there were ugly WAGs.

Nice breasts. Sweet hips. A childbearer. She could've had some beautiful children.

He took out his cellular. Took a photo of the WAG. Sent the image to his client.

Damn shame, he thought. *Damn shame.*

He undressed her. Dropped her smelly clothes in the compact washer.

He started a load of laundry. Then mopped up the piss in the bathroom.

He left the floor spotless. He was anal. Liked things clean and in their place.

Then he took out the map of London, wanted to see how far he'd be from a different tube.

The type was too small, but he tried to comprehend the tubes. London confused him. Always had. Frustrated, feeling vulnerable, he sighed when he had to put his reading glasses back on. Glasses he'd bought at Hartsfield International for $10.

He'd left his prescription reading glasses at home.

He reminded himself to go ahead and make that appointment for LASIK surgery.

IRS wanted money. Attorneys wanted money. Kids wanted money. Church wanted tithes. He didn't have an extra three thousand for LASIK, but he had to do what he had to do.

Mortgage had to be paid. The gardener had to be paid. He needed the money.

He dressed nice, but being broke and looking broke were two different things.

That's why he had left working at the university and gone back to picking up contracts.

For the money. The tax-free kind of money you got under the table.

He had come back because he needed the cash.

His ex would get the kids, the house, half the pension.

All he'd walk away with would be the memories.

And he wished he could let his soon-to-be ex take those bittersweet memories too.

The first few years had been good. New was always good. New was always exciting.

Having kids changed her for the worse. She was a horrible mother.

Being a parent had been the best thing that ever happened to him.

He was a great father. He did what he had to do to make sure his kids had what they needed. He just needed a woman in the house. A man was supposed to take a wife.

He picked up his self-help book. He'd find a new wife, he hoped, before long.

He dragged the WAG's naked body down the hallway, Jacksonville on his mind.

Then he passed by a black dress, saw it hanging in her bedroom, the clothes the WAG had no doubt planned on wearing this morning, saw that blackness, and his thoughts shifted.

To the beautiful woman he'd seen on the plane. The one who had been crying.

He would've stayed another day just to have a ten-minute conversation with her.

Divorce for Dummies in his pocket, dragging a dead WAG across the tile floor, he wondered where the woman in black was right now. He wished he had asked her her name.

He wished he had given her a handkerchief to dry her tears.

Ten

woman on the run

Myhotel. Third floor.

Hotel rooms in Europe were diminutive, but my suite was decent, big enough for a king-size bed, a desk, and a small contemporary sofa that was against the wall between the two windows. The sofa was one step away from the bed. The windows were two steps away from the bed, double windows starting three feet above the floor and extending to the ten-foot ceiling. The dark curtains were thick enough to make a red dress for Scarlett O'Hara; both of those curtains pulled back, still open, the gray skies and London's Victorian architecture peeping, a thousand windows facing this room, two thousand eyes acting as spies in the house of love.

Above the desk, a Sony flat-screen television was anchored to the wall, it now being on a music station, Corinne Bailey Rae singing, her voice wonderful any time of the day.

Mrs. Jones sat on the bed. Crossing, uncrossing her legs. Hands smoothing out the already perfect bedspread. Her eyes going to the dresser, to the CD player, to the television, looking at everything but me. I went to her, put my fingers in her thick hair. The texture of her mane was strong, had a wonderful scent, fresh, maybe jojoba oils. Her eyes came to mine.

She asked, "How do we do . . . how do we negotiate this?"

"The times you committed adultery, how did you do it?"

"Those men . . . we weren't total strangers . . . not like this."

"Where did you meet them?"

"One . . . we were in law school together."

"The other."

"At Starbucks. Used to see him . . . we talked a lot . . . became friends before . . . it happened. It wasn't my intent. But it happened. To my regret. He was intense . . . so needy . . . bought a house near mine . . . cars . . ." She took a breath and shook away that memory. "Let me be quiet."

I whispered, "How would you like to do this?"

"Don't know." Her voice thinned. "I don't know how to do this."

"Yes, you do."

"Should I get . . . should I undress now . . . what?"

"Do you want to get undressed now?"

"Damn you, Gideon."

I stood over her, my groin at her eye level.

She opened, closed her hands.

Her lips barely parted as she whispered, "I am so wet, so marinated right now."

She leaned into my body, took a lungful of air, then shifted toward me, turned her face to the side, rested her face on my groin, took a deep breath, and released a soft growl.

The beast inside her was waking up.

She breathed on me, the warmth of her gasps moving through the material of my sweats, her heat giving me an abrupt hardness as she rubbed her face on that sudden erection, did it with passion, exhaled on that rigidity, took shallow inhales and curt exhales as she moved her lips side to side, as she leaned forward and moved her mouth deeper into my groin, over and over the sweetest moans escaping her full lips.

I whispered, "Take your panties off."

Her hand pulled up her dress, did that in increments, exposed flesh up to her thigh, and that hand went underneath all of that blackness and mystery, tugged as she shifted to her left side, then tugged as she shifted to her right side, her ass shifting as she uncovered her secrets, her face still on my crotch, her warm breath on what was hard, creating an unexpected fire.

In her hand, her panties were black, dangling from the ends of her fingers.

Mrs. Jones dropped that soft blackness to the floor.

I looked down at the silver cross resting in the swell of her breasts.

She gazed up at me, swallowed, her chest rising and falling at an anxious rate.

Tears sat in her eyes.

I leaned into her, undid her bra, dropped it on her panties.

Mrs. Jones lay back, her eyes closed.

I put my hands at her knees, pushed her legs apart.

Then.

She moved my hand away and closed her legs. Not a hard move, very gentle, and I complied. I moved away from her, took a step backward, gave her the right to choose.

She sat up, eyes now wide, wiping unhappiness from her eyes, shaking her head.

Mrs. Jones stood up, adjusted her dress, found her underwear, stuffed her unmentionables inside her purse, moved across the room, leaving without announcement.

Hands clenched, teeth tight, still shaking her head, her wild hair moving as if it were a tree in a breeze; she stopped at the door, struggled with herself, then gazed at me.

I went to her, kissed her chin, raised her head. My lips went to her cheek, to her salty tears. Then her tongue eased out, greeted me, awkward and desperate all at once. She dropped her purse and devoured me. Greedy sounds came from her, sounds so primal they almost scared me.

I whispered, "Slow down."

"Okay, okay."

But she didn't slow down. Then we were tugging at each other's clothes, kissing, unable to get undressed fast enough, fighting to get undressed, both of us giving up, my hands squeezing her breasts, her hands squeezing my ass, my mouth sucking her neck, her nails digging into my skin, breathing and panting hard.

The phone rang. She jumped. It disrupted her pace, caused her to pull away.

She asked, "You need to get that?"

"It's the Hanso Foundation. They'll call back."

She came back to me, came back in a hurry.

My hand went between her legs, first raising her dress again, then two fingers finding what was wet, moving inside what was hot. Mrs. Jones was on the bed. Mrs. Jones was whimpering, moaning. Mrs. Jones wasn't crying anymore. Pleasure dominated sadness.

We moved around, touching each other, shifting positions until I got behind her. I entered her. Not all at once. Moved deeper with invitation. It was a subtle invasion of the kingdom that belonged to another man. A land, based on what she had told me, he no longer wanted to rule.

"Where are you from, Gideon? How old are you? Were you in the army or any other branch of the military? Have you done time? Tell me something about you . . . anything . . ."

"This is all you need to know, Mrs. Jones."

"No fair."

Mrs. Jones was on her left side, her right leg in the air, her limbs loose and lithe, fluid and ambitious, as I moved in and out of her, her body lean and more flexible that it had appeared, her pretty face craned back for a kiss. She sucked my tongue like she hadn't been fed sensuality in a long time, maybe was used to sex without the kissing. Mrs. Jones still had her expensive black dress on, parts of that top-shelf material pulled up, parts of it pulled down, most of if bunched up around her midsection; she still had on her high-heeled shoes; my sweats were dangling from my right leg; everything we had carried to the room had been dropped between the bed and the front door.

Mrs. Jones frowned when she cried but smiled when she was getting fucked. She shed her aristocratic demeanor and made wonderful sounds, never said a coherent word.

The bed rocked. The wind blew. The heater hummed. The moans grew. In the few minutes we'd been here, the room had moved from ten below freezing to ten degrees above hell.

The clothes got in the way and we struggled to get that dress up over her head, it getting caught up on her wild hair, that moment causing her to release a nervous laugh. Mrs. Jones was so damn beautiful when she laughed. She was a girl at heart, her laugh told me that.

She kicked her off expensive shoes, put her legs up high, and I sucked her pretty toes. Wildness invaded her, convulsions had her grabbing the sheets. I sucked her toes and slid a finger inside her. Then I sucked her toes and slid two fingers inside, first deep, then rubbing that part of her that felt like a magical button. That had her pulling the sheets to her, her back arching.

My tongue moved from her toes to her knees; she responded to that with twitches and shudders, then to the back of her knees, down her thigh, and settled between her legs. My tongue made circles, I sucked on her clit, licked figure eights, gave her the sweetest torture. Her head moved side to side, jerked and moaned like the devil inside her was fighting for freedom.

I turned her over, put her ass up high, her beautiful face in the white pillow, and from behind I rubbed my energy up against her dampness. Moved it back and forth until she reached for me, until she stroked me, until she put my energy inside her. She moved against me hard, then I slapped her backside, spanked the right side, then the left cheek, did that over and over, made her cringe and stop. I moved slow, kept control of my own pleasure, didn't want my energy to spill too soon, moved from lovemaking to a straight-up mean fuck, tried to see what speed she liked, what she loved, tried to have fun and find out if she wanted the smooth or rough.

When I pinched her nipples, she closed her eyes, she moaned that she was coming.

I watched her. Felt her. Enjoyed her orgasm as much as she did.

I sat up, my back against the headboard. She straddled me. Wiggled until I slipped back inside. Moved with me. This dance between strangers working so well. She held on to me, her cross swaying as she moved up, then her cross sticking to her damp skin as she came down on me hard. My thrusts were hard, almost brutal and unkind, but she came down on me with equal or greater force each time, clenching her teeth, growling, challenging me, telling me to give her all I had, grunting for me to bring it on and give her the best I could for as long as I could.

Mrs. Jones was insatiable, couldn't tell if I was fucking her or if she was fucking me.

I turned her over, flipped her around again, had to change positions, break that devastating rhythm before I shot my load. She frowned back at what was going in and out of her, stared at it with moans and detachment, moved like an exhibitionist but had the gaze of a woman who was a voyeur at heart. She moved like the freak in her had died and she needed me to give it major resuscitation. Sharp noises. Short words that made no sense. Mild shrieks. Tight-eyed groans.

On her back, head tossed back, her skull deep inside the pillow, she panted and jerked as I moved my tongue up and down that narrow slit.

Then with me on my back she held my balls and licked the sides of my handle, then took me in her mouth. I smiled and played with her hair, moved my hips up, went deeper inside her face. She worked magic.

She told me she wanted me back inside her.

Sharp breathing came from both of us. Her hands pulled at

her hair, making what was untamed even wilder. I understood her bohemian mane now. It didn't match the high-street clothes she wore, wasn't intended to complement the professional part of her personality. That hair matched this part of her, the part she kept hidden, the part she let shine behind closed doors.

Missionary. Her legs around my back. Moving slowly. Going deep. Stopped when it felt too good. Kissed her lips, sucked her tongue, and delayed the inevitable.

She stared at me, but her eyes were out of focus, seeing something else.

Or somebody else.

I asked, "What was that look?"

She smiled, came back to the here and now, found her focus, found me.

I asked her again.

She whispered, "Lola Mack."

It was my turn to smile.

Her eyes closed, her voice less than a whisper now. "She made me come."

"On the plane."

She groaned. "Had a goddamn orgasm at thirty-six thousand feet in the air."

I moved slow, felt her body start to quiver again, that right leg shaking, mild convulsions.

I said, "I'm inside you and you're thinking about Lola Mack."

"Yes."

"Imagining Lola Mack?"

"I'm not going to answer that."

I fucked her harder, fucked her and growled, "Are you imagining her?"

She surrendered. "Yes."

"Did you like that? When she made you come, did you like that?"

"God, you're . . . you're . . . your . . . it's getting so hard."

"Did you like that?"

"Imagining me and Lola . . . imagining us . . . that turns you on, doesn't it?"

"Did you like that?"

"Would that turn you on?"

"Answer me, dammit."

"Fuck you."

"Answer me."

"So damn hard. You are so damn hard."

"Did you like that?"

"God, you are fucking—"

"Answer . . ."

"—the shit out of me."

"Answer . . . answer . . . me . . . answer me."

I slowed down, caught my breath. She did the same. Her eyes opened wide, not blinking, as if she were gone to some ethereal place far away.

She whispered, "She made me come . . . when she massaged me . . . she . . . I came like a river . . . was too embarrassed to get up and . . . or make her stop . . . so I pretended to be asleep."

I asked, "On the plane . . . you come good?"

"Not as good as . . . as . . . as I'm about to come now."

She was shaking, holding me. Her nonstop whimpers were so sensual, so arousing.

I was grunting, mixing my sex sounds with her orgasmic squeals.

Pleasure was about to rush out of me. I pulled out, told Mrs. Jones that I was about to come. She lay back, waiting, panting like she was in heat, licking her lips, her eyes on my penis, watching, wanting to see, wanting to see, wanting to see. It was taking me too long to come. She took my penis and stroked me. Stroked me and took me over that ridge. I grunted as my seeds left me, as they spilled and decorated her stomach, as they created a river between her breasts.

Now she had a pearl necklace to go with her diamond ring.

She ran her fingers through the river of lifeless life, closed her eyes and played with those unborn children, children with nowhere to swim, children who would not hunt for an egg at breakfast time. Mrs. Jones licked her lips, hesitated, that urge rose in her face, that urge she couldn't suppress any longer, the urge she had to give in to. She sucked her fingers.

She hummed and licked her fingers like she was finishing a bucket of KFC.

Eleven

deadly is the female

Mrs. Jones had become an exotic vampire.

I smiled; what she was doing was so damn erotic. She grinned at me in return, now feeling safe with what she was doing in front of me. When she was done, she closed her eyes.

I said, "Lola Mack made you come."

She shook her head in disbelief, gave me a shallow chuckle, her eyes getting tighter.

"I couldn't look at Lola when we got off the plane. Hated her happy ass. Tried to avoid her after customs. Thought she would get her damn luggage and run to her boyfriend's hotel."

I chuckled. "She looked happy when she got in that taxi."

"That's how a woman smiles when she's horny and knows it's about to get handled."

"You have the same smile now."

She licked her fingers. "I know."

I lay down on her, that river becoming our glue, and we kissed. We moved from deep kisses to softer kisses as we cooled down, like two athletes at the end of a workout. She moved away from me, got her own pillow, put her back to me. I put my arm around her. She shifted and I took that as a hint, so I moved my arm away. Reached for the remote, hit the ON button.

I changed channels and stopped at TV6. Every few minutes they played that irritating opening for the *Simpsons*, this one using real people instead of animations.

She whispered, "Horrible. That's just plain horrible."

"That a woman made you come?"

"No, that *Simpsons* intro thing. The cartoon is much better. That's horrible."

A moment passed.

I changed the channel, found Prime Minister Tony Blair in the middle of a loan scandal.

I looked at Mrs. Jones. She stopped staring at my backpack, looked at me.

Mrs. Jones said, "Blair sucks."

I agreed. "He's just another Bush."

"Blair has a better vocabulary."

"Bush has better teeth."

"Tell me about your backpack."

I pretended she didn't faze me, surfed BBC1.

Pictures of Big Bad with birth and death dates lit up my room. Clips of his videos and interviews played in the background. The news had put together a package. In big Vegas-style lights BIG BAD. White Adidas to the bone. Shaking, doing the *Boom Boom Click* dance moves that came out of the Dirty South. Doing the walk-it-out. Pool Palace. Lean-wit-it-rock-wit-it. Rag Top. Everybody in the video dressed like they were his clones.

He said, "I'm *bling-tabulous* baby. *Bling-tabulous*."

The reporter said that this gang killing had left a trail of destruction only rivaled by the Japanese beetle. A thousand police lights and coroner vans were behind that strip club.

The news called it a gang war.

Fans were showing up with flowers and candles and testimonies.

They had his wife and kids on the news too. She was crying, so were the kids.

Two days ago the members of his former group were interviewed.

Sans Sledge.

Yesterday Sledge's publicist had issued a heartfelt comment.

They said Sledge was too shocked and broken up by the loss of an old friend to speak.

I changed the channel, moved on to BBC2, ITV, Channel 4, and Channel 5. One station was showing *Friends*. *Will & Grace* and *Just Shoot Me* were warming up, next at bat. Another channel had news, said that there was a thirty-minute delay on some trains in some areas. That was followed by a special report giving props to the area that had the worst teeth in the UK.

I changed the channel again. Leeds University students were demanding the resignation of Dr. Frank Ellis for supporting the right-wing "bell-curve" theory, which said black students were genetically inferior. Not exactly the kind of shit I wanted to hear about right now.

I thought Mrs. Jones was going to sleep, but she kept shifting positions, bothered.

I asked her what was wrong. She said her entire life was on her mind.

She said, "Thinking about . . . I had an interesting childhood."

I muted the television, turned and faced Mrs. Jones.

She whispered, "My first sexual experience . . . was unexpected. Like this."

"This reminds you of that."

"Was with a girl." She chuckled. "Never told anybody that. Not even my husband."

"What happened? How did that come about?"

"It started off . . . we called ourselves practicing . . . for the day we were with a boy. We practiced . . . kissing our hands . . . then each other . . . first lips closed . . . then French . . . then touching . . . what to expect boys to touch . . . and it . . . it became something else for a while."

"Did it?"

"After school we'd . . . be together. Do things. Things we thought boys would do."

"Like?"

"It was innocent. Tried to teach each other how to kiss. Learned about our bodies."

"How did it end?"

"Our parents found out . . . it got ugly."

"So you're bi?"

"Not at all. Was just something I did when I was a young girl, experimental, that's all. With that one girl. No one else. Something that happened . . . decades ago. A lifetime ago."

Silence from me while she shifted a lot.

She said, "Can't believe I told you that. My husband doesn't . . . didn't know that."

"Really?"

"There is . . . was a lot he doesn't . . . didn't know about me."

It was too quiet. I turned on the radio. I searched for Miles, or Wes, or Trane, stopped surfing at Choice FM. Beverley Knight's remake of an old Al Green song was going off as Corinne Bailey Rae took the floor with her original music and told the UK to put their records on.

I closed my eyes. The bed moved when Mrs. Jones got up. My hands ached. So did my face. Pins and needles were under my skin. All of those sensations were reminders. Days had passed and my insides still rattled with nervousness, like it did before a job. It was so vivid.

Wondered how many Hail Marys a man like me would have to say to see glory.

Corinne Bailey Rae went off and Amy Winehouse came on. "Moody's Mood for Love."

I opened my eyes; Mrs. Jones was preoccupied, trying to clean her black dress.

I walked to the window, pulled the thick, red curtains back. London was gray and overcast, the same mood Mrs. Jones had been in before we crossed that line, and she was drifting back toward the land of melancholy. She wasn't crying. That was good.

My thoughts stayed back in Tampa.

Mrs. Jones remained in her own world as well.

She said, "My dress is ruined."

"Come stains?"

"Jism blots all over. This dress cost four hundred dollars. Now it's ruined."

"Now it's a Lewinsky."

"It's fucked-up, that's what it is."

She got back in the bed.

Never should have brought her anxiety and problems up to my room.

I went back to the bed. Mrs. Jones had pulled the cover up over her petite butt.

"Lola made you come."

"Damn that talkative bitch."

I said, "Doubt if she's talking right now."

"She's probably fucking the shit out of her boyfriend."

We laughed hard, me because in that moment, I heard the ghetto rise up and walk out on the tongue of a sophisticated woman. The timbre of hard times and ruthlessness in her tone.

For a moment I imagined Mrs. Jones being my woman.

I asked, "What if your husband went away?"

"He's already left me."

"No . . . what if . . . if . . . what if he ceased to exist?"

"Died?"

I let that idea sit for a moment, then asked, "Would that make you happy?"

Silence charged into the room, followed by the muffled return of Mrs. Jones's tears.

She hurried into the bathroom, closed the door hard. I heard sobbing, water running, then the shower. She came back out wearing a towel, covering all she had shared with me.

I thought about Thelma.

Mrs. Jones said, "When he was a teenager, my husband used to rob banks."

"Your husband was a bad boy."

"He ran with gangs. And his older brother. Yeah. He robbed banks."

"You don't say. And here I am using an ATM to get my money."

"Your sense of humor is awful."

"Have to work on my timing, that's all."

"My husband. He doesn't know I know he was a stickup man."

"How did you find out?"

"His mother told me. Before we married, his mother told me."

"And you still married him."

She went into a trance.

"Gideon."

"Yes, Mrs. Jones."

She looked unnerved.

I asked, "Do I scare you?"

"You made me wet. On the plane, in the galley, when you were flirting, you made me wet."

"Did I?"

"You made me wet, then Lola put her hands on me. She fanned the flames you created."

Mrs. Jones pulled her dress on, tried to smooth away the wrinkles, and picked at the jism stains, sat at the end of the bed, not blinking, eyes glued to the wall.

She wiped away her tears, whispered, "How much would something like that cost?"

"You talking about a new dress?"

"No. The other thing. To make someone . . . cease to exist. What's the going rate?"

"What would it be worth to you?"

Then the whispers ended and she was blinking again, crying harder.

Her voice turned ragged. "Are you fucking with me, Gideon?"

I remained calm. "I'm not fucking—"

"Are you testing me—"

"—with you."

"Then what are you doing?"

"I'm just asking a question."

"To see what kind of person I am?"

She went on breathing hard for a while, tugging at her hair, shaking her head.

She said, "I come from a long line of bad people. I'm not proud of it, but that's who I am."

I looked at her, waited for her to say more or shut down. Either way didn't matter.

She said, "My father . . . he made money in Jamaica. He did illegal things."

"Drugs."

"I'm not saying."

"Jamaica is between where they manufacture the drugs and the people who buy drugs."

She nodded. "Lots of kidnappings. Lots of murders."

"And Kingston has a murder rate that ranks number one, I do believe."

"So you've been to Kingston?"

"Saw a lot of beautiful things, met some beautiful women, but what's up with the brothers walking the streets with their dicks hanging out of their pants? Is that a fashion statement?"

She almost smiled.

"I'm serious. Why do they walk around with their dicks hanging out?"

"Because they can."

"Is that against the law?"

"I didn't study Jamaican law." Her smile vanished. "My father, he took us to America."

"From Jamaica."

"He came to my room. I was a child. I was six, maybe five. But I remember his fear. He came and picked me up. In the middle of the night. Picked me up fast. He had me in his arms when he ran to get my mother. She was sleeping. Rushed us to an airfield. We left everything behind. Left abruptly, in our pajamas, my mother in her housecoat and house shoes, and I never knew why, but I did know why. The suitcase filled with money told me some of the why."

"That's wild."

"I'm telling you things I never told my husband. Things I've never talked about."

We exchanged expressions.

I asked, "Did you change your names once you got here . . . I mean there, to the U.S.?"

She smiled a life-weary smile that was a mask for her swift embarrassment.

"We changed names, changed everything." She whispered to herself for a moment. "Maybe I inherited my father's old ways. Maybe anger and revenge live in my blood."

"Meaning what exactly?"

"Meaning I'd better get away from you before I make someone cease to exist."

I shrugged. "We were just being hypothetical."

She whispered, "Contemplation is prelude to commission."

"Is it?"

"Like we contemplated fucking."

"Then we were fucking."

"Now we're two people contemplating murder."

Silence moved between us, wedged us further apart, put us back in our corners.

She whispered, " 'For what I am working out I do not know. For what I wish, this I do not practice, but what I hate is what I do . . . but now the one working it out is no longer I, but sin that resides in me. For I know that in me, that is, in my flesh, there dwells nothing good. For ability to wish is present with me, but ability to work what is fine is not present. For the good that I wish I do not do, but the bad that I do not wish is what I practice . . .'"

I said, "And she quotes the Bible."

She went on, her voice a perplexed whisper, the good and bad inside her fighting like rabid pit bulls, her face showing her inner struggle, revealing her angst. "I find, then, this law in my case: That when I wish to do what is right, what is bad is present with me . . ."

Somebody tapped on my door. We both jumped, only in different ways, for different reasons. Mine was the mild panic of a man worried about the law. Mrs. Jones jumped like a married woman who realized she was in the bedroom with another man, his come still on her breath, his seeds drying on her skin.

I asked who it was.

"Housekeeping. You would . . . do you like your room to be serviced, yes?"

We heard workers giggling in the hallway. Their accents thick enough to cut with a blade, maybe Polish or Romanian, could've been some other Eastern Bloc tongue.

I told them to go away, nothing was needed right now. They sounded like grown women but giggled like naughty teenagers. They apologized in chorus. That giggle meant they had heard us moaning. Their accents faded into the room across the hallway.

Mrs. Jones said, "My name was Henrietta Kellogg. That was my birth name."

"You changed it."

"My parents changed it. I woke up in America with a new identity."

"So you know how to leave an old life behind."

"Where I was from, money fixed all problems. Everybody had a price. Everyone from the police to the neighbor. You paid them off, made your problems go away. You made people go away. And if they didn't have a price . . . if they didn't have a price . . ."

"They slept under the dirt."

"My father . . . he tried to kill someone for me . . . he tried . . . his old ways came back."

"Why did he try to kill someone for you?"

"Because I asked him to." She paused. "Because I *told* . . . *begged* him to."

She wiped her eyes with the back of her hands.

I nodded.

She said, "It didn't happen. He tried. It went wrong. It went bad for all of us."

"Your husband? Your father tried to kill your husband for you?"

"Someone else. I don't want to talk about that. Not ever. I want to forget it all."

I listened.

"So, yesterday, I did just like I did when I was a child." She took a breath. "I ran away. Got on a plane. Left my name. Clothes. Everything I owned. I ran away from my life."

"Sounds traumatic."

"We shed the skins of who we used to be."

"Can't imagine what you went through. What you're going through."

"I'm going through . . . my life. Once again uprooted from friends. From my culture. From my world. Only when I was a little girl, I had my doll to comfort me. No doll, not this time."

She stared out the window for a moment. Looked like she was counting raindrops.

She whispered, "I can be someone different every day. I can become a new woman every day until I like the woman I become, then I can become her for a while, if not forever."

She finished dressing.

Mrs. Jones said, "Too bad I didn't know you last year."

"Is that right?"

She walked toward the door.

She asked, "Have you slept with a lot of married women?"

"Only the ones who have given up on their husbands."

"Then you have slept with a lot of married women."

I didn't answer.

"I saw you exchange backpacks. Your bag is heavier."

"What does that tell you?"

"You're a criminal."

"And you're an attorney."

"Not any longer."

"What are you now?"

"I don't know."

Mrs. Jones didn't look back at me, just left the room.

Twelve

this gun for hire

Mrs. Jones had bedded a contract killer and walked away.

I went back to the window.

The skies were darker, the rain coming down with the same silky cadence, a tempo that was steady but not urgent. Down on the cobblestone walkway it was about four degrees Celsius, which translated to about forty Fahrenheit. To my right, an Asian man wearing a bright yellow raincoat was out on the corner holding up a big sign that advertised his Chinese buffet was the best in the area, marching back and forth in the rain as Europeans and Africans hustled up and down Tottenham Court Road, umbrellas held high, most dressed in dark colors, casual and cosmopolitan, this metropolitan section of the world that housed Protestants, Catholics, and followers of Islam, looking like a mixture of Seattle, Rittenhouse Square in Philly, all of that with blended architecture, the historic and outdated along with the contemporary and chic.

I waited. It was cold out there, freezing by L.A. standards. Too bitter for the thin dress Mrs. Jones had on. All the other women who had on skirts wore black leggings, some with funky patterns, but Mrs. Jones's legs were bare. No way would she take to the cold dressed the way she was. Without a coat. Expected to hear a tap at the door, any second I would hear her taps.

The phone rang again.

I took my time, answered on the third ring. Expected to hear Mrs. Jones's jet-lagged and disheartened tone. Wanted it to be her. The voice on the other end was fresh. My work calling.

My instructions were curt. "Walk Tottenham Court Road until you see Freddie Mercury."

"You're in London?"

"Freddie Mercury will be on the left."

"Why can't I just walk until I see Tupac and Biggie?"

Then I was talking to a dial tone.

Time to go to work.

My attention went to the blue backpack. The one the Dutch woman at Gatwick had traded for mine. I unzipped the bag. Old Navy sweats and underwear were packed on top, white socks there as well. Under the clothing was a computer, a TX series Sony Vaio that weighed no more than two pounds. The three-prong power cable was made for the U.S. They had been kind enough to throw in a dual-wattage international converter set.

What had the most weight was a white box. I opened it. Inside was a sweet piece of hardware, a nine with its silencer packed off to the side. A SIG-Sauer was in the bag too, as I had requested. After the incident with the reverend I started using a bigger gun with a bigger bullet.

Other tools were in the backpack. Ice pick. Piano wire. Custom gloves.

I touched the guns and once again I was seven years old. Saw that big, ugly man beating my mother. A big man they called Mr. Midnight. He was choking her. Screaming at her and killing her. Had her by the neck, her body raised up sky-high, my mother naked and kicking wildly as she suffocated, her feet banging against the wall as he rag-dolled her around the room, my mother's feet knocking over lamps as she clawed at his hands.

Like Mrs. Jones and her family had fled Jamaica, me and my mother fled Charlotte. My mother took the cash out of that dead man's wallet and packed our clothes. He was my first kill. Not for profit, the ones that came later were put in a different category, at least they were in my mind.

While we sat in the back of a Greyhound bus, she held me in her arms, that smoking Smith & Wesson in her big purse, and told me who my father was.

Before that day, I never knew I had a father.

My mother told me that my father was an army man. He bragged that he used to jump out of planes, took sniper training, made Delta Force. While they drank and got high, while he paid my mother to do the kind of things a man paid a woman in her profession to do, he ran his strong hands through her long hair and held her close, treated her like a lady, a cigarette in his hand and liquor on his breath, and told her his secrets, told that young woman that the government still needed mercenaries. He was being sent to Latin America, somewhere in Honduras and Nicaragua, so he could deal with arms traders.

He met my mother on his sojourn to South America. He needed to relieve some stress, made a stop at a brothel in Montego Bay, where all the tender-legged women lined up for inspection, and picked the prettiest woman in the whorehouse, sweet girl from Charlotte, North Carolina. Nine months after that I was born in the city named after King George III's wife, the queen being a woman from Germany, Mecklenburg, hence the name of the county of my birth.

My father was strong, used to fight bulls bare-handed, beat them every time.

That was some of what my mother told me; I've added to the truth she gave me.

Like James Frey, in my own omniscient voice, I have embellished my own history.

As far as I know, my entire history, including what my mother said, could be a lie.

I hurried back to the window, hoping I hadn't missed Mrs. Jones.

She was leaving the hotel, moving into the streets, not looking in the right direction for traffic. She was in the middle of the road when a Smart car whipped around the corner; the driver slammed on his brakes and slid fast. Mrs. Jones was almost run down. In America, traffic came from the left. In London, a world that was reversed, traffic assaulted pedestrians from the right. Mrs. Jones had looked the wrong way, her mind now realizing this world drove on the opposite side of the street. Barely in London for three hours and she was almost killed, almost run down like Natalie Portman in the opening of the movie *Closer*. Mrs. Jones stood in the middle of the street, shaken, the driver blowing his horn as he struggled to maneuver around Mrs. Jones.

Mrs. Jones looked up at the window. She saw me. Stared. Then, without expression, turned her head away. I no longer existed in her world.

Forty-degree wind made her dark dress sway. Purse on her arm, she lowered her head, took quick steps to beat the traffic and negotiate Tottenham Court Road at the Odeon. Again she stood in the rain, pondered both directions like she was trying to ponder the rest of her life.

Then she looked down. At every intersection were markings on the pavement, big and bold, white lettering, telling pedestrians which way to scan for traffic: LOOK RIGHT. LOOK LEFT. I wonder how many Americans and Parisians were run down before they came up with that idea.

Mrs. Jones went left toward the high-tech district, passed by the red phone booths, phone booths that had business cards from every whore in the area posted inside.

The night I killed that evil man, my mother remained calm. Unbelievably calm. He'd almost murdered her and she never fell apart. She was calm to the point of being cold. She put a sheet over his body while we ate, packed, wiped our prints away from everything in that rented space, then left before the sun made friends with Mecklenburg County. My mother didn't shed a single tear. Neither did I. I read my comic books and became the echo of her emotions.

I asked my mother, "Where we going?"

"Quebec. On the island of Montreal."

I asked, "We have friends on that island?"

"My only friend died a long time ago."

"You have any friends?"

"Only one I ever had died. She was killed by one of her johns."

My mother was smoking, sweating.

I asked, "How am I supposed to make friends if we keep moving?"

"We'll stop moving one day. But right now we have to leave before the police come."

Once again I'd have to become someone else.

I asked, "Why we have to go this time?"

"Because they will take you away from me. They will lock me up and put you in the system. I grew up in the system. The system is no place for a child to be. There is no love."

I looked down at my hand. I moved my trigger finger back and forth. Felt the weight of that .22 in my hand, even though I wasn't holding that weapon. Smelled the cordite on my skin.

I asked my mother, "Did I do a bad thing?"

"Some people deserve to die." She shook her head. "Your daddy told me. Bad people need to die. It makes the world a better place."

I told myself that by killing that man and saving my mother, I was a superhero, that I had made the world a better place. I was still making the world a better place for someone.

Below me, on Bayley Street, over on Tottenham Court, nothing but crowds and strangers.

Mrs. Jones had vanished underneath a dark sky that was a doppelgänger for her mood.

Disappeared like her wicked family did on a terrifying night in Jamaica.

I smelled my fingers, the sweetness of her vagina still living on my tongue.

Thirteen

the woman in white

His broken nose ached.

He was sitting at a bistro table, Starbucks Coffee at Tower Bridge Piazza.

The area around Shad Thames and Horsleydown Lane looked like the old country.

He was only a few yards away from where he had dropped the WAG.

He had done as he was ordered. The WAG's estranged husband wanted her dropped on the spot he had proposed to her. He had paid a lot of money to make sure that happened.

People were mumbling about a body that had been found in the Thames this morning.

People thought it was suicide. London was a dark and dreary, depressing place that had plenty of self-killings. But the man with the broken nose knew the truth.

Glasses on, he was reading *Divorce for Dummies*, drinking a tall house coffee. No cream. Sugar. With his cellular up to his ear. Frustration was crawling up and down his spine.

Jaw tight, he told his soon-to-be ex-wife, "I'm in London. Left a message on your cellular."

"I'm leaving you. I'm moving on with my life."

"Let's not go through this again. I can't handle this right now."

"And I'm taking our daughter. I'm taking Melanie. Skeeter can stay with you. Boys should be with their fathers. You can teach him things I can't. No child support. Agreed?"

"I'm tired of the threats. Let's get this divorce over with, can we? This is worse than that crap Alec Baldwin and Kim Basinger are going through. You need to calm the fuck down."

"Don't tell me to calm the eff down. Don't you dare tell me to calm the eff down."

"You're killing me over here, you know that? It's what, still the middle of the night in Texas and you're blowing up my phone. Why do you do this to me? Why harass me?"

"I'm leaving you."

"Don't talk about it. Be about it."

"I'm leaving you."

"And I want you to leave. I was served. I signed. What else do you want?"

"But I'm not taking Skeeter. I can't deal with Skeeter. I can't handle Skeeter."

Pressure at both temples. He wondered if Paul McCartney was this stressed.

He snapped, "Don't do this to me, not right now."

"Two weeks you've been gone. When are you coming back?"

He took a breath. "Trying to get back to Katy sometime tomorrow."

"I can't handle Skeeter. Come get him. He should be with his father."

His cellular rang. Not the one in his hand, the one in his pocket.

The hotline.

He told his soon-to-be ex-wife to hold on.

She asked, "Hold on? I'm falling apart. Why should I have to hold on?"

"Business call coming in. Need to take it."

She hung up on him.

He almost called her back. But there was no need trying to put toothpaste back in the tube. That was both futile and messy. He flipped one phone closed. Flipped the other one open.

He answered, "Talk to me, Sam."

"Got another job for you."

He grunted out his frustration. "Where?"

"London."

"Need to leave. London's going to be on fire in the next few hours."

"Top dollar on the next one."

"Top dollar? What's top dollar?"

He listened. What he heard caused him to put his book to the side.

He said, "That's a lot of money."

"Can get you half in the next day or so."

"What's the job?"

"Cleanup. High-profile."

High-profile. People liked to clean up after big jobs, jobs that drew too much attention. The contractors liked to assassinate the contract killers to prevent them from testifying or even spreading rumors about who hired them. Rotten business. Profitable, but rotten to the core.

Everybody was expendable in the name of self-preservation.

The man with the broken nose asked, "From what job?"

"Can't say."

"Well, is it a European cleanup?"

"Something back in North America."

"North America runs from Mexico to the North Pole."

He sipped his coffee. Cleanups were the most dangerous. Killer against killer.

But wives cost money. Kids cost money. Coffee cost money.

He asked, "Who is the package on? Who is the hit on, Sam? Man or woman?"

"Don't know. Not like there is a Hit Man's Registration Act to keep you guys in line."

"Save the jokes. Get me a package."

"Will do."

"If I'm staying, I'll need some perks. And I need some additional hardware."

"Place your order. I can get almost anything."

"Had my eye on a Desert Eagle .50. Titanium finish."

"Israeli gun. Big bullets. Loud bang."

He said, "Hadn't planned on staying. Need money. Not to be held against my fee."

"Use the American Express that came with the passport and tickets."

"Need suits. And you know what kind of suits I wear."

"Then buy the kind of suits you wear."

"Need a place to hole up."

"Get a hotel. Use the AmEx. Get some rest."

"I don't want to be in London no more than another day. Get me that package."

He hung up that cellular.

Then flipped opened the other one. Started putting in the 713 area code to his soon-to-be ex-wife's cellular. Made it to the last number and paused. He hated her. He really did.

He wished he had thrown her into the Thames.

Now he was stuck in London.

He had planned on returning to Gatwick. An hour trip. Go through customs. Another hour. Wait for three or four hours to board a flight at British Air. Take a nine-hour flight back to Atlanta. Again through customs. Then wait for another plane. After that a two-hour flight to Houston. Drive the forty-five minutes to Katy. Get Mexican food for dinner.

Then listen to his soon-to-be-ex bitch about how much she hated her life.

Listen to her brag about her new boyfriend. How he takes her out.

He hung up the phone.

He didn't want to rush home to that. He'd take a nap, buy a couple of suits, maybe head out to the Brick Lane Market and take a glimpse at the Bengali culture. He'd picked up a travel guide. *London in 24 Hours.* Had circled a few things that looked interesting. A restaurant on Portobello Road looked nice. Brochure said it was across the street from a famous tattoo shop that had been seen in the opening of a Julia Roberts movie, one she had done with some wimpy British guy. Might find his way over to the Ten Bells pub. Maybe just relax for a few hours and do like the brochure recommended, become a tourist and take in some of Dickensian London.

He picked up a newspaper. Morning edition. Front page announced that Europe had 55 million hard drinkers, a third of them women who had started drinking by the age of thirteen. No wonder they had some of the unfriendliest faces on the planet. Hard to smile with a hangover. Next page was about a man who had been served divorce papers, and minutes later he poured gasoline around the house, lit a match, and damn near blew up the neighborhood.

He understood that man.

Women. When they didn't have a man, unhappy. When they had a man, unhappy. Not married, unhappy. Married, unhappy. No kids, unhappy. Had kids, unhappy. Go figure.

He was done with women. With dating. With marriage. For a long while.

Then.

A woman walked in dressed in all white. That color out of season, at least it was out of season by Texas standards. No white after Labor Day was the rule in the South. In the blacks and grays, she stood out. But she would've stood out anyway. She was bald, for the most part.

Stunning woman. High cheekbones, round face, full lips.

Dark skin. Small breasts. Small waist that lead to a healthy, round backside.

He looked at her, her bald head and angelic colors hard to ignore on a gloomy day.

Especially since she had to be at least six foot three in her heels. She was so damn vertical, tall enough to walk up to a man of average height and stick her breast directly in his mouth. She smiled at him, her features too astonishing to be obstructed by hair.

His voice vanished.

But he nodded at her. Then he looked away. Then he wished he hadn't looked away.

A moment later she was standing near his table, looking around the room, coffee in hand.

All the seats in Starbucks were filled. Except the one in front of him.

She smiled. "Is this seat taken?"

He stood up like a gentleman, motioned at the seat.

She got comfortable in her chair, took off her coat, put her purse in her lap.

He asked, "What are you drinking?"

"Caramel Macchiato. I'm addicted. Have to have one as soon as I wake up. Then I have to have a blueberry green-tea Frappuccino before I go to bed. Starbucks gets my money."

He motioned at his coffee. "Same here. One in the morning. One at night. Addicted."

Then she asked, "What are you drinking?"

"Coffee in the morning. Black with sugar. Triple grande mocha with nonfat later on."

She checked her watch. "Was crazy getting here. You see all the police and news stations on the bridge?"

"What's going on? Filming a movie or something?"

"You didn't hear about the woman who jumped off the bridge?"

"This bridge?"

"You're joking. You're sitting here and didn't know what was going on out there?"

"Just got to London. Literally. Walked in jet-lagged and got a cup of coffee."

She sipped. "Here on holiday or business? I'm guessing business."

"The suit gave it away, huh?"

"That and being near the financial district. How long you here?"

"Looks like I'll be here a couple of days."

"What brings you here? What business?"

He remembered all the real estate businesses that had lined Shad Thames. He said, "Looking at real estate investments. Had a meeting with agents at Rive, another at Cluttons."

"You like the area?"

"Yeah. It's calm. Kind of secluded. Peaceful. Queen's Walk looks like a good place to take a jog. Was looking at the terrace houses. And apartments. For investment."

"I love it over here. Bakeries. Wine merchants. Indian restaurants. Everything."

She looked at him, her eyes focused on his broken nose. He waited for her to ask.

He was ready to lie. Amazed him how he kept track of all of his lies.

She said, "You're American."

He nodded. "American. You?"

"I'm Motswana."

"What country is that?"

"Botswana. Miss Universe was from Lobatse, Botswana."

"Didn't know that."

"When Mpule Kwelagobe won Miss Universe, it was ecstatic at home, never before have we won such a coveted prize. She really represented us. Look her up on Wikipedia."

"I'll make sure I do that." He smiled. "So you're Motswana from Botswana."

"Sure am."

"Is that where they are razing the villages, killing men, women, and children?"

"I think you're thinking of Darfur. I'm not from there. It's tragic and horrible there."

"Not good with African geography. Sorry. Where's your homeland?"

"Southern Africa."

"Never would've guessed you were African. I mean, South African."

"Hell no." She laughed, but she had some attitude. "Not *South* African. Botswana really hate being referred to as South Africans just because people don't understand the difference between South Africa and Botswana, or that they don't know none other than South Africa."

"So it's Southern Africa."

"Not South Africa."

"Educate me. I like to get things like that right. I don't know much about Africans. But I can relate, in some ways. People over here think all Americans are the same and we're not."

"The way you call me African. It's funny."

"What's funny about that?"

"I wasn't African until I left Africa."

"Sorry? What were you in Africa?"

"At home I am Motswana. I leave home and they call me *African*. They talk about Africa like it's a borough. Africa is a *continent*. So, that irritates me to no end. No matter where you are from—Ethiopia, South Africa, Niger—we lose our identity and become African. Like when you leave America, they call you American. I'm sure in America they call you something else."

"Texan. Live in Texas. So I get called a lot of names. Not many flattering."

She laughed a little. "I've heard of Texas. Is that near California or New York?"

"Neither. Middle of America, as far south as you can go before hitting Mexico."

"My American geography . . . sorry. All I know for sure is New York and California."

"Texas is in the south. Right above Mexico. Texas is the second-largest state."

"What's the largest?"

"Alaska. About twice the size of Texas. Alaska is north and west, next to Canada."

"How big is Texas?"

"Takes two days to drive across Texas."

"Two days? To drive across one state?"

"Two days."

"Good Lord. I could be in ten countries in two days."

"Well, when Texas was founded, they had a provision that it could be broken up into ten smaller states, but I guess they never got around to it. Yep. Two days to drive across Texas."

"I'd go crazy if I were in a car that long."

They laughed.

He said, "I don't know anything about Botswana."

She told him that she had gone to Our Lady of the Desert Primary School from ages six to twelve, then to Mater Spei College until she was seventeen. After that, Botswana Institute of Administration & Commerce, then to Birmingham College of Food.

He said, "Birmingham, Alabama?"

"Birmingham, England. It's north of here."

"Food college?"

"I wanted to be a chef. Wanted to have my own restaurant. And I will one day."

"So you can cook?"

"Of course. Now I work and go to Bournville College on the weekends."

She told him she was on the way to work. He offered to walk

her out. He followed her across the rugged roadway, streets made of uneven brick, maybe to give that cobblestone feel. They took to the stairs, went up, came out almost at the spot he had dropped the WAG.

It was amazing.

Above, all across the bridge were police cars and ambulances. News reporters as well.

People were looking over the railing like it was a tourist attraction. Yards away people lined up to visit the Tower, where hundreds were executed. Murder was entertainment. He wondered if he had earned a spot on that tour. Wondered if soon people would come from all over the world to see this spot, if they would have cameras and pose in front of Death's handiwork the same way other tourists lined up to visit the horrors of the London Dungeon. Almost twenty pounds to watch re-created gruesome events, scenes of gory torture, murders, atrocities, group rates available. He could only hope his work would one day be included.

She said, "Did you hear what they said when we were walking by?"

"What did they say?"

"That they think the woman was dead before she was in the water."

"Thought you said she jumped."

"I did. People jump from the bridges all the time. A man jumped from London Bridge last week. They never found his body. Now they are saying she was killed and thrown into the river."

"That's horrible. What is this world coming to?"

"Crazy things happen here. Did you know on the tubes, people jump in front of the trains all the time? Especially on New Year's Eve. So many people kill themselves that way."

Dark skies and chilly winds, they walked toward the tube, commotion behind them.

He looked down at the muddy waters. An old fear rose up inside him.

Old horrors never died.

He remembered when he was a child. His father had thrown him into a lake. To teach him how to swim. He remembered that terror. Drowning. Remembered thinking he was going to die. He held his breath. Suffocating. Remembered thinking that was a horrible way to die.

He remembered waking up, coughing the water out of his lungs.

He remembered how he cried.

He remembered how his brothers and sisters laughed.

He remembered how once he caught his breath, his old man threw him right back in.

He hated water. He hated rivers. He hated lakes. He hated swimming pools.

She asked, "Where are you going? Business meeting?"

"No business for a while. Looking for a hotel in this area."

She pointed. "Over there. Novotel. That hotel is nice. It has a very nice gym."

Then an awkward moment. How to say good-bye. He didn't want to say good-bye.

He asked, "Where do you work?"

"East London."

"Anyway I can . . . uh . . . call you or . . . something."

"Depends."

"On what?"

"Where am I from?"

"Batswana."

"*Bots*wana. Not *Bats*wana."

"Botswana."

"I should give you a lashing."

"So I messed up a vowel."

She laughed. "What do they call me at home?"

"Motswana."

"What part of Africa am I from?"

"Southern Africa, not South Africa."

"Impressive."

"Do I get a gold star on my paper?'

"You have to stay after school and write *Botswana* on the board a thousand times."

"Bummer."

She handed him one of her cards. The Bank of New York. One Canada Square.

He saw that she had already had the business card in the palm of her hand.

Her name was Tebogo Otsile. Assistant treasurer. Corporate trust.

She said, "Tebogo. But they call me Tebby."

"My name is Bruno. And people call me Bruno."

He smiled. She smiled.

She said, "Call anytime. Or e-mail. If not, it was still nice meeting you, Bruno."

"I'll call you, Tebby. Just tell me when is a good time."

"Anytime, Bruno. Call if you need something, call if you just want to call."

"Maybe we could meet at Starbucks and chat."

"That would be lovely."

"You could tell me more about Botswana."

"And you can tell me more about America. I plan to move there one day."

"Do you?"

"Yes. I want to become an American. I want to have my own restaurant. I'm desperate to leave London and move to America. I'd go to the airport and leave right now if I could."

There a pause between them.

She said, "I love your American accent."

Then she waved good-bye and headed into the Tower Hill tube station.

The last thing he saw as she vanished was her smile.

And that angelic whiteness in a sea of dark and dreary colors.

His cellular ran again. Not the personal one. The hotline.

He answered, "Talk to me."

All the shyness in his voice now replaced by brutal harshness.

"Located a Desert Eagle. Titanium finish. Found it in Banglatown."

"That was quick."

"Everybody knows everybody in this area. Made a few calls. Called a guy I know out at the military base and he put me in contact with a supplier I know in Brixton. Found what you need in the East End. Sure you want a Desert Eagle? Weighs five pounds. Supplier is getting it, adding a markup to stay in the loop. So pricewise you're looking at about seventeen hundred pounds."

"How do I get it from your contact?"

"Already arranged pickup."

"How will I know the contact?"

"My contact will recognize you."

He touched his nose. "What about the cleanup job?"

"Will have information on that job later today. No later than tomorrow."

"If you don't have it tomorrow, I'm on a plane."

"Understood."

He was told where to pick up the Desert Eagle.

He hung up, then looked at the white-and-gray business card in his calloused hand.

Tebby never asked about his broken nose. But he had never mentioned her bald head.

His other phone rang. The friends and family line.

He answered, "Hello. This is Edward Johnson."

"And this is Melanie Marie Johnson."

"Melanie." He laughed. "Hey, baby. How's daddy's little princess?"

"Mommy told me you were in London."

"Yeah. You mad? I'm going to have to stay a few days."

"No, it's cool. I want the all Harry Potter books."

"You already have all the Harry Potter books."

"Not from London. I want them with the London publisher's cover and the price tag in pounds. I want it authentic. In hardback if you can find them. Please, Daddy, please?"

"Okay. I'll try and find them."

"I want to make all of my friends jealous."

"That's not a guarantee. I'll do my best."

"And magnets. Buy me Harry Potter magnets. I'll pay you back out my allowance."

"You always say that."

"And take a picture of the *Cutty Sark*. Kisses. Love you, Daddy."

"Love you too."

They hung up.

Damn shame how a ten-year-old kid had him doing flips for her.

He smiled. If only buying Harry Potter books could fix all of his problems.

So little joy in the world. He'd make sure his ten-year-old got as much joy as possible.

He checked into Novotel. He had wanted something more discreet. But the woman he had met. Tebby. Maybe she lived in the area. She was at that Starbucks, after all. Maybe she'd meet him at Starbucks again. Or in the area for dinner and drinks. He checked in, got his room key but didn't go up to his suite, instead he came right back out for the tube.

He wanted to have on clean clothes when he saw her again.

Maybe a nice European suit with one-and-a-quarter-inch cuffs.

No way he could wear the same clothes and see her again.

A Motswana woman from Botswana. That in itself was intriguing.

His phone rang again. The hotline.

He answered, "Talk to me."

"The contract is on a guy who uses the handle Gideon. He calls himself Gideon."

"That's it? Just Gideon?"

"That's it."

"Was expecting something more menacing."

"Well, Bruno isn't exactly gruesome."

"It's Italian. It's Mafia. I like the *Godfather* movies. Bruno is a kick-ass name."

"Well, this guy calls himself Gideon."

"What else you got for me?"

"Got more information coming in later."

"Don't keep yanking my chain."

"I assure you that a package is being sent to me as we speak."

"Could you be a little more vague, Sam?"

"My apologies to you, Bruno. They are dragging on the other end."

"Well, tell them to be professional. Respect my fucking time."

"But I should have the info soon."

"When is soon? Thanksgiving? Christmas?"

"Within the hour. In the meantime, my cranky friend, get some sleep."

He rubbed his jet-lagged eyes. "Call me when you get the package."

He hung up.

Harry Potter books.

He had to find Harry Potter books.

If his princess wanted Harry Potter himself, he'd kidnap the boy, take the bastard to her.

He was anxious to take this contract, kill the target, then go back home, eat some authentic Mexican food.

As far as he was concerned, Gideon was already a dead man.

And that was nothing but business. He was in the business of killing.

Fourteen

like oil on my skin

I was inside Benjy's deli.

The dead entertainer I was supposed to look for was standing across the street.

I was on the edge of the theater district, six lanes of insane traffic separating me from the Dominion Theatre. On top of the Dominion a larger-than-life-but-smaller-than-legend-size golden statue of Freddie Mercury was on the roof. The Queen Musical, *We Will Rock You*.

I was waiting between Chinatown and Bloomsbury, underneath the shadows of Centre Point Tower. Next door was a grungy-looking theatre-club that advertised Betty-somebody and some punk-rock-looking group whose name was the acronym GAY. I sipped on a green tea, reading Metro.Co.UK, an article about poor areas having the fewest free ATMs. The poor getting scammed, being once again penalized for being poor.

I looked up, didn't see her, checked my watch, went back to the paper.

Channel 4 was planning to screen Britain's first marathon masturbation event, called Wankathon. They were giving prizes to people who could have the most orgasms and masturbate the longest. Faking an orgasm could get you disqualified, and the record for the longest masturbation session was eight and a half hours. The Brits were special people.

Saw nothing about Tampa. Had to let that go. Was getting obsessed.

I looked at my watch and yawned. Sleep was trying to invade my body.

The people next to me were speaking French with a distinctive accent and vocabulary, "Secret Lovers" was on the sound system, Atlantic Starr sounding twice as popular here as they did on the other side of the pond. No matter if I was at a club over in Brixton or walking through one of the shops in Oxford Circus, I always heard more American music than I did British.

Above me, a small television was on. Still on the story about the dead WAG.

I looked across the street at the tube exit. A Filipina with skin the hue of sunrise over Ipanema was over in the crowd by Freddie Mercury, coming up from the tube.

She put her cellular up to her face.

My cellular rang.

I answered, "I'm inside Benjy's."

She hung up.

Black jeans. White sweater. Long black coat. Umbrella up high.

First she crossed in front of Centre Point; that left her one more intersection to negotiate before she made it to me. She passed by a man with a sign advertising Internet access at the cost of one British pound per hour. She passed by two police officers. They don't carry guns, just handcuffs. Hard to be afraid of a gunless cop. A cop with no gun was a security guard.

London was filled with thieves. On the tubes and in stores were continuous announcements to watch out for pickpockets, who preyed on the inattentive. Cafés had signs posted telling patrons to beware of thieves they called slashers, nimble-fingered crooks who would cut open your bags and catch the goods as they fell out. Plenty of nimble fingers in the UK lot who worked in groups and had mastered the art of distraction and blocking.

The woman coming my way would put all of London's criminals to shame.

Her name was Arizona. People in my dark world knew her as Queen Scamz.

I fell in lust with her the moment I laid eyes on her, as most straight men did. That was in North Hollywood, when she was young girl who had nothing but ambition in her eyes. Back then she was in love with Scamz, the man who slapped her silly, the man who had made her his number one, then, in the blink of an eye, replaced her with her own sister. Back then Arizona was a flight attendant, using her job pre-9/11 to be a mule for some of Scamz's illegal ventures, and her sister was working as a teller at a Wells Fargo in Hollywood. Arizona had brought her in on a job. Once her sister met Scamz, she had ambitions of her own, and her desires paid no mind to upstaging and dethroning Arizona.

We had that in common. Both of us had been betrayed by people we cared about.

Arizona crossed the street. Two men were about ten yards behind her, had been behind her since she exited the tube. Both of those men wore thick coats on top of black hoodies.

Arizona came in the door, umbrella at her side, bags under her eyes, lips tight.

I watched the men who were keeping up with her.

They kept going toward Leicester Square, now looking at other women.

I rubbed my temples, released my paranoia, let it float up toward the ozone.

Arizona made her way to where I was sitting, said, "You're early."

"Early is on time. On time is late."

She nodded. "And late is unacceptable."

I stood to hug her, but she extended her hand.

I said, "So it's like that."

She nodded once, her hand still extended, firm in her decision.

I extended my hand for a curt handshake, all business.

Last time I saw her we did things that would make porn stars take notes.

She opened the *Evening Standard* newspaper in her hand. Once again the Big Bad Wolf stared at me. It was international. Nothing to be proud of. It had followed me across the pond.

I said, "Already saw it."

She said, "This place is too small, too crowded. Let's walk and talk."

We fought the crowd, passed by Borders. Soho Original Books. Blackwell's. Lovejoys. Murder One. Henry Pordes. One look down any street and it was obvious that the British were literary. Bookshops were every ten feet, if not less, each one filled with book-hungry customers.

She asked, "WAG job?"

"Wasn't me. Sounded like a crime of passion. That was a hit?"

"Heard somebody was looking for somebody to take that contract."

"And you didn't refer me?"

"Needed you for horse-and-grass country. Need you to handle Lakenheath."

Brazilian. Indian. Chinese. International food was everywhere, just like hiking down Broadway in New York, or being on South Beach, minus the palm trees and sunshine. There were enough Burger Kings and McDonald's and Pizza Huts to make every foreigner feel at home. But it was the other shops I always noticed. In my world Starbucks ruled; here Starbucks was outnumbered by both bookshops and alternative coffee spots like Caffè Nero.

I said, "Why you pick me for this job?"

"Got fucked over on a Katrina scam."

"You know what I mean. I know him."

"He's afraid of you."

"And I'd be a fool to go after him."

"Asshole owes me a lot of money. No one else I can send to make my point. Everyone else is afraid of him. He knows you. Respects you. He'll be cool with you. He'll listen to you."

"How much he get you for?"

"The amount is irrelevant. But it's a lot. I taught him how to work FEMA like FEMA was nothing more than a pigeon drop. He made a quick grip. Refused to pay my percentage."

"Double cross on a Katrina scam? Scamming a scammer?"

"You know? Motherfuckers still don't think I'm for real. Some of them misogynistic pricks still refuse to take a woman seriously, Gideon. Looks like I have to send out another message."

"Hard business for women. Maybe you should get out and slow down. Have babies."

"I'm not the type for being barefoot and pregnant."

"Too bad. You have pretty feet."

"I was going to call Switchblade Molly in on this one, but she's too messy."

"She did some good work for your boy Scamz back in the day."

"She did. But that was ten years ago. When she was younger. She earned her moniker one hundred times over."

"I'll ride up to Lakenheath Village and take care of it."

We hurried by theaters, coffeehouses, bars, and Internet cafés, put her umbrella up high, dodged puddles, and headed toward one of the busiest spots in London. She told me there was a nice Starbucks across from the Odeon, this location being the home of the UK movie premieres, the UK version of Holly-wood's Grauman's Chinese Theatre. The area had been cleaned up. The small patch in the center of the square used to be a haven for junkies. Now it was safe to wander through the grass without tripping over piles of old, used needles, and still-damp condoms.

She asked, "You been back to New Orleans since Katrina?"

"Nope. Just saw it on the news. How bad was it up close?"

"Ninth Ward looks like a bomb was dropped on it. Houses stacked on top of houses. Cars on top of cars. Insurance companies don't want to pay. That's the scam right there. They blame the flooding on the levee, not Katrina. Don't get me started on that crap. Material cost has shot through the roof. And gas prices are crazy. And they are still pulling dead bodies out of the buildings. Hell, most of the evacuees are running scams. Half of them weren't doing anything before Katrina, then they were getting two a grand a month from FEMA, so they came up big-time."

"FEMA. Bet you tapped into that and made a mint."

"FEMA stands for Fuck Everybody with Melanin in America."

"Of course."

"And, yeah, I hit FEMA harder than Katrina hit New Orleans."

We passed by several spots to buy theater tickets. Saw a big poster for *One Flew over the Cuckoo's Nest*, Christian Slater starring in that one. *Stomp* had huge posters too.

I spied the TKTS booth, the only freestanding building in the square, but didn't see any ads for *Rent*. So many productions were posted. Impossible to notice everything.

I held Arizona's umbrella up over our heads as we entered the square and passed by all the tourist traps and souvenir shops, made our way across the cobblestone walkway leading to the center of the square and went inside Starbucks. Arizona ordered a latte. I went to the counter, ordered a house coffee, then found out that they didn't honor the U.S.'s Starbucks gift cards in this country. The man behind the counter apologized, and I paid in pounds and pence.

I told the server, "Lots of coffee drinkers. Thought Brits liked teas."

"There are no real Brits left in the London area. Immigrants have taken over. And immigrants bring their own tastes with them. I'm a Brit by birth and I only drink tea."

I thanked him and moved on.

This Starbucks was large, most of the seating being in the back of the space. By the time I had put four sugars in my tall cup of joe, Arizona had a table in the back of the room, away from everyone, but still surrounded with enough noise to keep other people out of our conversation.

She said, "Did you see the statue of Shakespeare out front?"

"Shakespeare was a master plagiarist. He stole Francis Bacon's work."

"Before we have that debate, let's get to the business I have for you."

Arizona opened her bag, took out a folder, a profile on my target.

She said, "Inside is a travel card good for all week."

"Why didn't you get me an Oyster card? I could've done a top up."

"Don't use an Oyster. It's an electronic card, just like the Octopus card in Hong Kong. Those cards leave electronic bread crumbs. So every time you touch in or touch out, Big Brother knows where you are. Use an Oyster and Scotland Yard knows your travel habits. They know where you get on the tube, where you get off the tube. They know where you get on the buses."

"You have an Oyster card."

"Mine was bought with a hot credit card. Under a fake name. A man's name. And I switch Oyster cards throughout the day."

"So you have extras."

"I'm prepared."

She dug into her bag, took out another Oyster card, threw it to me.

I said, "You think like a man."

"I'm too smart to be a man. That's why I'm a woman."

"Did you go to terrorist training school or something?"

"I'm too smart to be a terrorist too."

I yawned. "All the CCTV cameras. London is starting to feel like one big-ass prison."

"Put up some barbed wire and it would be. Surveillance cameras are both underground and on the platforms. Cameras are on the buses. Bobbies walking the street like guards."

"Are you a terrorist?"

"Just letting you know. If you're traveling, if you're trying to not be seen, trying not to be found, pay cash for a travel card, ride the tube, blend with the crowd, and vanish in the system."

Then she handed me a passport, this one deep red. It had the same photo as my blue one, the one made in the U.S. For the next few hours I would be a British citizen named Clive.

I asked, "This clean?"

"From a newborn. That's the best way to do identity theft. Not from the dead, but from a newborn. Takes years, since a newborn or a kid won't apply for credit anytime soon."

She tapped the information.

She said, "Handle Lakenheath as soon as you can."

Her fingers lingered on the information. I reached for her hand. She jerked it away.

I asked, "Why the attitude?"

"As soon as it's done, the rest of the money will be transferred to your account."

We sat there, Arizona finishing off the last of her coffee.

The moment reminded me of sitting at the kitchen table and watching my mother drink Folgers coffee in the morning. We used to leave our rattrap in the heart of the neglected

Dalton Village, abandon West Charlotte, and ride through the sweet, much loved areas like Myers Park, ride by those homes in South Charlotte screaming and pointing like I was on a ride at Six Flags Over Georgia. Looked at big homes the way people admired art at the Louvre. Loved them in the wintertime. Didn't really snow in Charlotte, but the ice storms would come and make all the bare trees look like they were silver master-pieces. So much beauty inside that danger.

When I gazed at Arizona, I saw the opposite, so much danger inside beauty.

Arizona spoke in a soft, almost vulnerable tone. "I started watching *Battlestar Galactica*."

"No shit?"

"Because of you, I watched that show because of you."

"You say that like it's a bad thing."

"Liked the Cylons. Love when slaves rise up and defeat the master. Racism. Battles amongst the classes. Sexism. Fear. So much hate wrapped around one television show."

"Like . . . life. Hate has put a lot of money in my pockets."

She said, "I have a theory on why people don't respect black Americans."

"I'm listening."

"Because black Americans never rose up and defeated their master. They were enslaved by the master and had to be freed by the master. There was no victory."

"The Cylons will be respected."

"No, the Cylons will be *feared*. That's *better* than being re-spected."

Her intense stare, it didn't wane.

Without transition she asked, "Who's the woman who went to the hotel with you?"

I took a breath. "A square. Met her on the plane."

"Don't mess with squares. What do you know about her?"

"She was looking for a room, checked out the hotel."

"Is that right? Where is she now?"

"Well, Arizona, I offered you first right of refusal."

"Keep it professional, Gideon."

"So New York and Chapel Hill didn't happen?"

"No idea what you're talking about."

"You're breaking my heart."

"When did you get a heart?"

"Why are you being so damn nasty to me?"

"Doesn't matter. I'm a bang-and-go kind of gal anyway. At least that's how you see me."

"Yeah, you're breaking my heart."

"Better yours than mine. Actually mine has already been shattered."

"Can't break what has already been broken."

"Abso-fucking-lutely."

"Hold up. How did you know someone came to the hotel with me?"

"Maybe I came to see you. Maybe I thought about Chapel Hill and New York and wanted to see you again. Maybe I was going to surprise you and get beans and eggs and toast for breakfast. Maybe I was outside your hotel room. Maybe I heard you fucking your concubine."

If water fell on her skin, it would sizzle away.

She dug inside her bag, took out three CDs. Miles, Wes, and Coltrane.

She put them on the table, slid those legends toward me, her anger controlled.

I had given her those CDs as a gift. Now she was rejecting the memory.

I said, "Keep 'em."

Arizona shook her head. I saw the tempest in her expression, the frost in her eyes.

That femme fatale owned beauty and more danger than an ice storm in North Carolina.

Then I saw another kind of danger.

I said, "Sit down."

"Fuck you."

I gave her a broad smile. "No, sit down."

"I'm not your whore. I don't work for you."

I added a light laugh. "We're being watched."

She hesitated. "Don't play with me."

"We're being trailed."

Fifteen

chinatown

That had Arizona's attention.

I told her that the men who had followed her from the tube were in the room. Their hoodies had been pulled back. I got a clear view of our present danger. One was bald, the other sported locks. They had slipped inside and posted up in the section of Starbucks between us and the front door. There was only one way in and one way out. They weren't that close. The coffeeshop was large, could be divided into three sections, us being in the back third. Neither had a coffee or a newspaper. They were waiting for something, and I knew it wasn't the tube.

I told Arizona all of that with smiles and laughter.

Arizona sat back down, did that real ladylike, crossed her legs, played with her hair.

Then she chuckled and smiled like everything was okay.

I did the same, kept the game going.

She asked, "You sure they're following me? They could be following you."

"They were behind you when you showed up at Freddie Mercury."

"Who are they?"

"Thought they might be part of the Tampa crew."

"Thought you handled them."

"Rappers are like roaches."

"Cockroaches."

"Can't kill 'em all."

"Not even with a nuclear explosion."

Between us, we'd offended so many people that death or justice could come at any time with any face. I'd been that death for many people, enough to earn me damn near a million.

Arizona tensed. Then she smiled again. "Okay, I'll leave first. See if they follow me."

"Which way?"

"Pass by Häagen-Dazs Café, get to Charing Cross, make a left, first narrow street turn left again, that'll take you off the main drag and into Chinatown. Head toward car park on the right."

I nodded. "Left out of Starbucks and two more lefts to car park."

"Gideon. If it's the police on my ass, let it go, okay? Let them take me and let it go."

That hurt my heart. "Just make it around the block as soon as you can."

"You know the rules. If it's the police and they're after you, I'll have to do the same."

"I know."

Arizona took a small package out of her bag.

She said, "Forgot to put this jewelry with your special order."

She slid that package across the table toward me.

Arizona picked up Miles, Trane, and Wes, held them in her hand, put on a sweet smile, blew me a kiss good-bye, got up, and walked away. I picked up a left-behind copy of *The Daily Telegraph*, pretended I was reading about the twelve who bankrolled Tony Blair into a loan crisis, then spied toward the front of Starbucks again, toward the two men who had raised my senses.

I wanted them to be after me, not Arizona. I'd lead them in the opposite direction.

But the second she walked out of Starbucks, they were hot on her trail.

As soon as they hit the front door, I was on my feet, grabbed what Arizona had left behind, opened it as I moved with quickness, walking fast enough to keep them in sight.

Brass knuckles. Arizona had given me brass knuckles.

Arizona was making her way through the sea of people crowding Leicester Square.

They were focused on her, gradually getting closer, keeping her in sight.

I was right behind them, separated by a decent crowd of tourists and locals.

I expected one—if not both—to look back. They never did.

They weren't pros. Not even close. But that didn't make them any less of a threat.

They got closer to Arizona.

I sped up, got closer to them.

The neon signs and Eastern structures of Chinatown rose up.

Two lefts and a right later, I ran into a wall of Chinese food.

The stench of egg fried rice and lo mein took me back to Tampa, turned my stomach.

Arizona moved through all the Asians on the plaza, strolled like she was about to pass by the car park and head toward the section of Soho dedicated to the queer and gothic, but she made an abrupt right turn, her casual walk changing into a fierce run.

That sudden change in direction and sprint surprised her stalkers.

The men broke into a trot trying to catch her.

Arizona was fast, moved like greased lightning.

She'd been chased before. She'd been chased and never been caught.

I broke into a sprint, cold and damp air in my face, trying to keep up with them.

They raced inside the covered lot, looked left and right, heard something, footsteps running, and they ran up the curved exit. When they made it to the next floor, they were winded. Confused. They looked between cars, then looked behind them, saw me standing there. Watching. Relaxed. Hands in my pockets, I faced my new dilemma eye to eye.

I said, "Amazing how she vanishes. Like smoke. Poof. She's gone."

A few automobiles and a motorcycle exited the car park with us staring.

We were up a level, away from the eyes of the public.

I took a step forward, my foot landing in a puddle, splashing water.

The one with dreadlocks was five foot eleven, the shorter of the two. His silent friend was taller, larger, owned the mean face. Obviously the enforcer.

I asked, "Who sent you?"

"Who the fuck are you?" Dreadlocks was the spokesman.

Hands in pockets, eyes on my new friends, I inhaled deeply, let it out slowly.

They came closer. Closer. I went numb. Detached myself from the moment.

Then they were close enough to hurt me.

The smaller one stayed back at least three steps.

The big one came at me ready to do damage. He came after me like I had gone after others. I held my position. Nervous. Scared. Excited. Sweating. Numb. I was all of that.

I knew twenty-two ways to kill a man with my bare hands. Buy only one way to die.

In an accented voice Dreadlocks asked, "Where is Queen Scamz?"

A car was zooming down the ramp. The car was half the size of a Mini Cooper, even smaller than the popular Smart car. It was one of the short and slender LUV cars big enough for two anorexic midgets. That car was quiet and moved like a bullet.

The car hit Dreadlocks dead on, flipped him, and knocked his ass to the side. His dreads whipped around his face as he grunted and slammed into one of the concrete pillars, went down headfirst, landed in a way that told me he wouldn't be getting up anytime soon, if at all.

Arizona put on her brakes, got out of that fuel-efficient weapon on four wheels.

The big one that had come up me with fists doubled, that crash had stolen his attention. Now he was suffering blow after blow, bending, grunting, bleeding, going down hard and fast. Ten hard and fast blows from my right hand to his face and ribs left his face broken beyond belief. I had slipped on the brass knuckles Arizona had slid me. He'd wake up in a London hospital, pissing blood, a tube in his nose, and a shit bag strapped to his hip.

Then I was surprised. The other one, after being run down, moaned and got up.

Head bloodied, dreadlocks swaying, he staggered toward the exit. His right arm looked broken. He was whimpering and limping like a monster out of a late-night creature feature. Moved like he was in "Thriller." Arizona's arms pumped and her heels clacked on the pavement as she ran after him.

He tried to speed up, but only made it to a slow, stumbling, pain-filled trot.

Arizona stopped running, walked after him, looking around, weapon in hand.

He must've been delirious, in shock, because he headed up the ramp.

Arizona didn't run, just walked after the crippled man.

I was a few feet behind her, made sure the one on the ground stayed on the ground.

They vanished around a curve.

When I caught up with the pandemonium, Arizona wasn't walking anymore.

She was focused, aiming, had her arm pulled back. Knife in hand. She slung her blade.

A painful sound echoed from around the corner.

Then Arizona was walking again, her steps a lot quicker.

Dreadlocks was on the ground trying to pull a five-inch blade out of the back of his thigh.

I told Arizona, "Your aim is pretty good."

"Was aiming at his neck."

"Your aim sucks."

"Fuck you."

"Thought I taught you better."

"Well, I'm not as good as you. But I'm good enough, dammit."

While Arizona stood over Dreadlocks and put pressure on the blade, I put my shoe stiff against the back of his neck, my weight pushing his face deep into the cold pavement. Fear rose up from the trembling man. Piss drained from between his legs and mixed with his river of blood.

Arizona frowned at me. "Do you mind?"

"Sorry."

I backed away, became her wingman.

This was her show. I kept a lookout and let her have it her way.

Arizona's voice filled with anger as she demanded, "Who hired you?"

He refused to answer.

She brought the blade out again.

For a moment I thought she was about to cut his throat.

He battled with the hurting.

She pressed on the knife. "See what I mean? Motherfuckers think I'm a joke."

Arizona brought the blade down into his arm; that improved his hearing and memory.

"Lakenheath. Call came from Lakenheath. Military guy. That's all I know."

He tried to scream, but the blade had been moved to his neck; that muted his agony.

Arizona fumed, "How much you get paid?"

"Twenty-five hundred euros."

Either way Arizona was insulted at such a low offering.

She asked, "Where you from?"

"Haarlem."

"You don't sound like you're from New York."

I interrupted, "His accent is Dutch. He's talking about Haarlem in the Netherlands."

Arizona snapped at me, "Do you mind?"

I raised my hand in apology.

She took her fury back to Dreadlocks.

"Holland? You came from Holland?"

He nodded again. "On the train. We came on the train."

"To kill me?"

He didn't answer. She pressed on that knife. Drew more blood.

He confessed, "Hurt you. Break your arms. Your knees. Cut off all of your hair. Rape you. But we weren't going to rape you. Honest."

"Just cut off my hair and break my knees and crush all my bones."

"That's all."

Her eyes told me she was about to become a murderer.

Then she backed away.

She asked, "Are we done? Or do I need to take this to the next level?"

Again he managed a nod, then he shook his head.

I looked at Arizona.

She shook her head. "Fucking amateurs."

Arizona knew what this was about.

Arizona took her blade, the blade that had her fingerprints all over the handle, and wiped the blood on the man's coat, dropped the weapon inside her bag, and walked around the curve toward the edges of Chinatown, headed back the same way we had come with a generous pace.

I called out to her, asked, "What about your car?"

"Not mine. Hot-wired it."

"That was quick."

"Used to be quicker. Leave it where it is."

A few seconds passed, enough time for Arizona to get to the first level.

I headed toward the big guy I had taken down.

He was fucked up, crawling across the pavement, trying to run away from his pain.

I walked by him.

I dropped the brass knuckles inside my pocket.

Looked back at the wrecked LUV and the men on the ground.

I buttoned my coat, adjusted my scarf, and walked away.

At the bottom of the ramp, hundreds of Asians were moving through the area, a few were looking at mouth of the car park. They looked at it all from a distance. Maybe they had heard the whole thing. I expected them to either point fingers or run away from me. But they stood, smoked hand-rolled cigarettes, and watched in silence. Like we were a show on HBO.

Arizona was standing to my left, the way we had come.

Head down, shoulders hunched, I headed that way.

When I got to her, she pushed the CDs back into my hands.

Two men lay bleeding on frozen concrete and we were back to that heated argument.

I said, "These were for you."

"Take them back to your hotel and give them to your concubine."

She moved on, shoulders hunched, her head down as well.

Arizona lit up a Djarum, walked away blowing smoke, leaving the scent of cloves behind.

I followed her. She'd become a female version of James Dean.

She sped up.

Now she was running from me, heading across St. Martin's Lane into Covent Garden, her cellular phone in hand. She was outside the tube station before she slowed down.

My cellular rang. I answered.

Arizona snapped, "Stop following me."

"I'm trying to make sure you're okay."

"If I need you, I will call you."

I pressed on, "When I finish here, I want to get away from all of this. I want to take you with me."

"Gideon, I'm not your girlfriend. Not trying to be. Never will be."

In a few words she stripped my heart down to nothing.

I hung up.

My phone rang. It was Arizona.

She said, "Look, on the business tip, I have another job for you."

"Outside of the work here in London?"

"Holland. Looks like I need to send a message to someone in Holland."

"The Holland boys said they were working for Laken-heath."

"Don't believe everything you hear."

"What do you know that I don't know?"

"Just handle Lakenheath. Holland will be there. Go do what you do best."

That put fire in my gut.

"Now on personal level, stop following me, Gideon. Please stop, okay?"

She stopped and faced me, stood waiting for me to leave her alone.

She said, "No expectations, no disappointments."

She hung up. I did the same.

Dark clouds clung to heaven's floor, rain fell, I turned around, went the other way.

Way down, at least a block away, thought I saw bandages on the nose of a bald man in a dark suit. The man from the airplane. He was turning around, hurrying away from me.

Like he had been following me. Following us. Now he had been seen.

I jogged to the corner and looked into the crowd. Didn't see him. Saw lots of men in suits. But none were bald. Too many narrow streets feeding into narrow streets to check them all. Maybe paranoia and tiredness were teaming up with my guilt and making me see things. I rubbed my eyes and looked back. Hurried back toward where I had left Arizona. She was gone. Didn't know if she had kept going through Covent Garden toward the Embankment or had hurried down into the tube station.

I called Arizona's cellular. Her calls were being diverted.

I left her a message. "I think those guys had a wingman. Be careful. Hit me back."

Rain fell soft and easy. I crossed into Leicester Square, heard the wail of ambulances roaring toward Chinatown, saw policemen on BMW motorcycles zooming the same way.

I kept going, made a right at TGIF, moved by theaters and pubs, zigzagged toward the red-light district, always looking back, or checking windows to see if I was being trailed. The way the city was laid out, all the narrow streets that fed into even narrower streets, with the number of tube stations and places to vanish in an instant, no wonder Jack the Ripper was never caught.

I stopped at the edges of the red-light district, an area that, in the middle of the day, looked respectable; vendors were out in the cold selling fruit, fish, odds and ends. People were inside Somerfield food-shopping. Other were at the various porn stores, shopping there too.

Men were slipping inside narrow doors that led to Russian and Asian pussy for sale.

I looked up, saw African whores, Spanish whores, red lights in almost every window.

I moved on toward Oxford Circus, Thelma on my mind.

I'd find her one day.

No matter where she'd run, I'd find her and finish what we'd started.

I stopped and bought warmer clothes.

Needed heavier jeans, thermals, a turtleneck, boots, and a short leather jacket that zipped. Had to dump what I had on, in case blood had splattered on me from the crime scene we'd just created. Thirty minutes later I came out in Soho looking brand-new from head to toe and in between, dumped my old clothes, then hit the main drag at Oxford Circus, an area as busy as Chicago's Magnificent Mile, blended with the crowd. I went down into the tube, waited on a Central Line train to take me to the Northern Line, would take that line one stop over to Goodge and get off there. I walked back to the room and grabbed my backpack.

Had to take the tube to the Liverpool station.

It was time to go visit a man on Arizona's behalf.

Like I had done for her when we connected in New York.

When that delinquent debt had to be settled.

Only this was somebody I knew.

We weren't the best of friends, but we were a long way from being enemies.

This was a merciless business.

A different kind of coldness came and hugged me.

The kind of iciness that came with my complex occupation.

It was time to bundle up and go to work.

My hands trembled again as I changed from the tube to the Stansted Express and headed toward horse-and-grass country. The place that in the summertime, with all the fertilizer in the air, they called horse-and-*smells-like-ass* country. My hands trembled the entire forty-six minutes I was on the train, trembled as the airport came in sight. They wouldn't stop trembling.

As I exited the train, that feeling of death moved through me, tried to cling to me, but I shook it off. In the middle of the terminal, people all around me, I stopped walking. A wave hit me. Coldness. Followed by numbness. Followed by an almost unbearable heat.

I looked down at the three CDs I still had in my hand.

Memories of New York clung to me. I thought about the fun we'd had in Chapel Hill.

I stuffed those CDs in my backpack and found my way to underground parking.

I walked until I found a row of motorcycles, stopped in front of a BMW 1200. Light blue, helmet attached to locking strap. Keys were in my backpack. I took out a black key and a red key. The black key opened the sidesaddles, where I found gloves. Two small bottles were there as well. One was a small bottle of Jack Daniel's. The other a special order. The same key also unlocked the helmet and started the engine. The bike was still warm. Hadn't been here too long.

Minutes after that, I was easing around the roundabout, getting a feel for the machine, then I was speeding down M11 north. Thoughts of Arizona, thoughts of Chapel Hill never left. As I changed from A11 to A14 and back to A11 again, as I zoomed down a two-lane highway by grass and horses and sheep, as I slowed for speed cameras as I entered Suffolk County, Miles, Wes, and Coltrane stayed on my mind.

Sixteen

contract killer

Docklands Light Railway.

Aboveground train. Heading toward Canary Wharf.

The man with the broken nose had been turned around all morning. He had taken the tube to Embankment. But he was supposed to be at Bank to catch the DLR. Embankment had sounded like Bank. When he realized he was at the wrong location, Embankment not Bank, he looked for Bank on the tube map again. That labyrinth of tubes was confusing. Didn't look like it was that far. Hoping to have better luck, he had taken to the streets, got lost again, ended up at Covent Garden, then hurried back inside the tube, took the Piccadilly to the Central Line, finally made it to Bank and the DLR.

Brits and their fucking accents. Felt like he was in a damn Harry Potter movie.

That reminded him. He had to find a bookstore. Had to buy books and magnets.

For a moment, when he was lost at Covent Garden, it felt like he was being followed.

But no one was there.

No one had boarded the train with him. No one on the platform shadowed him.

The ride was shoulder to shoulder.

People were forced to touch other people.

His personal space no longer existed.

He hated public transportation. One look and he could tell the tubes were a breeding ground for germs, people coughing and sneezing and blowing their noses all over, breathing the same germ-ridden air stop after stop, nasty hands touching the same seats and holding the same contaminated rails, everyone forced to be right up on each other in flu and cold season. Two hundred and seventy-five tube stations. Two hundred and seventy-five places to get contaminated. Maybe a million people crammed on the tube each day. If bin Laden dropped a virus at Victoria, London would be extinct in two days, the rest of the free world in less than a week.

He understood why people in Tokyo wore those Michael Jackson–style surgical masks.

The DLR was better. He had his own seat. A grubby seat, but he had his own space.

And he had a better view to see if he was being trailed.

The WAG had become the talk of London.

He had to make sure someone hadn't targeted him for cleanup.

That being-followed feeling he had had at Covent Garden had stayed with him.

Until now.

He let it go and took out his over-the-counter reading glasses, opened his self-help book.

He had his glasses on, adjusted over his bandaged nose, again reading pages in *Divorce for Dummies*. He didn't look up. His contact would know him. Hard for him to not be recognized, broken nose and all. Still, for some reason, even with that, he was invisible to most people.

No one ever noticed Clark Kent until he became Superman.

That always worked in his favor.

He put his book down and picked up a discarded *London Lite*. A sex-slave market was being operated out of Heathrow. Young Malaysian women were being tricked into coming to London, ending up working at brothels in Campden Hill Gardens, Notting Hill, and Hyde Park, a few feet from Tony Blair's swank Connaught Square property.

He shook his head. Would kill them all if they even glanced at his little girl.

The DLR stopped at West India Quay.

A small crowd rushed on the train. Men. Women pushing strollers. Boys with backpacks. Four teenage girls boarded last. One took a can of Red Bull out of her backpack. Another took out plastic cups. A third took out a bottle of Scotch and became the bartender.

They made drinks and moved to the front of the car. Like it was no big deal.

The fourth young girl was staring at him. He nodded. She stood up. Thin kid, five feet tall, if that. Black parachute pants with a thousand silver zippers. Black military shoes. Black hoodie with a white smiling face on the front. Red-and-black fingerless gloves, fingernails the color of midnight. Her hoodie was pulled down over her head, only parts of her face showing. Her eyes as red as week-old ketchup that had been left out in the sun. She had a copy of *The Voice* in one hand and a green backpack in the other. The backpack had some weight. A black iPod was on her narrow hip, headsets were on, hip-hop blasting. Sounded like British rap.

The girl looked him in the face, exchanged a slight nod, then sat next to him.

The girl said, "Sam I am."

Her tongue ring showed.

He nodded. "Green eggs and ham."

She looked Cherokee Indian. Her accent very London, like everyone's.

Her breath smelled like hard liquor, cigarettes, and beans.

He moved to the back of the train. No one was there.

She followed.

They sat at the same time.

She asked, "What's happened to the nose, mate?"

"Nothing I care to talk about."

"Looks like you got in a row and got your bloody ass kicked."

"You have my order?"

The girl nodded. "Need anything let me know. I have a connection at Scotland Yard that's pilfering a mad load of guns from the Operation Trident program. Guns they take from minorities. Right now I could supply Iraq. Revolvers, machine guns, MAC-10 if you want to do a spray-and-pray. Crack cocaine, cannabis, CS sprays. I can get anything you need."

"How old are you?"

"Fourteen. If you need some Charlie, I can get you a deal."

He nodded. Wondered what his daughter would be like in four years.

He said, "I need clean barrels for the Eagle."

"How many?"

"Half a dozen."

"Have drops in Colindale and High Barnet, then I'll get you what I can. François might have them. Tell Sam to tell me and I'll get you what you need. Remember. Handguns. MAC-10. Cocaine. Crack. Cannabis. I'm the one you need to go to. Ask Sam. He'll tell you."

The train slowed down. The next exit Mudchute.

"Or if you know somebody chav or stoosh, I can get you gold, Burberry, anything bling."

Cellular up to her ear, the girl exited at the next stop.

The girls who were drinking Red Bull and Scotch exited too. They handed her a cup of their mixed drink. They all walked away like nothing they were doing was a big deal.

He wondered what *chav* and *stoosh* meant.

The green backpack was left behind. So was a newspaper. He

looked at the front page. Article on the new trend sweeping across the nation, rich trailer trash going to third-world countries and buying black and brown babies like they were shopping at a pet store. The things rich trailer-trash people did when they were bored. The newspaper had no messages, no significance. It was tossed.

He pulled the backpack closer to him.

Then he pulled out one of his cellular phones. Dialed.

A man answered. "Talk to me."

"What kind of shit was that?"

"So you met Zankhana."

"What kind of name is that?"

"Hindu."

"Shouldn't she be in school playing tetherball?"

"Guess you haven't heard about the kids over here. They are the worst."

"This gunrunning teenage alcoholic know what she's doing?"

"Big shoot-outs in London over the last few weeks. Albanians' card club in Park Royal, three dead. Guy shot up a McDonald's in Brixton. Another man shot in the face at Harlesden."

"And London doesn't have a death penalty."

"Abolished in the United Kingdom under the 1965 Murder Act."

"So you're telling me that fourteen-year-old Zankhana supplied all the guns."

"Zankhana is a piece of work. All the gangsters know her. She supplied guns in both sides of a shoot-out in Colindale. Then supplied guns to the crews who went in for vindication."

"Fourteen years old."

"Will be lucky to see fifteen."

"What's her connection with the Trident thing at Scotland Yard?"

"Indirect connection. She works for somebody older. Druggie named François Bertin."

"Fucking Frenchman."

"You've got issues with the French?"

"Just the Frenchmen who spit out bullshit poetry."

The man with the broken nose thought about his soon-to-be ex-wife, took a breath.

He asked, "What else you have for me?"

"Still working on the second one. Contract is coming in from the States. The buyer has the funds but is having a problem moving the funds at this time. But the money is there."

"They're being watched."

"Not sure. But if they are, not our problem."

"Don't waste my time. I could be on a plane right now."

"Worse-case scenario. Would you be interested in bartering for a Benz?"

"You shitting me?"

"Client has a brand-new CLK63 AMG Cabriolet."

"Cabriolet. A convertible."

"AMG."

"An AMG?"

"V-eight engine."

"Get out."

"Lovely car. Would look good in Texas."

"What year?"

"This year's model."

"What's that cost on a piece of work like that?"

"Off the showroom floor?"

"What's this one worth?"

"Almost one hundred thousand."

"Uh-huh. And how would that get into my possession?"

"Client would report it stolen. I'd arrange for the new paper-work and IDs."

"Oh, yeah. Why don't you just send me to jail? Just get me the money."

"Bruno, the car is brand-new. Look it up on the Internet."

"They have brand-new prisons filled with dumb fucks too. Don't waste my time."

"Just thought I'd ask. Promised the client I'd put that out there."

"This contract." He took a breath, touched his nose. "You have the package?"

"The information on Gideon is coming."

"Don't bullshit me, Sam."

"I assure you it's coming."

"Don't fuck me around, Sam. You don't want to fuck me around."

He hung up. He exited the DLR at Cutty Sark for Maritime Greenwich. Needed to get souvenirs for his daughter. And there was this other thing on his mind. As he walked he took out the other phone. Dialed.

His call was transferred.

She said, "Good afternoon."

"Tebby. Bruno. The guy from Starbucks."

"I know who this is. How are you?"

"Is this too soon to call? Was trying to wait, but I wanted to call you."

"Did you?"

"Is this too soon? I mean, I can call you back if this is too soon."

He heard the smile in her voice. "Not at all. I wanted to chat with you as well."

Butterflies in his belly, he stood to the side talking to her.

He asked, "Are you available to get together later? Only here a couple of days and I—"

"I love the cinema."

"Cinema?"

"Movies. We call them the cinema here."

"Oh, movies. Nice. We could do that. I like the cinema too."

"Well, the Prince Charles Cinema has some nice movies. Or if you like theater and want to know more about South Africa, there is a wonderful play about South Africa at Stratford."

"Haven't been to a play in a while. What's it called?"

"*Township Stories*."

"Is that like *Lion King*?"

"Not at all. But it's a good crime thriller that shows the gritty reality of South African life. They say Zenzo Ngqobe is excellent. Think he plays a cold-blooded assassin in the play."

"A cold-blooded assassin." He smiled. "Let's go see that."

"That would be lovely."

"But I have to tell you one thing. More like two."

"Yes."

"I'm going through a divorce. It's not over, hasn't been finalized, but that's weeks away. And I have two kids back in the States. A son and a daughter. Just wanted you to know that."

"Bruno."

"Yes."

"I'm divorced. And I have two children. Their father does not send a dime to help them. Two boys. Back in Botswana."

There was a long pause.

Bruno said, "Really?"

"Really."

"Well, I'm on my second marriage. My first wife died. Breast cancer."

Another pause.

The silence on the other end of the line told him that he had said the wrong thing.

Had said too much too soon.

The past should be given in measured doses, not all at once.

Tebby said, "Should I meet you at the theater? Or would you prefer to not be seen with a divorced woman who has two children? Would you rather be with a woman with hair?"

He hadn't blown it. He smiled.

He asked, "What theater and what time?"

She laughed. He laughed too.

Tension dissipated.

She told him where to meet her, then said, "I will meet you there, Bruno."

"Okay. Would you like to go for dinner before the play?"

"After would be better. That way we don't have to rush before the theater."

"Okay. Dinner after the play."

"I love your voice, Bruno. Love the way you sound so . . . American."

"Love your accent too."

"Have to get some things sorted out here at work."

"Have a good day."

"Cheers, Bruno."

She hung up.

His smile refused to end.

While he walked by all the shops that led to the *Cutty Sark*, he felt free.

He didn't think about his divorce.

Or the IRS.

Or buying Harry Potter books.

Or his son.

He only thought about Tebby.

He was happy.

Seventeen

murder by contract

Back at his swank hotel room, the man with the broken nose took his coat off.

He put the souvenirs from the *Cutty Sark* on the dresser and took off his Italian shoes.

Then he put the backpack on the queen-size bed.

It felt like Christmas. Like he was opening a Christmas present.

He unzipped the backpack. Took out a box.

He took his time, opened the box with patience. And there it was.

Desert Eagle .50. Not a regular Eagle. This bird was dressed in titanium.

He had owned one years ago, but not with this finish.

Almost five pounds. Not many men could control an Eagle's recoil. Its thunder so loud indoor ranges prohibited them. The Eagle was all about the big hunt. It was made for a real man.

There was a tap on the hotel room door.

He put a pillow over the Eagle, left his bird within reach. Adjusted his pants. Looked through the peephole. It was the man from concierge. He was bringing up a small FedEx box.

The package had arrived. He took the package, gave a tip, closed the door.

He opened the box as he walked across the room.

Stacks of information and photographs.

And a book.

He pushed the book to the side. Stared at the photograph.

He put his glasses on and took a better look.

He muttered, "No way. No fucking way."

He took out his cellular phone. The hotline.

Sam answered, "Talk to me, Bruno."

"This is the Gideon son of a bitch?"

"That's Gideon."

"No fucking way. I was on the plane with this guy."

"What plane?"

"The plane I just took to London."

"You're kidding me."

"Same fucking guy."

"They say he did the job in Tampa last week. Big bloody mess. All over the news."

"Haven't been watching the news. So, this hit . . . this about the thing he did in Tampa?"

"Let's pretend I didn't say as much as I already did."

"So he's a psycho."

"Be careful. He's a smart one. He's sneaky and brutal. I'll get you photos from this thing that just went down in Tampa. If you get on the computer, I can send you a link to YouTube, they have it out there too. A two-minute clip. This Gideon guy took out eight or nine guys by himself."

"What weapon?"

"No gunshot wounds. No knife wounds."

"Military background?"

"Nobody knows. For all I know he was raised by the Shaolin monks."

"What's the James Patterson book for?"

"Show him the book."

"What, he in a book club or something?"

"Show him the book. Look at his eyes. It'll mess him up."

"Will he go ballistic?"

"Not in a public place. Do it and exit. That will fuck with his head. Get him off-balance."

"So this is a cleanup and it has to do with the Tampa job."

"Need anything else, call me."

They hung up.

He studied the package. Studied Gideon.

Saw Gideon's credentials.

A few pictures from a bloody crime scene in Tampa were in the package.

He was glad he didn't have a weak stomach.

This business had been profitable for Gideon.

Very profitable.

Another knock at the hotel door.

He looked out. Saw a short, old man in a nice suit. He opened the door.

The old man said. "Mr. Bruno Brubaker?"

He nodded.

"You need me, no?"

"Who are you?"

"Friend of Sam. I brought you suits to try."

The Russian Jewish man, his back mildly crooked, his suit impeccable. The old man entered pushing a tall rack filled with suits and shirts, each suit in its own suit bag, everything else new and in the box. On the rack was a bag filled with belts and ties. Another had shoes.

Bruno found two suits to his liking. Four shirts. Two belts. Two pairs of shoes.

Bruno handed the old man his American Express card.

The man sat at the small desk and closed out the transaction.

Each suit cost a £1,000. Two thousand U.S. dollars.

The belts were £200. The shoes were £600 a pair. The old man charged him £100 for two shirts, gave him two for free.

He'd paid a fortune for his clothing. But he'd pay five times that much today.

There was a woman he wanted to impress. A woman who looked like a queen.

The Russian gathered the rest of his things. Handed Bruno a business card.

"In case you need anything else while in London."

He nodded. "I do need one more thing."

"Tell me what you need, my friend."

"Underwear. Boxers or briefs."

"Sorry, no boxers and briefs. No socks. Only what I have on. You want to buy?"

He shook his head. "Well, thanks anyway."

"With a good salesman, everything is for sale."

"Well, I don't know how they do it where you come from, but where I'm from, men don't wear other men's underwear. Sorry, but I'm not one to wear another man's underwear."

"Stores all over. Get to any high street."

"High street?"

"Any main street. Any big street."

"Okay. I'll find a high street."

"Cheers to you, my friend."

"Cheers."

The old man left, back bent, pushing his cart of wares toward the elevator.

Picture of his next job in one hand, gun in the other, the man with the broken nose went back to the window, looked out at the sideshow. He loved the weight of the Eagle in his hand.

He wouldn't need the gun tonight. His hunt would begin tomorrow.

Eighteen

path of the unrighteous

I burgled my way inside a single-story Tudor home.

I'd traveled north and engaged in criminal acts right outside Royal Air Force Lakenheath. Eyes burning, in need of rest, I sat and waited for my contract to come home.

American flags decorated the walls of the modest home. Not one thing in the place was expensive, nothing was beyond his military income. Nothing was out of character. Plaques praising the sergeant's marksmanship, leadership, and dedication, all sorts of commendations took up every inch of one wall in the living room. Pictures of his six children were on another wall. Not a single photo of either his first or second ex-wife. His oldest kid went to USC. The kid below that one was stationed at Lackland. His youngest was almost in middle school. Had pictures of him and his kids out at Thetford Forest working out on the Go Ape obstacle course. Pictures of him on the Breckland Pines Golf Course. From a glance everything looked ordinary.

Six kids, one of the six in college, four young enough for child support, all that and two ex-wives latching onto your pension, that was enough to keep a military man bankrupt.

Enough to make a man walk on the other side of the law to earn his bread and butter.

I looked in the two bedrooms, the second bedroom filled with golf clubs and weights, 350 pounds on the bench press. I looked in closets, made sure no one else was here hiding out. I was inside the home of a warrior. I expected somebody to jump out and strike like a rattlesnake, knife or a gun in hand. The modest home was empty.

I went to the kitchen, pulled out a chair.

Leg bouncing, I rubbed my face, slapped myself, sat and waited with the patience of Job.

My mind remained on Chapel Hill.

Chapel Hill had been a month ago.

Before Tampa.

I closed my weary eyes. Remembered what I needed to forget.

But North Carolina had good memories too.

I remembered that day.

The sun was going down when Arizona called my hotel room. I was on the bed, reading *The Daily Tar Heel*. My work hadn't made the news. That was good. The news talked about rape and Duke's lacrosse team, then about a West Charlotte prostitution exclusion zone, showed poor people getting arrested for buying sex. Maybe the lacrosse team should've been hanging out in that zone. Saw that Damego Lee was charged with stabbing his girl-friend to death. Other news was about an immigration rally be-ing sponsored by the Carolina Hispanic Association.

Arizona got to the point, said one word, "Lobby."

"Okay, boss."

"Smart-ass."

"See you in a sec."

I dropped the paper on the bed, that article about the prosti-tution zone staring up at me.

The good people of North Carolina were being locked up for buying pussy.

Buying pussy.

Less than a minute later I was in the lobby.

Arizona was looking studious and collegiate, sporting a beat-up Carolina-blue backpack. Everybody in the area wore Carolina blue. From skies to clothes, that was the only color for miles. I offered to carry her backpack, but she shook her head.

I handed her a package.

She asked, "What's this?"

"Luwak coffee."

"Wow. For me?"

"For you."

"Thanks."

The gourmet coffee I handed her was rare and exotic, labor-intensive and time-consuming to produce, made with the help of the marsupial Luwak of Indonesia, and cost more than most hard drugs. With a schoolgirl smile, she stuffed her present inside her backpack.

In silence we headed down the one-way street, took Columbia Street toward Franklin. She lit a Djarum cigarette, but didn't smoke it. Lit it, took that initial puff to get the fire going, just inhaled its exotic, clovelike scent, then dropped the Djarum, used her foot to put out the fire.

We went to the Top of the Hill, a local restaurant and brewery, sat up on the third floor facing the Varsity Theater, sipping beers and looking out over Kerr Drug store, Starbucks, Subway, Wachovia Bank, and all the mom-and-pop shops lining Franklin. The outskirts of campus were like Mayberry. With the area that housed the brown- and black-skinned minorities being miles away, minorities that built these colleges and businesses being out of sight and out of mind, this area was a regular Pleasantville. The drugstore sold popcorn for fifty-nine cents. The movie theater had two screens. It was a Dockers, Old Navy, and backpack world. I had on dull gray sweats. Dark shades. Baseball cap turned backward. Arizona was dressed in plain jeans and a Carolina blue hoodie, hair pulled back, a simple ponytail, white tennis shoes.

I was close to my birthplace. Felt comfortable under skies painted Carolina blue.

Arizona said, "You did a good job yesterday."

"Thanks."

"The bell tower? You dropped him from the bell tower?"

"Didn't drop him. Just encouraged him to fall."

She nodded in agreement. "The message has been sent out."

"Effective?"

"Misogynistic assholes who owe me are paying up. That put fear in their hearts."

"If they don't respect you . . ."

"Make them fear you. And truth be told, fear works better than respect."

A group of strangers passed by. One of them stopped, asked Arizona if she was a member of No Entry, a South Asian dance group.

One of the men asked, "Ain't you Chinese?"

"I'm Filipina. Not Chinese." She shook her head. *"Kantutin mo ang nanay mo."*

He asked, "What was that?

"Puputulin ko titi mo."

Confused, as if in their eyes there was no difference, they went away.

I asked her, "What did you say?"

"Told that redneck asshole to go fuck his mother. And threatened to cut off his dick."

Back to her perfect English. No hint of a Filipina accent. When she switched gears, her Tagalog was authentic. But her English was clear, perfect, and neutral. Owned no race, creed, or color. Like mine. We'd both studied hard at becoming neutral. Neutral people were never remembered. Neutral people were invisible to the rest of the world.

Arizona sipped her brew. "You never exterminate the same way twice, do you?"

"Try not to repeat myself. Don't need a signature."

Last time I saw her she was in New York, room 3607 at the Parker Meridien, wearing a $2,000 suit and a watch that made a Rolex look like a dime-store gift, and shoes that were so sexy they made me get an erection. Now she looked like a grunged-out college student, Wal-Mart and Target to the bone. Always so different. She was a chameleon, always dressed so she would fit in, taught how to blend in and go unnoticed, schooled by the best of grifters.

I said, "You should come to Atlanta with me. I have some business to take care of."

"What kind of business?"

"Sledge. Decided to meet with him. On the strength of your referral."

"He laundered some money for me."

"I hate rappers."

"Me too. But I owed him a favor."

"Come with me."

"I'll pass. But thanks."

We drank. We relaxed.

I said, "Want to catch a movie?"

Arizona whispered, "We're not squares, Gideon."

"It's just a movie."

"Last time it was just a play."

"So you remember New York."

"I remember New York."

I said, "Come on. My treat."

We hit Starbucks, then caught *Basic Instinct 2*. Ten minutes into the movie we thought about walking out, laughed, and called that fiasco of a film *Basically It Stinks, Too*. Movie was so bad that only four people were in the theater. A huge, dark theater that didn't have the latest sound technology. Like I said before, only two movies played at that local spot. Mayberry. And those two movies only played twice a day. Very Mayberry. No discounts for students. No wonder all the bars along the strip were full. Inside the dark theater, the other people were on the right side, close to the front. Old Tar Heels with bad vision. We sat in the back, far left side.

Arizona's hand came to my lap, rubbed, then she brought her other hand over, undid my sweats, fished inside, took out my penis. She stroked me. She watched the movie and stroked me until I started to rise. Then she paused. Shifted. She leaned, put her face in my lap.

She did what naugthy squares would do at a moment like this.

Arizona stroked me while she looked at the movie, not impressed with what was on the big screen. She put her head back in my lap, took me in her throat with small, slow thrusts.

She said, "This movie is horrible."

Sharon Stone continued getting sexed as Arizona opened her soda, sipped a little, took some ice inside her mouth, then leaned over, took me inside her jaws again. One of my hands gripped my seat, the other held the back of her head. She worked me good, worked until I came, then kept working me until I was almost hard again.

While I caught my breath, Arizona ate popcorn and sipped on the last of her soda.

Arizona smiled. "That's payback for what you did to me in New York."

"Is that right?"

"So that debt is paid in full."

We left the sorry movie and went back to the Top of the Hill. More beers. Loud and obnoxious college students were getting wasted. Sober X hangover patches were on every other arm, and condoms were in just as many pockets. Meaningless sex was on the horizon.

The Terry Wiley Band was playing the best soul, funk, and blues, a serious party band. I convinced Arizona to mix with the blue-blooded crowd and dance with me. She was the queen of the grifters, but at the end of the day she was still a woman who loved to feel the groove.

I whispered in her ear, "Let me eat you out."

She pushed me away from her. "All about control, Gideon. You know that."

"What are you afraid of?"

"I lost control once . . . with Scamz . . . can't afford to get caught up like that again."

"You haven't gotten over him."

"It ended abruptly. There was no closure. No real closure."

"Want to talk about it?"

She didn't answer.

The conversation disconnected for a moment. Her lips turned down almost as if she were experiencing some sort of a love-hate relationship deep inside her soul.

We left the party, took a slow stroll down Cameron Avenue, cut through campus between Phillips and Memorial Hall, her hand in mine, me holding her delicate fingers as we headed toward middle campus, taking in her softness as we headed toward north campus.

She stared at the buildings. "I never went to college. I never made it out of high school."

"And you're smarter than most."

"Got my Ph.D. in the streets."

"And richer than most."

"Made my money hustling. Like my mother did. And my mother's mother."

Temperature was dropping. Had made it up to the midsixties, now it was nose-diving toward the low forties. We strolled back toward my historic, five-star hotel. The good old Carolina Inn. Up and down Columbia Street there was enough foliage to make a forest, nothing but easygoing trees and that peaceful feeling surrounding all the bricked structures.

We went inside the lobby, chilled out in the chairs next to the concierge.

She said, "I have the same nightmare over and over."

"What nightmare is that?"

"Watching Scamz get shot in the chest. Keep hearing the shotgun blast. See the blood."

"Heard it was nasty."

"I was inside the pool hall. We had just left a club. Me. Scamz. My sister."

"Your sister."

"That backstabbing, jealous bitch."

"Tell me how you really feel."

"We'd all been out. We were waiting on him, standing right next to him. He got into an argument with this guy. Shotgun went off. Me and . . . my sister . . . we saw him die. I saw him take his last breath. That sound . . . life leaving him . . . hollow look in his eyes . . . I see it in my dreams."

"How does it make you feel?"

"Happy. Sad. Depends on the day."

She thanked me for the Luwak, gave me a one-arm hug, as if what had happened at the Varsity was just a way of thanking me for the exotic coffee from Indonesia. She was always about fair exchange, never robbed me. Arizona adjusted her backpack and went toward valet parking and got her car. A simple Saturn. Dents in the side. Nothing to write home about.

The doorman held the door open for me, gave me that Southern service that made this historic hotel so enviable. I went back inside, headed down the hallway, went to room 160.

I showered. Decided I'd drive around town, revisit my old childhood haunts in West Charlotte, maybe ride as far as Greenville, Asheville, or Spartanburg.

While I was drying off, there was an urgent banging at my door.

I eased into my bag, pulled out my friend, a Beretta Elite,

stood to the side of the peephole, kept my voice even, and called out, "Who is it?"

"Open up."

Weapon down at my side, I took a deep breath, relaxed, opened the door. Arizona was sitting on the carpet. Her back to the door. She looked back, saw the weapon in my hand, saw my naked body. She stood up. Still she was unnerved, had a stressed expression.

I said, "Thought you were gone."

She shifted from foot to foot.

Her backpack was gone. She had left it in her car.

That meant she was back for a moment. To tell me what was on her mind.

I saw it in her face. Bad news. Angst. I had done or said something to offend her.

She said, "There is something . . . me and you . . . it's rough . . . like Tracy and Hepburn."

"Just when I thought it was smoothing out and becoming more like Bogart and Bacall."

"This thing between us . . . it bothers me."

"Well, it really bothers me too."

She held her strained expression as if she were living in the middle of a moral dilemma.

She whispered, "What would you do with Arizona . . . if she came inside your room."

She spoke of herself in the third person. With detachment. Inanimate object. A divided soul.

I played along. "My favorite scenario is giving you a candlelit bath, washing your hair, drying you off, Miles Davis playing in the background, having your legs apart, giving you some serious mouth passion, and putting you to bed . . . then watching you sleep."

"You have any Monk?"

"And I have Miles. *Kind of Blue*. Got Coltrane. *Equinox. My Favorite Things*."

"You're making me weak."

"I was trying to make you wet."

"You did that when we were at the Top of the Hill."

"I did? How?"

"They way you look at me. Same way you're looking at me now."

"My look bothers you?"

"Monk and Coltrane."

"I have Miles and Wes too."

"Yeah. You're making me weak."

"Good."

"Don't know if I'd be able to handle all of that."

"We can always start with Monk, ride the Trane a few Miles toward Wes."

She didn't move.

I said, "Come on in."

"So far as my personal life . . . I'm very discreet . . . require total discretion."

"Don't worry. I don't kiss and tell."

"It's bad for business."

"I understand."

I went back to the bed, put my Beretta back in my bag.

She stood at the door, staring at me. Right then she was no different from all the college girls we had passed by tonight. I saw how she could've been a square, saw the normal in her.

She made a frustrated sound. *"Malibog ako. Gusto kitang kantutin."*

"Translate that shit."

"This is a booty call, Gideon. Just a booty call."

"A booty call."

"You're a male whore. It can't ever be more than a booty call."

That stung. Not in a painful way. Just introduced a reality, a part of me that might be coded deep into my DNA. My father, a man on the move. My mother, a whore.

I said, "You're a thief."

"I'm not a low-level thief. I run scams. I'm a businesswoman. I am the queen of my industry."

"I stand corrected."

She said, "I don't romanticize my existence. Not any longer. My eyes are open. The world is like *Lord of the Flies*. All about survival of the fittest. Survival of those who aren't afraid to be cruel. I don't care if you're a clergy or the president of a Fortune 500 company, don't care if you're homeless or a trust-fund baby, being good, following the rules, that shit doesn't work."

"Cool. I won't bullshit you and you don't bullshit me."

"Please. You tell me you want to make love. Save that rhetoric for the squares. They love that shit. First off, you don't know how to make love. You know how to fuck. Which is ironic. The better a man fucks, the more a woman will be convinced that he is making love to them."

She reached under her hoodie, hand going to the small of her back, fumbled with a strap, and pulled out a Ruger Mark III. She put her cold steel on the nightstand.

She glanced at me, swallowed.

The weapons were gone. Her shield was down.

She said, "So let's stop talking and fuck."

I held her small head in my hand, moved to her slow and easy, eased my lips on hers, moved my tongue around her lips, then eased my tongue inside her mouth, slow-grooved her with my tongue, my kiss a long and easy song, pure jazz, like I was Trane, Wes, Monk, and Miles.

"Stop being all romantic, Gideon. Fuck me means *fuck* me."

Then I dropped the romantic notions and fucked her.

I yanked most of her clothes away, did the same with mine, entered her doggie style, had her bent over the dresser, her holding the dresser while I fucked her booty-call style.

Over and over she moaned, "*Gusto kong kantutin tulad nito . . . susmariosep.*"

I wasn't nice. I stopped being pretty. I fucked like I wanted to hurt her.

"Isa pa . . ."

I pulled her hair and fucked her the way a thief needed to be fucked.

"Sigi pa . . . do that . . . *gusto ko yan . . ."*

I tried to fuck the arrogance and pain and rejection out of her.

"Sigi pa . . . do that . . . *gusto ko yan . . .* again . . . *isa pa."*

I tried to fuck her to me.

I tugged the rest of her wrinkled clothes off her, took her to the bed, eased her down, put my weight on her, made the bed sigh, eased back inside her, and kept the party going.

Arizona's moans told me she wanted more.

I said, "Keep talking to me in Tagalog."

"Why?"

"It turns me on."

She smiled a little. Said things I didn't understand, things that excited me.

I held her breasts and kissed her, pinched her nipples while our tongues danced.

Kept sucking her breasts.

Then my tongue craved to taste what was between her legs. I licked the edges . . . just around the edges . . . circles . . . tongue moving slow and easy like a Sunday drive down Route 66.

She stopped saying things in Tagalog. Nails in my back, she begged for me to stop eating her out and fuck her.

"You're trying to control me with your tongue."

"Come for me."

"No."

"Come for me."

"No . . . no . . . shit . . . oh . . . damn you."

"Coming?"

"Don't stop . . . don't stop."

I did stop.

Left her hanging at the edge of orgasm.

Left her twitching.

"Damn you . . . Gideon . . . damn you."

"Open your legs."

I got on top of her, broke her skin a little at a time.

She said, "You're driving me crazy."

"Then we're even."

I kissed her like I had wanted to kiss her for a decade. Sucked her neck like I was madman in search of sanity. The touch of her breasts magnifying my madness.

I teased her and drove myself insane.

Then I backed away. Left her suffering.

She clawed at me, begged me to not back away.

She said, "Stop playing and fuck me."

I didn't fuck her, not right then.

I was in control.

I wasn't going to let her control me.

I'd never let a woman control me.

I turned her over, put her on her knees, her face in the pillow, pulled her ass back toward me, my hands on her waist, made sure she kept her ass up high.

She said, "Gideon, give it to me. Please."

I rubbed my length against her over and over, let her feel what I wanted to give.

"That feels good. Shit. That's making me come."

She looked so feminine. So vulnerable. So damn sexy.

Then I went inside her. Went deep. Held her waist.

And I stroked her.

Didn't want it to end. Even if that was all we had. Wanted to make it last.

I tried to grab the edges of forever and make it stretch beyond eternity.

She came.

And the way she moved, I couldn't hold on any longer.

I came.

I came and kept moving until the well was dry.

I moved away from her, panting.

She did the same, running her fingers through her mane.

"Damn you, Gideon."

"Yeah. Damn you too."

A few minutes later Arizona sat on the edge on the bed, unlit Djarum in hand.

Djarum. The brand of clove-smelling cigarettes her dead lover used to smoke.

He didn't matter to me. Never did.

I told her, "Love you. Mean it."

She dragged her fingers through her hair, sighed, didn't look back at me.

I said, "You hear what I said?"

She shifted until she was sitting in profile, frowned, put the Djarum down, shook her head. *"Tahimik ka na."*

"Something wrong?"

"Don't say that. No love talk. Please. Don't do that."

"Took me ten years to get you to make love to me."

"We've had sex twice. We flirted and things . . . we crossed that forbidden line in New York. We mixed business with sex. Don't make it sound like something it's not, okay? We had sex. And today . . . we both needed this and so we got this from each other. Maybe I needed this. That's all. Just sex. Keep it real. Don't get foolish. Love talk is for squares, Gideon."

"Why did you come back?"

"You caught me at a good time. I just needed to . . . I needed some sexual healing."

"Sexual healing."

"I'm horny."

"Queen Scamz gets horny?"

"Ain't I a woman?"

"Yeah." I chuckled. "You're a woman. Best of the best."

She leaned back, kissed me. Growled as she sucked my tongue. She asked, "Are we done or can you go another round?"

"Still horny?"

"Very. Get like this when it's close to that time of the month."

"Not done. Was letting you catch your breath."

"Well, let's get this party started."

"Staying the night?"

She shook her head. "I can stay a little while longer."

"Make me feel special."

"Fuck me again, Gideon. Like you just fucked me. Pull my hair, fuck me like that again. Don't be so gentle. I like gentle, but I don't want gentle right now. Fuck me like that again."

Coltrane adding to the soundtrack created by her moans, I pulled her hair and fucked her from wall to floor, made her stand up and touch her toes while I fucked her senseless.

Then I took her to the bed, again missionary, tongue to tongue.

She came.

She came again.

"Give it to me . . . that's it Gideon . . . give it to me . . . don't stop . . . that's it."

I kept going until I couldn't fight it anymore.

I came.

She laughed.

I laughed too.

We stayed like that awhile.

Nothing was said after that.

Sweat dried.

North Carolina winds blew against the windows.

The room went from being hot to cold.

Then we pulled the covers up over us.

She whispered something in Tagalog. Something soft, emotional, and sweet.

I didn't know what she said.

I didn't ask.

All I know was I put my arm around her, pulled her to me, kept her close to my heart.

In silence she held onto my penis.

I fell asleep.

But the next morning she was gone. Had left like she was my overnight whore.

Or had left like I was the whore.

I jerked awake. Jumped to my feet. Spun around. Disoriented.

I had fallen asleep. Had my head down on the kitchen table.

That was fucked up. Dozing off, even for two seconds, could've sent me to the Big Sleep. I stretched, bounced up and down, splashed water on my face.

Took me a moment to remember I was eighty miles from London.

A vintage military jeep was pulling up out front.

The engine shut off.

My breathing shortened. Heart rate increased tenfold.

My palms were wet as rain. I took a few deep breaths.

He was here.

Sergeant was home.

It was time for the dance to begin.

Nineteen

one false move

I took another hard breath and wondered which way this was going to go.

Peaceful. Or with a hellified row.

I wanted him to see me when he came in. Wasn't going to hide.

A key was put in the door. My heart crept up my chest and stopped in my throat.

The door opened.

He came inside. Dressed in military fatigues. Rough face. Looked like Sergeant Rock.

He paused when he saw me sitting at his table, *Stars and Stripes* newspaper in my hand.

He frowned at me for a moment. A long, hot moment.

He spoke right above a whisper, "Gideon."

"Sergeant."

He looked like a sixty-year-old Sergeant Rock and sounded like Johnny Cash.

I kept my hands where he could see them. "Sorry to sneak up on you like this."

"This a social call?"

"Arizona asked me to stop by."

He nodded, said, "The slant-eyed bitch raised the stakes and sent Gide-fucking-on."

"Guess you could say that."

"She tell what it was about?"

I nodded. "FEMA scam. That's all she said. Don't need the details."

"Why didn't the bitch bring her narrow ass up to horse-and-grass her damn self?"

"Probably the same reason you sent the guys from Holland to talk to her."

"Guess that didn't deter her." He almost smiled. "Of all people she sent Gideon."

I nodded.

"Well, Gideon, so far as the boys from Holland, those weren't my men. Arizona has her own problems in Holland. She knows who sent those boys over here. Don't let her fool you."

"Does that matter?"

His frown deepened.

"I should've sent some military boys down. Never should've let her send Dutch boys."

"Who is the mysterious *her* that hired the Dutch boys?"

"Arizona knows. Oh, she knows. I should've handled that problem myself."

"You should've. But you didn't. And now I'm up here trying to smooth it out."

"The Dutch boys hurt her any?"

"Not at all."

"Too bad."

"Sorry to disappoint you."

"Too fucking bad that slant-eyed cunt didn't get any justice."

"The Dutch boys will be crippled for life. If that makes you feel any better."

"I don't need this in my home. Don't want this battle on my territory."

"I understand. Your being military and all. Could be hard to explain to the higher-ups."

"Is that right? How do you see this, Gideon? How do you see this playing out?"

"News of a military man's investment in a FEMA scam ever hit the paper . . . can't even imagine what that would do to the country. Or to a man's career. No matter how much paper he has stacked. Family shamed. All because of a little Filipina girl. Wouldn't look good at all."

"Your advice? So I don't end up falling on my sword, your advice?"

"Cut your losses. Pay your bills. Walk away clean. With money in the bank."

"Money in the bank."

"I'm not the one, but you know Arizona will send somebody."

"So I'd best make a call to my moneyman and rectify this little problem."

"That would be my suggestion."

"Is that a threat?"

"Only a suggestion."

His hands were trembling, shaking worse than mine.

I was scared. He was scared. That meant everything was normal.

He said, "Some entertainers were massacred. Back in the States. Saw it on CNN."

"Really?"

"Some rapper. Happened in Tampa. Heard it was a mess."

"Didn't hear about it."

"Last time you been to Tampa?"

"Never been to Tampa."

"When you get here?"

"Few hours ago."

"You been to visit a WAG since you got here? They just found one floating in the river."

"Wasn't me."

He took out a cigarette, popped it in his mouth, used his lighter to fire up the cancer.

He asked, "Do you mind?"

I shrugged. "Your house."

"I take it that if I don't make a call, we will have a problem."

"There is already a problem, you know that."

He said, "You know that Arizona bitch, you can't trust her. Didn't care for her when she was Scamz's bitch. Don't care for her now. Scamz was a fair man. She's stolen Scamz's name. That evil bitch, nobody can afford to work with her, not and make a profit. Everybody hates her. She'll double-cross you, do you know that? She'd double-cross her own mother to turn a profit."

I didn't say anything.

He inhaled, spoke when he exhaled. "Never should have gotten in bed with that cunt."

He looked at me, put the cigarette out, and dialed a number. He was put on hold, while he waited he stood up, never took his grimace off me. I didn't move an inch.

He asked, "You fucking her?"

"Maybe I should be asking you that question."

"Don't let pussy come between men. Pussy starts wars and good men die."

"What about Iraq?"

"George W. Bush is a pussy."

"And Blair must be his twin."

"I'll remember that one. Twin pussies. The boys'll get a good laugh out of that one."

He said some things to whoever was on the phone, nodded, cursed, hung up the phone, then he sat down.

He wasn't happy. Not at all.

Sergeant said, "Be careful. Men get fooled by sex. All men do."

I nodded.

We waited.

I took my eyes off him for second, long enough to open my backpack.

In the blink of an eye, he made an M&P .40 appear. Smith & Wesson's military gun.

Everything slowed down.

I asked, "You going to shoot me?"

"What's in the bag? Show me. Use one hand. Your left hand. Move slow."

I showed him that, except for the pint of Jack, the backpack was empty.

"Somebody called one of my friends this morning. Looking for a Desert Eagle."

"Wasn't me."

"Wasn't you?"

"Nah. I'm nine guy. Beretta time to time. A SIG. Maybe a .22. Nothing that big."

"My friend didn't know who the guy was. Told him he would have to look elsewhere. You're here in London and somebody happens to call up looking for a large-caliber, gas-operated semi-automatic pistol manufactured in Israel. Hope you're smarter than that, Gideon. For your own sake. Piece like that is too easy to follow back to the source. Hope that wasn't you."

"You know I'm not a show-off."

"Whoever it is, watch it, bet they trace the gun to find him . . . arms dealer selling off a .50-caliber gun dressed in titanium. That's over-the-top. That's six-o'clock news if ever I heard it."

"Titanium?"

He nodded. "That bitch will be easy to find. A big-ass loud gun. Whoever he is has to be a loose cannon. A man who has to have the biggest dick that screams the loudest orgasm."

"No insecurities over here."

"Just looking out for you. I have always been partial to you, Gideon. As a friend."

I nodded back at him, keeping my hands where he could see them at all times.

"If that was you buying the Eagle, take my advice, throw it

in the river and walk away." He kept his eyes on mine. "Too easy to trace, too showy, too loud."

"Wasn't me."

He put his S&W on his lap. His piece smiled at me.

He said, "Pardon the lack of trust. Somebody calls up for an Eagle, then you show up . . ."

"I showed up after you sent a hurt squad after Arizona."

"Like I said, what a coincidence."

"You say we're friends and you still have that barrel aimed at my gut."

"If I didn't like you, you'd be on that floor with two in your chest and one in your head."

"Make sure we exchange Christmas cards this year. Since we're friends."

"You got a weapon on you?"

"Just a pint of Jack."

"Sure about that?"

"You can search me."

"Don't need to be that close to you. So I'll take your word on that."

"I'm just the messenger."

"So the slant-eyed bitch just wants to play it like this. Who does that cunt think she is?"

"Queen Scamz. She thinks she's Queen Scamz."

My phone vibrated.

He jumped for his gun again.

Then he relaxed. Wiped his forehead with the back of his free hand.

The money he owed Arizona had been transferred.

I said, "See how easy that was?"

"Tell the bitch to suck my dick. You can quote me on that. And tell her to lick my balls while she's at it. Quote my ass on that too. Jacking me for my goddamn retirement money."

My phone vibrated again.

The money Arizona owed me had been transferred as well.

He stood across the room from me.

Again he asked, "You ain't fucking her, are you?"

"Let's keep this business."

"You know you ain't the only one she fucking. Get you a regular girl if you have to have a steady one. A girl like Arizona will be the death of you. Regular girl might break your heart and take your money, might even take your house, but they leave you breathing in the end."

I remained across the room from him, kept my hands where he could see them.

He asked, "You fucking her? And that is a damn business question, if you must know."

I shook my head.

He said, "Two hundred. I'll give you two hundred to put a bullet in her head."

"Pounds?"

"U.S. dollars. She ain't worth half what I'm offering you, and you know that."

He was talking two hundred thousand.

In this business a nickel was five thousand and a dime was ten.

I said, "Thought you'd spent your retirement money."

He gave me a one-sided grin. "FEMA supplemented my never-rising income. You know the exchange rate is killing us over here. Can't afford to buy shit off base. Not a damn thing."

I sat down. He did the same, his gun at his side, finger on the trigger.

My hands were damp, throat dry, heart maintained a steady gallop.

I said, "Two hundred is a lot of money. You must have a nice wad stashed away."

"Don't worry about what I got." He nodded. "You want the contract or not?"

I said, "Let's take a drink and talk about that."

I took the bottle of whiskey out of my backpack. Jack Daniel's. The brand we drank.

I sat the bottle down.

I asked, "Coke?"

He went to the small refrigerator.

I asked, "How you like living over here in England?"

"Either cold as hell or hot as hell. Gets hot as hell and ain't no air conditioners in England. No dryers, so when it's cold as hell, you can't hang your clothes out to dry. In the summertime you have to hang clothes on the back porch to dry."

"I was here once in the summer. Never came up here and went on base."

"On base, black women have light-skinned babies with curly hair. White women have brown-skinned babies with curly hair. Black is fucking white and white is fucking black. This is about as kum-ba-yah as it gets. Just like it is down in London. Same all over Europe. America is the most advanced country and still refuses to acknowledge the natural course of evolution."

He put a liter of Coca-Cola down.

He said, "This is the *real* thing. From home. Not that NutraSweet shit from London."

I said, "Glasses or straight from the bottle like winos in an alley?"

He went back to the cabinet, never taking his eyes off me, gun barrel aimed at the floor.

He said, "London kills me with that eat-in/takeaway bullshit. They add a surcharge to your meal if you eat at McDonald's or Pizza Hut or anywhere. All those mayonnaise-eating bastards. They put mayo on everything. I got some mustard here if you want some. You won't be able to find mustard in London. Hot sauce either. Got a few bottles if you need some."

"Thanks."

He sat in front of me.

I poured him a shot of Jack.

He thanked me, then asked, "You drinking?"

"Probably shouldn't. I'm on a motorcycle. Streets are damp. Not a good idea."

"Have a word with Jack before what I'm holding has two or three words with you."

He stared at his glass. Smiling. Waiting. Trembling. His fear controlled.

I said, "You think I put a little something extra in Jack?"

"Talk to Jack, not to me. Better hurry up 'cause my trigger finger is getting twitchy."

I eased the bottle up to my lips, took a hit.

A minute went by.

He said, "Sip a little more. For good measure."

I did. Another minute went by.

He relaxed, but he never moved his hand away from his military gun.

I said, "For two hundred, if you're serious, I'll celebrate and drink the whole bottle."

"So you'll take the contract on that slant-eyed bitch?"

"I'd kill that slant-eyed bitch and my favorite whore for two hundred."

"Your favorite whore." He chuckled. "How is Thelma?"

"Have no idea."

"You ain't seen her?"

"Saw her in Amsterdam a few years ago."

"That why you in London?"

"What do you mean?"

"Guess you didn't know. She's in London."

"London?"

"Thelma's been working in London for at least two years. I see her from time to time."

"Where in London is she working?"

"Down in W1. A few doors down from a store called Le Pig something or another."

"Didn't know that."

"She's on the Internet. She's got herself an ad on craigslist. org under erotic services. She had a nice ad out at eros.com in the classifieds. Think she's still out at halfprice.com too."

"Sounds like she's keeping busy."

"Sent some business her way a time or two. Military is prison and so is marriage. Few married guys up here like to get away from their families and go down to the city for a day trip."

"Thought Thelma had run to Brazil or was hiding out some-where in South America."

"She got in trouble down there. Then, from what I hear, she was over in Berlin for a while. Since the wall came down and prostitution became legal, all the girls are going there."

"Yeah. Heard all the whores were running to Germany."

"They have damn near half a million sex workers. Half a million. Wall-to-wall pussy. And for the man on the move, they have drive-through sex stalls in Germany. I shit you not."

"So Thelma went to Germany."

"She was over there working twelve-hour shifts. The young girls are lucky to get five to ten guys a day. Thelma said there was too much competition. After that she was working in Den Haag, Spijk, and Apeldoorn for a while. Then she came to Lon-don. Smaller market."

"Had no idea."

"You ain't been in touch with her?"

I shook my head.

He shook his head. "Damn shame."

"It is what it is."

"Look her up. If you go visit her, tell her Sergeant said hello. When I make it back down to Central London, tell her I'll visit her. Would love to buy her a drink and talk old times."

For a moment I smelled that whore's perfume on his skin.

"Let's talk contract," I said. "Have to hit the road. Almost a hundred miles to London."

I extended the bottle to him for a toast. His glass clinked my bottle.

I said, "Half up front. Other half when it's done. I'll send visual confirmation."

"SOP." That meant Standard Operating Procedures. "Where's that cunt Arizona hiding?"

"She's in London. Not sure where she's hiding out. But she's in contact."

"Sending somebody after me." He sipped. "She has a lot of nerve, you know that?"

He drank his shot. He looked around his modest life. Looked at all the flags and trophies and commendations. Looked at the sum of his military career in a single glance.

He said, "Six more months with Uncle fucking Sam and I'm out of this bitch."

"Where to?"

"Retirement. Gonna chill out and retreat to a small island. Some place peaceful. And away from everything that's going on in the world. Sit back and watch countries destroy each other. Take on an exotic wife. Get the best wife with the sweetest pussy that my money can buy. Even if she doesn't love me, she'll love the lifestyle I can afford. Dick can still hold up an American flag and squirt, so I'ma have as many children as her body can handle. Maybe take on more than one wife. A man should be able to have as many women as he could afford."

"Only takes one to make a rich man broke. Only takes one to steal all of your money."

He rubbed his eyes. Blinked a few times.

I took a small hit of the Jack. Did the same as it burned my throat.

I said, "This is some good shit."

"Jack has a nice kick. Top-shelf?"

I sipped a little more. "Only the best."

He poured himself another shot. Tossed it back. "I'ma grow a beard like Jerry Garcia. Let my hair go long like John Lennon. Work out twice a day, run five miles every morning and swim naked in one of God's beautiful bodies of water every evening.

Read the Bible from cover to cover. Repent. Find Jesus and get to know the Lord like my mama knew Him."

I smiled at him. Watched him throw back another shot.

He said, "But I'll have to go down and visit Thelma before. On a weekend. No congestion fees on the weekend. Goddamn robbery. You know about the congestion fees?"

"I heard they were about to go up. Heard the congestion zones were getting wider."

"I mean, you know about the checkpoints and the cameras that record you as soon as you hit the zone? They are on you as soon as you hit the city. And it's a rip-off. Eighteen U.S. dollars a day to drive into Central London. Parking fees not included. That's more than my car note to drive there a week."

"I heard."

"But what I'm telling you, Gideon, it's bigger than the fees. It's Big Brother's never-blinking eye. Be careful. Cameras track all moving vehicles. As soon as you hit the congestion zone, they run your plates and hit you with a bill for congestion charges so fast it could make your head spin, so that means Big Brother knows your every move. I park at Epping, catch the train down. Takes all damn day, and if the Central is down, I'm fucked, but I ain't paying no . . . no . . ."

He rubbed his eyes again. Coughed and smiled.

He refilled. My bottle clinked his glass, another toast.

He said, "But before I get religious, I want a bullet in that slant-eyed cunt's head."

"We're talking about Arizona now."

"Damn right."

"However you want it done, it's done."

"Always running her hand through her goddamn hair. And cut her damn hair off. Make gook-looking bitch bald." He rubbed his eyes. They were out of focus. "But don't cut it until after she's apologized and transferred my damn money back to my . . . not until she's sent every last dime of my money back . . . back . . . back . . . my money . . . my . . . money . . . back . . ."

Then his smile turned upside down. Panic lines grew in his forehead.

His vision was blurring, his breathing shutting down at a rapid pace.

I said, "Thanks for telling me where Thelma was working. I'll pay her a visit."

"Son of a . . . you son of a . . ."

"Sorry. This is business. Just business. I hate it, but this is how it is."

Eyes wide, he looked at his glass, maybe saw the film inside, and frowned at me.

His gun went off. Shot where my stomach would've been if I hadn't moved. The gun came up over the table, followed me. The next bullet exploded where my chest had been two seconds before. The third shot hit where I was a half second before that.

By the fourth explosion, I was across the room. I was nervous. Scared. Alert.

No way a man could dodge bullets and not feel his own death dancing in the room.

Agony seized him. He dropped the Smith & Wesson and grabbed his throat.

Death was charging his way. I kicked the gun out of his reach.

Sergeant convulsed. Wet his pants. A river of fear ran from between his legs.

I didn't poison the Jack. That would've been expected. I'd laced his drinking glasses with the tasteless, odorless venom. No matter which glass he'd picked up, it was poisoned.

I'd sipped from the untainted bottle.

Face red, he tried to get up, but crashed to the floor face-first, eyes wide-open.

His legs kicked, twitched, finally stopped moving. His bowels released, stenched the air.

I couldn't let him live. Not after he said he'd kill Arizona.

He had sent men to cripple and rape her.

My heart thumped inside my chest. But I didn't have time to wait for it to slow.

I put on rubber gloves and picked up his glass. Grabbed the one I didn't use. Picked up the bottle of Jack too. I washed his glasses out. Washed them all to prevent collateral damage.

I dried the glasses, put them back in the cabinet, stood over the sink, waiting for that nauseous feeling to go away. I was sweating and numb. I was living in my own darkness.

Had to remain on task.

In a couple of hours the poison in his system wouldn't be detectable.

Natural causes. It would look like death by natural causes.

I wiped down the bottle of Jack, then put the bottle in his hand long enough for his fingerprints to take. I put the bottle on the table, let it turn over and spill. Jack rained to the floor. Wanted it to look like he had knocked it over. Wouldn't make sense to empty the bottle, no need to toss it. I left his weapon where he had dropped it.

Had to.

Bullet holes were everywhere.

I'd let the police explain the bullet holes.

Maybe they'd think he'd gotten drunk, gone mad, started shooting, had a heart attack.

I didn't give a shit.

Better him than Arizona laid up in a hospital, raped and beaten.

I couldn't allow that to happen.

Five minutes later I was on A11 doing seventy, horses at my side, sadness in my heart.

The sadness went away when the anger returned.

Thelma was here. Right up under my nose.

Twenty

erotic gherkin

Hours had gone by.

The grayness of London had changed to a mild black.

The coldness remained, most of that chill surrounding my heart.

Not many tall structures polluted London's skyline, so the contemporary Erotic Gherkin could be seen from almost everywhere. It was actually the Swiss Re Tower, but the locals loved calling it the Erotic Gherkin, maybe because it was smooth and looked like an exotic vibrator rising from the ground. Hard to believe that Foster got away with that architectural design.

If he had put two round buildings at the base, it would've been a dick pointing at the sky.

Arizona said, "Good job. What you did in Lakenheath, good job."

I didn't say anything. Didn't want to rejoice in my wrongdoing.

She said, "After what happened this morning in Chinatown, I started thinking."

"And those thoughts were?"

"Come work for me. Exclusively."

"Other shit is on my mind right now."

"I'm listening."

She had boarded the Stansted Express at the Seven Sisters platform. She smelled top-shelf. She had on an expensive business suit, long black coat, boots, hair pulled back in a bun.

I told her, "If I wanted to work for somebody, I'd get a nine-to-five."

She flipped me off.

I said, "You get my messages?"

"I get a lot of messages. Remind me of your messages."

"Guy from the plane. Red shirt. High-end suit. Broken nose. Saw him again."

"That guy. Where?"

"After Chinatown. You ran away and when I turned around, he was behind me."

"The wingman you left me a message about."

"You thought I was bullshitting?"

"What happened?"

"I went after him. Lost him. He vanished somewhere in Covent Garden."

"So he was behind me."

"He was behind us. He could've hid out in the market."

She bounced her leg.

I asked, "How many people are after you?"

"About half as many as should be after you."

I repeated, "When you ran away, I turned around and he wasn't too far behind me."

"We'd just straightened out the Dutch boys. Maybe Sergeant used him as backup."

I shook my head. "Doubt it. He was on the flight from the U.S. with me."

"Maybe it was Lakenheath. Maybe Sergeant tried to get to me before I got to him."

"Wasn't Sergeant."

"Why so sure he didn't put a hit out on me too?"

"Because he offered me a contract on you."

That broke her pace. She saw the seriousness in my eyes. "How much?"

I told her. She remained poker-faced, but her leg bounced a little faster.

She said, "The guy in the suit, black, white, European?"

"Could be all of the above or none of the above."

"Bald."

"Yeah."

"A hit man shaves his body to get rid of DNA."

"Wait. Sergeant said he had a partner. A woman."

Arizona didn't say anything. Her face told me she knew.

She said, "His partner, the bitch he was dealing with, she's in Holland."

"So she arranged the Dutch boys?"

"The bitch did. She sent them to rape . . . she sent them."

Arizona was nervous. Her discomfort was as subtle as the sweat on the tip of her nose.

She said, "I need you to go to Amsterdam."

"Get me a package."

Her cellular rang. She looked at the number and took the call.

She frowned a little, then frowned a lot, then looked at me.

When she hung up, she cursed and shook her head.

I asked, "What happened?"

"Sledgehammer was murdered a few hours ago."

That got my attention.

I asked her when that happened. She told me that it was this morning.

He'd been killed after I made it to London, around the time I was bedding Mrs. Jones.

I asked, "How?"

"My contact said Sledge's van exploded." That was her answer.

"Sledge and his family were having a family outing in Trinidad. At least ten members of his family were inside the van."

"His family? His wife and kids?"

"Wife. Kids. Parents. In-laws. Everyone was piled in the same van."

Fear was in her eyes. Or maybe that was just a reflection of what I felt at the moment.

She said, "Consider my offer. Work for me. It would benefit both of us."

"I get it. You need me. You need protection."

"I fear no one but God."

"You're afraid. If I hadn't been on it and saw the cats at Starbucks, you're worried about what would've happened. You're scared because right now you'd be laid up in London Hospital. Every bone in your body broken while the police asked questions and brought a rape kit."

She swallowed. Had never seen her this rattled before. She said, "Be my partner."

"Answer me. How many people are after you? Who else would come after you?"

"All business. Without the sex. I think I need a male partner so these ignorant fools will take me seriously. And you, Gideon, would be perfect. People hear your name and know they are about to take a shortcut to hell. Hey, what's that puzzled expression all about? I lose you?"

"So those days are behind us."

"Draw your own conclusions."

"You're killing me over here."

"We'd have to be professional. Anything else would be a disaster."

"And how would a man with my impeccable résumé fit into your fine organization?"

"You could travel with me. I have a lot of business going on. I'd school you, bring you up to speed on the various operations I have going on with this aspect of the business."

"While you're playing one-minute manager, would I get to wear high-end suits?"

"I love a man in a suit. You know I do. I can get you the best. Only the best."

"I'm not interested in being your replacement for Scamz."

"No one is Scamz, Gideon. Scamz is irreplaceable."

She reminded me of Lil' Kim, still obsessed with Notorious B.I.G. We stared at each a moment, then she looked away. My contempt wouldn't let me turn my head away.

She said, "Your reputation is growing, becoming almost mythical. Come work for me."

I shook my head.

My throat tightened. After what the Dutch boys said they had been paid to do, felt like I was betraying her. She'd get over it. Everyone betrayed in this business.

At Liverpool we dropped that conversation, left the train, and found our way to the tube.

As we breathed polluted air, the train rocked and pitched. One commuter stumbled. Others held on. There was enough noise to keep our conversation away from other ears.

I rubbed my hands together, touched Arizona's leg, said, "I'm close to a million dollars."

"Your point?"

"This girl I met at this pool hall in North Hollywood, back when she was half-naked and hustling, trying to feed her mother, hustling to take care of her sister, I had a thing for her, and I was bold enough to ask her to be mine. She told me if I had a million dollars she would be mine."

"I bet that young girl was broke and needy, probably had low self-esteem."

"Or would've done what it took to take care of her mother."

"Bet her mother is dead now. Bet her mother died with a needle in her arm."

"I heard she took care of her little sister too."

"That's what a big sister does when her mother is in the gutter smoking crack. Somebody has to grow up. Somebody has to become the adult. Somebody has to sacrifice."

Arizona turned away. People boarded the train and our conversation died.

I asked, "You have more work for me?"

"I do. And I need your help on the Amsterdam problem."

"And all of this madness and drama is connected to the same FEMA problem?"

"Need you to take the contract without question. Want that part of my life over."

"Without question."

"Yes. Without question."

"It sounds more personal than business."

"Sometimes there is no difference."

"Like I said, get me the package."

"It's forthcoming. Give me a day or two."

"Problem?"

She hesitated. "No problem. No problem at all."

"Guy from the plane. Let's assume you're being followed. How you want to handle it?"

"Need to make a few calls. See what I can find out about a contract man."

"His nose is broken."

"A contract man with a broken nose."

We rode, the tube rocking the crowd ever so gently. Next to us a group of professional Chinese women were talking, all of them had cockney accents. Black people were talking in French across from us. I'd been in America too long. Some things I'd never get used to.

A couple got on, carrying an infant. Arizona looked at them, almost smiled.

I moved over and sat next to Arizona.

I asked, "You ever think about having babies?"

"This isn't . . . I'm not living the have-a-baby lifestyle."

"You ever think about getting out of the business and being a full-time square?"

"Too late. I'm too caught up in the world I'm living in now. This is who I am."

I nodded.

She said, "I want children. Love. I want the things that make a woman feel beautiful."

"If the time was ever right, down the road, would you want that beautiful life with me?"

She sighed. My words aged her a hundred years, put stress lines in her forehead.

She said, "I care about you, Gideon."

"You say that like it's a bad thing."

"I want to *not* have these feelings for you or any man."

"What are you afraid of?"

"I will not let you come into my world and dismantle me."

"I told you I loved you. You rejected me. You're the one doing the dismantling."

"I will not allow you to break me into pieces. And it hurts me to say this . . ."

"Say it."

"Anong gusto mo sa buhay ko?"

"In English."

"You know we can't be together."

"Tell me why."

"Not like regular people. We're not regular people. We're damaged. Gideon, you and I have that in common. We are both damaged. Beyond repair."

She was a con artist. I killed people.

She asked, "The woman you met on the plane, what do you know about her?"

"Why?"

"Not trying to get personal. Trying to protect you. You're thinking with your dick and I'm trying to make sure your dick doesn't get you killed, the same way leaving the dick in charge has buried so many other men. With that said, what the fuck do you know about the woman?"

I took a hard breath and exhaled. "Nothing."

"Was she with the man with the broken nose?"

"Not at all. She sat next to me the whole flight."

"Same flight."

"Yeah."

"She made herself available to you as soon as your plane landed."

"Yeah."

"Eight hours after you met her."

"Yeah."

"And you fucked her."

"Yeah, I fucked her. You want the details?"

"You have to be careful."

"I am careful."

"When it comes to this business, soft legs and pussy is a great disguise."

"I am careful."

"Bullshit. Sleeping with strangers will have you waking with enemies."

"Which are you?"

Her lips turned down. "Unbelievable. You are unbelievable."

It was my turn to look frustrated, my turn to age one hundred years.

I thought about how Sergeant had offered me a ton of money to put Arizona to bed. For a moment, I imagined her gone, dead by my hand, the longing I owned dead as well.

She snapped, "How do you meet a bitch on the plane, end up fucking her as soon as you get here?"

"How do you fuck me, then say we didn't? How do you vanish for months at a time?" I threw my hands up. "Don't get mad at me for doing my own thing while you do yours."

"Let's not . . . let's remain professional."

"Fuck being professional. Let's be personal."

She leaned forward, looked in my eyes, remained calm. "Sure. Let's."

"I've worked hard, bent over backward because I wanted to be with you."

"Who asked you to?"

"Who asked me to?"

"That's what I said."

"I tell you I have close to a million stacked up and you blow me off."

"Because I can't be bought. I'm not a whore."

"What?"

"You asked me how much it would take for me to be with you, like I'm some sort of a whore. I'm not for sale. *I'm not a goddamn whore.* I'm not your mother. I'm not my sister. I don't go running to the highest bidder. I'm not my own mother. I am none of those people."

My laughter was gone. I gritted my teeth.

She said, "I'm not for sale."

"*You* said a million dollars. Those were *your* words, not *my* price."

"Of course. I said an amount that to me, at the time, years ago, was unreachable."

"So, in other words, you've always been unreachable to me."

"Maybe it's the other way around."

"What are you talking about?"

"Like a fool I came to you, came to surprise you, but you had that woman in your bed."

"If you were in my bed, would you be there when I woke up the next morning? Would you decide it didn't happen again, file it away with Chapel Hill and New York?"

She nodded. "This is why business and pleasure should not mix."

I nodded back. "You don't want me, so what difference does it make who I'm fucking?"

She reached into her bag, took out a package, tossed it, made it land next to me.

Luwak coffee. The present I had given her in North Carolina.

I said, "You're giving that back too?"

"Don't bring me coffee, talk to me for hours, walk around holding my hand, make me start to feel things I haven't felt in years, don't be nice to me, do the things in bed . . . the things you do . . . don't do all of that then take some whore to bed with you and act like it's no big fucking deal."

"You run hot and cold, push me away, tell me whatever we did didn't fucking happen—"

"Why in the hell do you think I came to London? *To see you.* I could've handled this business with you over the phone. Same goes for the business in North Carolina and New York."

"I tell you I have damn near a mill saved up and you—"

"Does it look like I need *anything* from any man? I'm not that destitute girl you met years ago. I have *hustled* my way through my pains and heartaches. A million dollars? Before long I'll have that ten times over. Your problem is that you're . . . you're . . . a whore. Just like your mother."

I dared her to say that shit again.

"Just like your mother. *Puta ka.*" She growled. "*Puta ka. Putang ina mo.*"

Then there were long, hate-filled stares.

The tube rocked. People around us. Nothing I could do. Arizona knew that.

I smiled. "Arizona, your mother was a cock-sucking, strung-out, broke-ass crackhead who fucked strangers and sucked unwashed dick to get high, and you're disrespecting me like that?"

"Son of a whore. That's all you are. The son of a whore."

"That's why Scamz used to smack your ass silly. Smacked you and fucked your sister because you didn't have what it took to keep a real man. And you still don't have what it takes."

She put her hand in her bag like she was about to pull out a weapon.

The female British voice announced we were approaching King's Cross. The train stopped. People rushed off as others hurried on, raced for vacant seats. Others stood, jockeyed for space, got between us with their backpacks and luggage, separated jealousy and anger.

I said, "How do you suck the Jesus out of my dick at a movie, get your nut, then leave like a goddamn whore? How do you do that? Learn that from your mother? Her mother?"

"Do I suck dick better than your mother?"

That shut me down. Flames rose in my eyes.

"Bitch." I gritted my teeth, my voice a deep growl. "I'll fuck your ass up."

Arizona said some things to me in Tagalog, and judging her expression they were vile and horrible things. She struggled by people, exited the tube, rage pacing her stride. I left the Luwak coffee on the seat, bumped around people, made it off the train just as the doors shut, more people separating us, chased her toward the WAY OUT sign, ran up the stairs after her like a damn square. She hurried away. Arizona knew I was there, heard me calling her name.

Both of us were beyond upset.

I was losing control. Not cool, not cool at all.

This was too damn volatile. Needed to turn around. But I chased her.

I was dynamite chasing a woman made of nitroglycerin.

She headed toward the escalator, got on, and moved with the impatient people on the left side, kept up with the ones who walked and ran to the top. Her slender legs pumped as she moved by people standing to the right, as she held her coat and bag tight to her chest, worked her heels and sprinted by advertisements for both the yellow pages and the theater.

Halfway up she slowed her pace and scowled back at me, her

small mouth tight, her body rising up toward the surface. We traded scowls until, once again, she vanished.

Grimacing, I went back to the tube, decided to let Arizona handle her own problems.

I battled London's cold and dreary weather.

London was a scandalous woman and I knew her sex-and-music district well, took to the small alleys with the clubs, places that were scary from the outside and not much better inside.

She was here.

I could smell her.

I'm surprised I didn't sense she was here.

The stench of Chinese food and heinous memories had battered my senses.

A boy in his late teens asked me if I was looking for girls, told me he had three upstairs. That there was no charge to look. I asked what his working women looked like. He described them, said all the girls were Russian. I shook my head, moved on.

Another man handed me a business card and walked on. The advertiser was half-naked, a dark-skinned African woman, her hair had dark roots, turned pink as it left her scalp, becoming fire red, wild hair that shot out like a fireworks show on the Fourth of July. The card said she worked in Central London, on Edgware Road; her rates started at £80 for half an hour, for full and personal service she charged £140, outcalls started at £250 for one and a half hours.

It wasn't her.

I dropped that card and moved on.

I was close. If she was still here, this would be her postal code.

Some places left their doors open, signs welcoming American money. Around £60 for half an hour of sex. Girls were selling themselves all over Chinatown and at Shepherd's Market.

I'd find her.

If she was here, I'd find her.

London was another hedonistic place, not the best, but far from being the worst, just had to know which rocks to turn over, which alleys to walk to rent pleasure.

I knew where to go. Outside of being Pleasure Alley, Soho had a strip of places for cultured businessmen to stop and buy hard-core porn before going home to the family.

Soho was where the whores went to work undisturbed by the law.

No matter how long it took, I'd find her tonight.

The anger I'd received from Arizona, it would get used before I went to bed.

I needed my own vengeance.

My personal anger had dug its claws into my flesh and dragged me to Soho.

My rage was looking for a whore.

A whore I should've killed in Amsterdam.

Twenty-one

women are trouble

Phone call from his ten-year-old daughter as he waited for the tube at Tower Hill.

"But, Dad . . . Skeeter is eating *all* the cereal. My *favorite* cereal. The *last* box."

"Melanie. Baby. What time is it over there in Texas?"

"It's one o'clock. And he's eating all the cereal. He always eats all the cereal."

She went on and on. In full-blown drama mode. Like her mother.

He took the phone away from his ear.

He was standing midway on the platform, District Line, when a couple, a tall and muscular black man wearing a BOSTON cap, and a woman, short and light-skinned, maybe a Zadie Smith–type, maybe an octoroon, he thought, stopped right by him. More like she stopped in front of him, her face tense with anger, and the tall black man followed her, his steps heavy, face laced with frustration. The guy wearing the BOSTON cap had on a leather coat, long and black. She wore an oversize black coat, about the size to fit the tall man she was with, and across the back of the jacket, in big red letters, was the word RENT. Her red scarf and red gloves matched the crimson marquee across her back.

She was upset. "You ran after her. Were gone an hour. Sneak off for a shag, did you?"

"No, I didn't sneak off and shag anybody."

Her accent was British. His accent wasn't.

"You prefer shagging her? If so, then go to her. Go to her now."

"Could you not do this bullshit right now?"

The man with the broken nose watched them. They were the loudest on the platform. Not screaming, but the only ones that could be heard, the British being a quiet lot.

"You pathetic wanker. Liar. You're still shagging her. If I hadn't come back from Birmingham with me parents, you would've been shagging her in our bed nonetheless."

She stormed away from him, her heels clacking across the concrete.

The tall guy waited a moment, took a few hard breaths, then he followed her.

They resumed their argument to the end of the platform.

The man with the broken nose stopped watching the show, put the phone to his ear.

His daughter was still ranting about her older brother eating all the cereal.

He asked his daughter, "Where is your mother?"

"I just told you Mom was in her room syncing her iPod."

"Syncing her iPod?"

"She's on iTunes downloading movies and videos and television shows and music."

"Tell your mother to stop syncing her iPod and make Skeeter stop eating your cereal."

"She yelled at me, told me to leave her alone, then she closed her door in my face."

"Geesh."

"Skeeter had cereal last night and this morning. I won't have any cereal for breakfast. What am I supposed to eat for breakfast, Daddy? He's eating the cereal."

He put the phone down again.

Glasses on, he checked his watch, saw it was seven, took his glasses off, tucked them away, looked up at the monitor, saw a tube was due in two minutes, then stood to the side of the crowded platform and looked over the tube map. The concierge had told him he could catch the District or the Circle. But he didn't trust the man's Romanian accent. He read the map. The Circle would take him to Liverpool, then the Central to Stratford. He was confused. He was at the District Line. He could run to the Central Line, but running would mess up his shower. Decided to take the District Line to Mile End, change to Central Line for one stop to Stratford Station. He hoped he was there in thirty minutes. He had to get to Stratford. To the Theatre Royal Stratford East.

The best seats cost £18 and he wanted to get the tickets before they were gone. This was his day off. No guns. No packages to take care of. No soon-to-be ex-wife.

No IRS. No lawyers.

He put the phone back up to his ear. Loved his kid, but wanted her off the phone.

He asked, "What do you want me to do about it? I'm in London, for Christ's sake."

"Daddy—did you hear what I said? I asked you about Harry Potter."

"Look, I'm on the tube platform and—"

"Harry Potter Harry Potter. Please please please get my Harry Potter books."

"Take the cereal from your brother."

"He'll slap me in my head if I take his cereal."

"Make him a ham-and-cheese sandwich. Cut the edges off. He'll like that."

"He'll throw the sandwich at me."

"I have to go."

"Last time he threw his cereal at me. The whole bowl. Milk was all on my hair."

"Look . . . you're going to have to be a big girl and handle the situ—"

"Daddy—I'm ten years old. He's fifteen. He's ten times bigger than I am big."

"Stop exaggerating."

"Daddy. Help me."

"Bang on your mother's door." He took a breath. "I have to go."

She hung up, screaming at her brother to stop eating up her favorite cereal.

He hopped on the tube. So many crazy people were on the tube. He'd never seen so many iPods and books in one place. Everybody wore earphones, crowded next to each other and disconnected from each other. The closer people were, the further they were apart. That's why he loved Katy. People were nice in Katy. People talked to each other in Katy. With all the books and iPods the tube looked like a cross between an electronic and a book convention.

The loud couple moved around looking for space, came his way, stopped next to him.

They were still arguing. It was obvious the woman wouldn't let the argument die.

The tall guy with the BOSTON cap asked the might-be-an-octoroon wearing the oversize RENT jacket, "Who did I help get the audition? Who has the part? You or Lola?"

"Did you tell Lola that? Did you tell Lola that you told them to not audition her? Does she know I'm Mimi? She's not Mimi. I am Mimi."

"Not now."

"*But did you tell her?* Did the words come from your mouth and go to her ears?"

"Please." He adjusted his BOSTON cap, infuriated. "Let's talk about this later."

"You left me looking like a fool and you chased her. Do you know how that makes me feel? You left me and you ran after her. You were gone almost an hour. You left me for her."

Boston didn't say anything.

The girl folded her arms, closed off body language.

She asked, "You still love her, don't you? You prefer her to me. Tell me. You pathetic lying wanker. Tell me. Do you prefer her? I bloody hate you. You know that? I bloody hate you."

Boston gritted his teeth, then grabbed the girl, grabbed her rough, five thousand pounds of anger in his eyes.

Looked like Boston was about to knock the bejesus out of the might-be-an-octoroon.

The man with the broken nose was about to say something, was about to get involved.

But the guy wearing the BOSTON cap pulled the might-be-an-octoroon to him and kissed her, tongue and all.

She fought it for a moment, twisted, struggled, slapped his shoulders, very theatrical, then went limp in his arms, again dramatic.

The man with the broken nose moved by them, went to the opposite end of the car, found peace and quiet, and an empty seat. On the seat was a newspaper. *The Mirror.* Special edition.

The front page was about the dead WAG.

He popped a square of cinnamon gum in his mouth, picked up the paper, fixed his $10 glasses over his injured nose, started reading about the heinous crime that had London in a choke hold. The papers said the crime was brutal. Done in public. With no reliable witnesses.

He looked down at the other end of the train.

That couple was still kissing.

Tebby smiled.

Still dressed in the colors of angels. Six feet tall, like a goddess. Standing out in a sea of darkness and gloom. He saw her when he stepped off the tube. She was waiting.

Tall and bald. Her long coat flowing like a cape. But the bald head.

She made being bald look chic and daring and beautiful.

He greeted her with a broad smile, asked, "How was your day?"

"Lovely because I thought of you all day."

He smiled. "I thought about you all day too."

She complimented him on his new suit, then extended her hand. He took her hand.

Her skin was soft. And warm. Very warm. And electric. Very electric. His throat dried and his voice tried to shrink.

Seeing her again was enough. Holding her hand was more than he had expected.

She took the lead and he followed her, maneuvered through the mostly black crowd toward Great Eastern Road. The tube station was huge. A DLR station was there as well. A freight yard not too far away. Across the street was a mall. She told him that the theater was on the other side of the plaza, but they could walk through the mall and come out right at the theater.

As he walked, one of his cellular phones rang.

The phone that chimed was the hotline.

Sam was calling.

Either with news on Gideon. Or a new contract.

But he didn't answer. Not while he was holding Tebby's hand.

Not while everything in his life was, for once, perfect.

Inside the small theater the actors were already onstage.

The stage set up to show different locations. The play hadn't started, but the actors were on stage interacting, ignoring the audience, already creating the atmosphere of South Africa. Men to the side drinking and gambling. A young man on a bed, resting between a younger girl's legs, a girl dressed in a school uniform. A mixed-race boy reading a book. Much more.

The actors moved with spirit, the set changed, the play began.

With a brutal rape.

He heard sobbing and looked at Tebby. Tears remained in her eyes. The play had moved beyond the initial rape and murder, eventually showed a schoolgirl fleeing her home after a lifetime of squabbling and abuse, only to find solace in the arms of a gangster, and Tebby was still crying. Not loud. Gentle tears. A serial killer was on the loose, the play was dramatic and brutal, but since the part with the schoolgirl fleeing, Tebby had quietly been sobbing.

The man with the broken nose reached over and took Tebby's hand.

The play ended as it began. With brutality and abuse.

The actors received a standing ovation.

Tebby looked at him as if she were saying this was her life, her world.

He put his finger up to her damp cheek. Then he kissed her cheek.

While the crowd applauded, Tebby moved closer, put her head on his shoulder.

He asked Tebby, "You need a moment?"

She nodded.

Inside his pocket, his cellular vibrated. The hotline was on fire.

Twenty-two

detour

Leicester Square was alive, crowded and lit up like it was Times Square.

The man with the broken nose hated the crowd, he hated crowds, preferred the easiness of Katy, Texas, over this craziness. Too many people. He had paused in front of the rows of people off the side of the three cinemas, artists sketching mediocre caricatures of tourists, hundreds of people filing into clubs and restaurants between the Leicester Square tube and the Piccadilly tube. They walked by Burger King, Starbucks, Häagen-Dazs, and steak houses.

He moved on with Tebby.

Tebby said, "You haven't said anything about the play."

"I didn't know what to say. Saw you were disturbed by the performance."

"I wanted a different ending."

"You didn't like the ending?"

She shrugged. "Yes. And no. It made sense. But I wanted something else."

He said, "Seemed appropriate to me. Made sense."

"The killer got away."

The man with the broken nose shrugged.

Tebby nodded. "Wanted a happy ending. We all want happy endings. Everybody does."

He thought about the scenes with the killing the most. How when dying, people clung to life to their last breath. Like they were suffocating. Like when he was a kid drowning in water.

He didn't asked Tebby why she'd cried during the scenes portraying rape and murder, more of the former than the latter. He just thought about his little girl. It was a brutal world.

Tebby led him by the Prince Charles Cinema in the heart of the square. Another Häagen-Dazs Café. Pizza Hut. Tokyo Diner. Cork & Bottle. All Bar One. New Diamond. Mr. Kong.

She asked, "See anything to your liking?"

He pointed at Bella Italia, an Italian restaurant between Baskin-Robbins and Club Metro.

The man with the broken nose took Tebby there. He was still holding Tebby's hand.

He said, "You haven't asked me about my nose."

"And you haven't asked me about my bald head."

"I figured if you wanted me to know about your bald head, you'd tell me."

"Same for your nose."

He wanted a table where he could keep his back to the wall, so he could watch whoever came into the room. Old habits that had kept him alive this long. Tebby told him she wanted to sit upstairs in the window, said that way they could see all of Leicester Square and people-watch as they ate dinner. Mild tension rose up inside him. The corner of his lips turned downward.

First date. In London. With a queen from Botswana.

He complied.

After they ordered he said, "So you say you're from Francistown in Botswana."

Tebby said, "Francistown. That's where I was born."

"Haven't heard of a lot of the places in Africa you mentioned."

Tebby asked, "Do you read? If so, what books?"

"I read. I lean toward Dostoyevsky. Kafka. What about you?"

"African writers. Bessie Head. Zoë Wicomb. Nelson Mandela. Coetzee. People like that. Oh, I'm reading Constance Briscoe's book. *Ugly*. Heard her mum is suing her over things she said."

"Connie Briscoe?"

"Constance. She's a judge here. Wrote her story. Abused as a child by her mum."

"Is that right."

"Her mum beat her, starved her, abandoned her when she was thirteen."

"Sounds . . . depressing, if you don't mind me saying so."

"She was physically and mentally abused. Now she is a judge."

"Amazing. But still sounds depressing."

"We can do anything when we decide to win no matter what. You should read it."

He wanted to order drinks. Tebby recommended shandy. Beer flavored with lemonade. Her favorite drink. So he ordered shandy.

Tebby asked, "Where were you born in Texas?"

"Moved to Texas when I was a kid. Grew up in a little city called Roscoe. Was born in West Memphis, Arkansas."

"Never heard of that West Memphis place. Is that similar to L.A. or New York?"

"Neither. Sounds like the place you grew up, to tell the truth."

"I doubt if it's anything like where I grew up. We didn't have electricity."

"No electricity?"

"No one did. It was no big deal. We didn't know we were supposed to have electricity."

He wasn't good at small talk. Wished he hadn't said the *Ugly* book sounded depressing.

Not like his life had been the source of inspiration for many.

A moment later Tebby asked, "Your father only had one wife?"

"Yeah. Yours?"

"Six wives, my father had. Maybe seven."

"Six or seven wives?"

"Africans. Polygamy. It still exists. Men have many wives."

"Brothers and sisters? You have brothers and sisters?"

"Of course. Do I know them all? Of course not."

The food came and they began eating.

He said, "So, why are you bald? Since you put it out there a while ago."

"My best friend back home, my childhood friend, her name is Lorato Modiri."

"Okay."

"She has cancer. She lost all of her hair."

"Sorry to hear that. I really am."

"That is why I shaved my head. I had long hair. Long, beautiful hair. So did Lorato. The chemotherapy has taken all of her hair. So I shaved my head to show her my love. My support."

That warmed him.

He said, "You're amazing."

"So are you, Bruno."

When they were done eating, Tebby went to the toilet.

His phone buzzed. The hotline.

He took out his phone. Voice strong and confident he answered, "Talk to me."

"Got another job."

"Pitch it to me."

"Gambling debt. Jamaican."

"The sponsor?"

"Jamaican that runs this betting shop in Croydon. Jamaican-on-Jamaican thing."

"Get me the package."

"Talk soon."

"Yeah. Talk soon."

He hung up.

Tebby was making her way back through the crowd.

He watched the way other men and women stared at her.

Tebby had her cellular phone up to her face.

He wondered who she had tipped away to call.

Her children.

An old lover who spoke French and spat out bullshit poetry.

A current lover that she would go visit as soon as she finished dinner.

He sighed. Killing was so much easier than dating.

He looked out the window. At the crowd. So many people in a small space.

Hip-hop boys were passing out flyers, trying to lure the pretty women into clubs.

A white man with a Bible was off to the side preaching the word to no one.

A hundred pubs and twice as many clubs were in the square. Thousands of people were passing by. He witnessed at least three hundred nationalities per minute.

Then he almost jumped to his feet.

Gideon.

He thought he saw Gideon coming down Bear Street, a street that angled in from Charing Cross and Trafalgar Square into the heart of the pandemonium. The man with the broken nose wasn't sure. *Im-fucking-possible.* His heart raced as he watched the man that looked like Gideon, spied him passing by the venues that sold half-price theater tickets. It was dark, it was crowded, thousands of people were down below, but he focused on that singular face as it came closer.

As if on cue, Gideon stopped right out front of Bella Italia, looked back toward Café Rimini and Vue, then moved by the long line of people trying to get inside Metro Club & Bar.

It was Gideon without a doubt. And he was alone.

He was in perfect position for a bullet to the head.

The man with the broken nose reached for his gun. But he didn't have a weapon.

His Desert Eagle was back in his hotel room.

He took out his cellular, started dialing Sam's number.

Had to know if the money was in place.

If the money was in place, he would handle that contract tonight.

"Bruno, are you ready?"

Phone in his hand, he looked up at this woman.

A tall woman. Dressed in white. Her smile as big as her earrings.

For a moment he had no idea who she was.

Then he remembered.

Tebby.

The woman was Tebby.

She said, "Ready to leave?"

He hesitated. "Ready."

He took her hand and rushed her out of the restaurant, headed in the direction Gideon had gone, looking for him in the crowd, then seeing Gideon again.

Tebby said, "Thank you for dinner."

"You're welcome."

He thought Gideon was heading toward the Piccadilly Circus tube, but Gideon turned down a side street that went toward Shaftesbury Avenue, moved through that crowd.

Holding Tebby's hand, the man with the broken nose paused, his heart still racing, palms damp, jaw tight, droves of people moving around him as he stared at his vanishing target.

He asked Tebby, "What's down there?"

"Wardour Street goes into Soho. Chinatown. Red-light district. Strip clubs."

"Is that right?"

"Harmony has a big store down there. Largest adult store in the area."

"Didn't know that."

"Want to go?"

"Actually, I'm tired, ready to turn in, so I'd better get you back to the tube."

"You're right. I need to get the tube south and find where to change."

"South? You're not going back to Tower Hill?"

"To Brixton. South London."

"Thought you lived somewhere up by Tower Hill."

"Oh, no. Can't afford that area. Was in the financial district looking for another job. I won't be able to afford to open my own restaurant with the job I have, not on this salary."

"Then let me . . . I'll walk you to the tube."

"Actually, I'll take the bus. Walk me to Charing Cross?"

Charing Cross was in the opposite direction, at least ten minutes. Longer with Tebby's slow and easy pace. By the time he walked to Charing Cross, stuck her on a tube, and ran back to Soho, Gideon's trail would be cold. Gideon's trail was almost cold now.

He could do this now. Get home to his children.

He was anxious. "How long will it take you to get to Brixton?"

"Depends. If I leave now, I should be fine." She checked her watch. "If I miss the last tube, then I have to catch the bus. And if the tube stops before I get home, I still have to get off and take a bus or a taxi. Getting to Brixton could be tricky. And that could take a while."

He was determined. "No, let me put you in a taxi."

"That's not necessary."

"I insist. Let me put you in a taxi."

He held her hand as they walked.

Desire.

He felt her desire.

It was subtle, but it was there.

With him trying to end the evening, that desire became more pronounced.

More obvious.

She said, "If you wanted to go through Soho, look at some shops . . ."

"It's late."

"I know. Just don't want the night to end so abruptly."

A six-foot-tall, beautiful woman from Botswana had offered to stroll into the red-light district and browse a porn store with him. The gods could be so cruel.

Tebby asked, "Everything okay?"

"What you mean?"

"You're . . . different all of a sudden. Did I do or say something wrong?"

He said, "I'm . . . it was a long flight. Six-hour time change. No sleep. Had a long day."

"And I didn't bring clothes. If I went with you, I'd have to leave in a couple of hours to get back home in time to change for work. I'd be exhausted. So I guess I need to go home."

He flagged down a hackney, gave Tebby £60, more than enough to get her home. He hugged her good-bye. He was trying to rush, but he felt her trying to make it linger.

She said, "I'm glad I went to Starbucks today."

"Me too."

She leaned forward. He leaned to her. She gave him her tongue. A slow, soft kiss.

When it ended, he felt light-headed. She looked intoxicated.

He said, "Tomorrow?"

"Should I bring an extra bag with me? Or would that be inappropriate?"

That frankness caught him off guard.

He smiled. "Yes. Bring an extra bag."

"Then I will bring an extra bag. Clothes for work. Just in case."

"Talk soon?"

"Talk soon. Cheers."

As the taxi pulled away, he sprinted back toward the street he had seen Gideon take.

He peeped inside porn shops. Passed by strip shows advertising American-style pole dancing. Then came out in heart of the red-light area. Saw men going in and out of doors.

Saw women up in the windows, red lights glowing as they smoked hand-rolled cigarettes.

He found Gideon. Spied him passing by two little boys who were in the streets playing soccer. He watched Gideon look inside the doorway that led to every working woman.

The man with the broken nose eased through the crowd.

Moving by the kids playing soccer, he watched Gideon, focused, searching.

He got closer. Twenty yards. Ten yards. Point-blank range. Without a gun.

The filthy soccer ball stole his attention, hit his leg. The little boys ran by him without apology.

Then Gideon disappeared inside the doorway of the house of whores.

The man with the broken nose slowed at the door.

The whore asked Gideon, "Blow job or full service?"

He saw the back of Gideon's head, the golden legs of the working woman who was up at the top of the stairs. The man with the broken nose moved on, lurked across the street from a queer porn shop, then found a better hiding spot in Tyler's Court, an alley that was about six feet wide and no more than thirty yards away from the door Gideon had entered.

He jogged down the alley, searched for something he could use as a killing device. Nothing. He couldn't find a bottle on the streets. Nothing to serve as a good shank.

He ran back to the end of the alley. Watched men walking in and out of doors.

The kids were still playing soccer, kicking a dirty ball up and down a street that smelled like shit. He stood in the shadows wondering if Gideon was armed, wondering if Gideon was in that flat on a contract, waited with his heart beating loud enough to mute all sounds, reminding himself that Gideon had massacred several men in Tampa, knowing Gideon had acted alone, that he had done what was impossible, had killed a small army without any weapons.

That meant Gideon was good at hand-to-hand combat.

This might not be the place. Or the time. Not for hand-to-hand.

A bullet in the head was always the best.

Hand-to-hand wasn't his ideal scenario.

He waited. People going up and down Berwick, some taking the alley, he waited.

He kept his eye on the whore's door, watching the boys chase the shitty soccer ball.

Gideon's package had been impressive. It seemed like Gideon had a reputation.

The man with the broken nose told himself he needed a larger reputation.

A larger reputation yielded more money.

He could kill Gideon and take his name. Take both his name and his fame.

Or just be known as the man who killed Gideon.

He waited wishing he had time to get his Desert Eagle and come back.

He waited thinking about Tebby.

Wondering, if he hadn't seen Gideon, how their night would've ended.

It didn't matter. He wouldn't call her again. It always started off nice. And ended badly.

When a man grew older, he grew wiser, learned to play the ending.

He'd learned from his own experiences.

He'd let the romantic evening with Tebby die with that first and last kiss.

His phone rang. The hotline.

Sam answered, "Talk to me."

"I found Gideon. And I'm getting ready to kill him."

He'd never see Tebby again.

He'd kill Gideon and catch the first flight back to Katy.

Twenty-three

valley of darkness

The green cardboard sign outside the first door I passed said
MODEL UPSTAIRS.

Hand-painted on the wall inside the next door was the same advertisement.

Berwick Street. Central London. Postal code W1.

Red lights were perched in almost every windowsill, red bulbs hanging inside dingy windows.

Openings to every door had at least one fading sign made from cheap cardboard, damp cardboard that had been cut by hand and warped by the elements, written on in block-style lettering that looked like it had come from someone who had a third-grade education at most.

A soccer ball rolled by my feet. Two young boys, neither any more than six, ran by me, chasing the ball. One had blond, curly hair. He had on yellow-and-green footballer's gear, Brazil's team, the number 10, and the name RONALDINHO across his back. The other boy had dark skin, maybe the darkest skin I'd ever seen, his footballer gear blue-and-white, the colors of Chelsea, the number 8 and the name LAMPARD across the rear of his jersey.

Five little girls stood to the side cheering them on. Miniature footballers and wannabe WAGS. Those preschool kids were out during the sexual hours, on their own. Not afraid of the night or the adults passing by in search of pleasure and drugs. They were at home in this world.

So was I.

Every door was open. They were waiting; women with working names like Michelle, Sarah, and Elena were in their windows waiting to show customers how friendly they could be for the right price. The doors that had cheap signs that said YOUNG ASIAN MODEL were ignored. Thelma wasn't Asian. Door after door, I searched London's red-light district, where the whores called themselves models. I doubted if any of these women would appear on Tyra Banks's show.

The sign was yellow. The handwriting familiar and as unique as her own fingerprints.

DIAMOND. SEDUCTIVE AND FULLY EXPERIENCED. ALL SERVICES. LOVES A&O.

Her cheap, wooden door was barely on the hinges of a small, indiscreet opening between British Sex Shop and Blue Boy Paradise DVD Shop, the latter having more than enough copies of blue movies with men being friendly with men in every square inch of its front window.

She was working on a narrow street lined with porn shops and peep shows.

I looked down the avenue. The blond kid was kicking the ball to his friend.

The children of whores were entertaining themselves in the midnight hour.

Nobody noticed me.

I could find my peace and sanity in five minutes. Maybe less.

A man rushed down the concrete stairs.

He hit the streets smiling, looking relaxed and anxious to get away before he was exposed. He made eye contact and

surrendered the red-faced chuckle of a man who had just finished fucking, then hurried down Berwick, not looking back
until he was down by Vinyl Junkies.

He looked back and gave me the thumbs-up.

That meant the pussy was good. Give it a shot. The ride was
worth the ticket.

I turned into the opening, a piss odor assaulting my senses.
Chipped concrete stairs led up to more chipped concrete stairs.
Dull white walls and more foul odors greeted me. Paint was
peeling away from the walls and ceiling. Exposed pipes and
crooked stairs were an eyesore. Handrail was about to fall free.
Light fixtures outdated, would bet the same for the electrical
throughout the building. Another step inside and I saw the ceiling was sagging. A handyman could spend three years on this
property doing modernization and improvements.

The stairway was steep. All I could see were her feet. And
from her angle all she could see were my jeans and boots. I recognized her feet. My heartbeat sped up.

I stepped up until I could see most of her body, from waist
down.

Then went up a few stairs until I could see her up to her
neck.

It was her.

She was at the top of the dingy stairway, in the cramped
space, sitting on a shiny barstool, a brand-new barstool that was
in contradiction with everything else. She sat there, reggae playing in the background, legs crossed, like she was a queen sitting
on her throne.

Bob Marley sang his redemption song. Everyone wanted redemption.

I wanted revenge.

She was on her cellular phone, finishing up a cigarette.
She released a quick exhalation that stopped short of exuding
boredom.

She asked me, "Blow job or full service?"

"Are you as good as the Russian and Asian girls?"

"First off, I'm better than the Russians. Or the Asians. I'm better than anything you'll find on Tisbury or Peter Street. And the Asians give you a awful blow job and the worst sex you ever had. They won't give you your money's worth. With me, you get a wicked time. And no up sale. My rate is all-inclusive. So, with that said, tell me what you need and I'll tell what it will cost."

"Is that right, Thelma?"

She stood up with quickness when I said her birth name, a name she hadn't probably heard or gone by in years. Her shiny barstool screeched across the rugged concrete landing.

I went up a few more stairs, until I could see her face, until she could see mine.

"What's the matter, Thelma?"

Disbelief widened her eyes.

I said, "Haven't seen you since Amsterdam. Not since you were in window 120."

She saw that it was really me and dropped her cigarette, fumbled for it, and dropped her mobile phone. Her mobile hit the stairs, came apart, the battery flying out. I picked up the phone, the battery, put it back together, took a couple of steps up, and tossed it back to her. She tried to catch it, but it fell again, this time near her feet. She left it where it was, not worried about reconnecting and finishing her phone call in the proper way. I took three more steps. Heard her deep breathing. If I didn't know any better, I'd think she was trembling. The red light over my head, darkness still shadowing most of my features.

Seconds slipped by with droves of witnesses hurrying down the cobbled road behind me.

She lit another cigarette. In a trembling voice she asked, "How did you find me?"

"I found you."

"You're angry. You're still angry."

I took another step up. "Very angry."

She backed away from me.

I asked, "You don't think I'd kill you, do you?"

"You're so damn angry." She touched her left eye, did the same to her lips and chin, made a terrified face, cringed like she still felt the pain. "You beat me up pretty bad."

"With cause."

"You went insane."

"You were gone when I came back."

"I was in the hospital pissing blood."

"You should've been in a mental institute."

"What I did was wrong. But I never struck you. Not once."

I was one step below her by then. Close enough to inhale her perfume. Smelled the scent of seven or eight colognes mixed into the sweat that had dried on her skin. The scent of many men lived on her flesh. Today had been a good day for her. I'd showed up after the rush.

She took my hand, pulled me closer, kissed both sides of my cheeks, then kissed me on my lips. Her lipstick was thick, red. I wiped it away. It stained my hands like blood.

She softened her voice, asked, "How've you been?"

"Was about to ask you the same, Thelma."

"Please, stop calling me Thelma."

"Your name is Thelma."

"You're my son. Please. Call me mother."

Twenty-four

prelude to fury

Her cellular rang.

Her ring tone was hip-hop. Beyoncé. Thelma picked up her cellular phone, looked at the number, pressed a button to divert the call, then sat back down on her barstool.

I leaned against the wall, left her potential customers a clear shot of her wares.

She asked, "What name are you using now?"

"Gideon."

"The name you had when we were in Montreal, that was the name I liked best."

"I don't give a shit what you like."

She paused. "You found me. You actually found me."

"Ran into Sergeant."

"He told you."

"Right before he died."

Her face lit up. She shook her head. Grief covered her face. Her eyes watered.

She asked, "You?"

I nodded.

Her lip trembled. She swallowed. "No. Not Sergeant. Why?"

"Because some people deserve to die."

Her grief magnified. As did her fear of me.

Looked like she wanted to run. Then realized there was nowhere to run.

Then she jumped.

Someone was sneaking up behind me.

I remembered Amsterdam, how she had sent trouble to find me.

I jerked around, ready to attack whoever was creeping up behind me.

I wouldn't be as nice to them as I was to the thugs in Amsterdam.

A man in a suit was standing in the ragged doorway. His face unseen.

Thelma called down, "What can I do for you today?"

He crept up the stairs, took slow steps, walked halfway up before stopping.

He said, "Diamond?"

"Yes."

"You were referred to me."

"By whom?"

"Ahmad."

"Okay." She said that like she had no idea who Ahmad was. "What can I do for you?"

He wore jeans, tie, and worn dress shoes. Eyeglasses with small lenses. Hair black and cut short. Thick and with so much body hair looked like he had the werewolf syndrome. His leather coat was open wide, his gut spilling over his belt.

He whispered, "How much for straight sex?"

"Twenty pounds."

"How much time?"

"Ten minutes."

"How much for a blow job?"

"Sex and blow job, thirty pounds. If you want multiple positions, forty."

"I would like to get the sex and blow job for thirty quid, please."

"Thirty pounds up front."

"How soon can I see you?"

"Catch me in about an hour."

"Have to get the tube home to the family. I don't have that much time to spare."

"Then come back in fifteen to thirty. You'll have enough time to make the last tube."

"You take Visa?"

"Cash. Until you become a regular. Then I'll accept credit."

"I'll go to the cash machine, be right back."

"A cash machine is right across the street at Somerfield."

"Somerfield is closed."

"Use the one inside Blue Boy. Tell them I sent you."

The man waved and hurried away, checking his watch.

It was hard to do, but I raised my head and looked in my mother's eyes.

We stared for a moment.

She said, "A son should never hurt his mother."

"And a mother should never do the hurtful . . . the damaging things you did to her son."

Again we stared. Two unfeeling, poker-faced stares.

She said, "You killed Sergeant."

I nodded.

Her grief magnified. "I was drunk. When that thing happened, I was drunk."

"And I was angry."

"You almost killed me."

"You did so many horrible things to me."

"I almost died that night."

"Almost."

"You're still angry."

"Very."

"You were so angry in Amsterdam. I'd never seen you look like that."

"This is what you created. I'm your Frankenstein monster."

She swallowed.

I had marched up to her door like I was the Cylons invading New Caprica. Had come to her filled with bile, hate poisoning my every thought. Hate was a virus. Revenge its only cure.

I said, "'You can't play God and wash your hands of the things you've created because sooner or later the day comes and you can't run from the things you've done anymore.'"

I had just quoted *Battlestar Galactica*, a speech Adama had given had hit close to home, stayed with me. That same quote reminded me of other whispers from a shallow grave.

Nothing was said for a moment.

Her eyes were blank, haunted. She mumbled, kept repeating, "Sergeant is dead."

She said that like there had been a deeper connection between them.

More than sex for hire. More than sharing drinks.

She said, "Ever since Amsterdam, almost every night, without fail, I've dreamed about you coming to murder me. I knew you'd come. I knew you'd find me. I knew you'd be angry."

"We'll get that taken care of before I leave London."

She shuddered.

"Diamond?" That British accent came from behind me. "Are you Diamond?"

A man in a leather jacket was down in the doorway. Tall. White. Dorky. Ugly as hell.

Her voice trembled. "Can I help you, handsome?"

"What you charge for back door?"

"Sixty quid. That includes blow job and multiple positions."

"Now a good time?"

"Why don't you come up here and wait."

The man passed by me, went up top, passed by my mother, went into her flat.

I smiled, my grin unadulterated anger.

She smiled in return, hers still laced with fear.

I terrified her. She had let that stranger up so she could feel safe. So I wouldn't do her harm right now. If I did, she'd have a witness to my rage. If I needed to, I could kill him easier than I could kill her, just as fast. In every war there was collateral damage. Somebody was always in the way of victory.

"Good to see you're still selling the hole I came out of."

She swallowed, almost came undone. "I have to go."

"One question before you go make that money."

"What, Son?"

"Don't call me Son."

"You are my son. I will call you my son."

I paused, then worked my way to one of the many questions that had been in my mind all of these years. "You stole from that man. Did you not steal from that man?"

"What man?"

"The man who tried to kill you. The man I killed for you. The first person I killed."

"Mr. Midnight."

"I think he caught you trying to steal from him."

"That's not what happened."

"His attack wasn't unprovoked."

"Shouldn't matter why he attacked me. You were supposed to save your mother."

"He tried to kill a thieving whore."

"Now you have become him."

"Bullshit. I became what you made me."

"My sweet little Frankenstein."

"I'll be back for you. Before I leave, I will be back."

"I know. I'll be here."

"One more question."

"Yes, Son?"

"Who was my father?"

"I told you. He was in the army. Special Forces."

"Where is he now?"

"Only saw him that one time."

"Then how do you know that man was my father?"

"Maybe I made sure he was your father."

"What does that mean?"

"I put his sperm inside me when he left. I took the condom and put his sperm inside me."

"Why?"

"Because I liked him. Because he was a real man. He was the kind of man I would've wanted to be my husband. Because I wanted part of him to stay with me."

"Why?"

"Because I wanted to have a baby. Because I was tired of being alone. After my best friend was killed, maybe I had a hard time dealing with life. I hated being alone in this world."

My anger had me blazing.

I said, "See you soon."

"How much time do I have?"

"Not much. Get your house in order."

"I'll be here. I'll be ready."

Then she backed away, eased inside her apartment, and closed the door.

Her perfume remained, mixed in with the toxic stench that was assaulting my senses.

I turned around, took the slimy concrete stairs to the cold and slimy rue, once again greeted by droves of strangers and neon signs advertising sex. I headed up the narrow road.

It was starting to rain again. Even if it stormed forty days and forty nights, it would never rain hard enough to wash away this scum.

Numb. I was numb. I slowed down between a cloth shop and

the Islamic Centre. I looked back, saw half-dressed women standing in dingy windows, cigarettes burning between their fingertips, lips painted, eyes done, boredom in their eyes, red lightbulbs over their heads.

"How much does she charge you for her services?"

Coming toward me, money in hand, it was the fat, hairy man I'd just seen in her doorway.

He adjusted his glasses, asked, "How much she charges you, mate?"

My eyes went to him. My hands turning into fists.

He asked, "I think thirty quid is a bit much for straight sex and a bloody blow job."

Darkness rose. I was about to lose my freedom and kill that man.

He repeated, "They all say she's good, but if you ask me, she looks a little worn around the edges. What you think? Was she worth it? Did she give you full service or only a blow job?"

"*Away from me.*"

"What was that?"

I shoved him so hard he stumbled and fell down.

He rolled side to side, got up, cursed me. I went toward him, hands in fists. He ran away. I scowled at the stiff-lipped people who were staring at me.

I marched away, shoulders hunched.

Like Frankenstein.

From time to time my mother used to send women to my room. I'd wake up and some beautiful stranger would be stimulating me, doing whatever my mother had paid them to do. The last time . . . I was sixteen. Maybe seventeen. Had dropped out of school by then. I had fallen asleep. Nocturnal emission. Might've been masturbating in my sleep. Don't know what I was dreaming about. Or who. Halle Berry. Vivica Fox. Nia Long. Maybe all of those heavenly creatures at once. Woke up when I started having an orgasm. Looked down and expected to see the

Filipina woman I had grown accustomed to, or maybe the face of a stranger from Ethiopia, or Russia, hoped to see the eyes of an exotic women smiling up at me, sucking my dick as her introduction. But I woke up with my drunken mother in my bedroom; the woman who had birthed me had taken me inside her mouth like I was a john from the streets.

I knew it had to be a mistake. She wouldn't do that on purpose.

Then she looked up at me. She looked in my eyes.

I wanted to push her away. But my orgasm had traveled beyond the point of no return, no matter how I wanted to, that overwhelming sensation had gone too far to turn it around.

I shuddered, cursed, held her head, pulled her hair. She made me come.

My drunken mother had assaulted me. Raped me with her mouth.

I yanked her up to her feet and hit her. The first blow was a backhand across her face.

She grabbed her bloodied mouth, tried to run. I caught her, threw her into the wall.

She tried to get out the door and I grabbed her leg, dragged her back inside.

Like Mr. Midnight had done, I grabbed her hard and quick, picked her up by her neck.

She scratched my hands, kicked her feet, gagged.

I was going to kill her and throw her dead body in the streets.

Was going to kill her quick and without mercy, kill like she had taught me to do.

I had already found out she'd been stealing from me, pimping me.

When she stopped moving, I yanked my hands from her throat.

I dropped her. I thought she was dead. Hoped she was dead.

And I left her just like that. I left her battered and bruised body in the middle of the floor.

That had fucked me up.

When I came back, she wasn't there. She never came back.

Left me there, a high school dropout, the only skill I had was the one she had taught.

Neon ADULT CINEMA and XXX signs lit up Berwick Street and Soho.

Soho. *So many Hos.* Maybe that's what *Soho* stood for.

I tried to move on, but I couldn't. I was stuck in my past. I looked back at Thelma's door. Saw another man standing in the piss- and smoke-smelling stairwell reading her cheap, handwritten cardboard sign, then saw that man lower his head and hurry up the filthy stairs.

I could've been done. Could've ended my misery. With the heel of my hand I could've hit her nose, shoved her bone back into her brain. It would've been quick for her. And over for me.

The soccer ball was kicked hard, bounced off one of the boys, rolled my way.

The kids were playing football as if they were in the middle of a park.

The damp and filthy soccer ball rolled by me. I caught up with it, stopped it with my foot, then looked back. Both of the young boys were waiting, jumping up and down.

I wondered if they understood what their mothers were doing in those disgusting rooms.

I kicked the ball back to them, the blond boy losing the race to the dark-skinned boy.

The blond boy looked at me, put his hands up and shrugged, then ran and chased his friend. I watched them battle for the ball awhile, overwhelmed by my own childhood memories.

Then they started chesting the ball, controlling the ball, passing it back and forth.

The blond kid was good, but the dark-skinned boy was a regular Pelé in the making.

I watched the boys play. Watched the innocent.

Thelma's red light was off. Like a black cab that had a paying customer.

I stared at my mother's window.

Tears in my eyes, I hurried away, headed down the uneven and damp streets that reeked of sin and shame, shoulders hunched like I was walking down the Boulevard of Broken Dreams.

I was leaving my revenge behind for one reason.

I was being followed.

I'd left her dilapidated flat and two minutes later I was being followed.

Like in Amsterdam. But only one person was following me this time.

I moved through the crowd, looking for his reflection in the storefronts.

I caught a glimpse.

Saw the man following me had on a suit. Saw the bandages on his nose.

Him again.

I was confused. Him being on the plane. My mother. Tried to put all of this together.

The pieces didn't fit. The dots wouldn't connect. But that didn't mean they didn't.

The stench of Chinese food assaulting me, I made a thousand turns.

He stayed behind me, kept a few people between us.

I didn't know if he was carrying. I only knew I was naked right now.

Then I ducked inside the tube station. Put hundreds of people between us.

Hundreds of witnesses. Which didn't mean much. A man got his throat cut while he rode the tube in Croydon. Got his throat slashed wide-open in a crowd. And nobody saw anything.

I got on the tube.

My wounded admirer did the same. Rushed on the same car, only at a different door.

I pretended I was reading a left-behind paper, saw him without looking at him.

He never looked directly at me, but at the same time he never took his eyes off me.

I tucked the paper under my arm, took out my cellular to phone Arizona, needed backup.

But there was no signal underground.

Death was riding this train, like it was the 309.

I was on my own.

I ended up leading my stalker to Knightsbridge.

I took to the crowded strip outside Harrods. Blended with thousands of shoppers.

He was still behind me. Had taken the heavily populated tubes along with me.

Big crowd. An ocean of people with bags in their hands going in every direction.

Lots of corners. I made a few turns and he lost me.

He lost me because now I was behind him. The rabbit had become the fox.

He gave up looking for me and I followed him back down into the tube.

He saw me in the crowd. He saw me without looking directly at me. I did the same without looking directly at him. My position let him see the mouse had become the cat.

I was near one door and he was at the door at the opposite end.

Then we killed the game and looked at each other.

I nodded. He did the same.

With those simple gestures, this had been confirmed.

We kept our eyes on each other.

He rode the Piccadilly Line down one exit and jumped off

at South Kensington, an area where a small flat went for over a million pounds, then rushed through the underground through-way. He started running. I did too. I chased him through an underground tunnel that extended the better part of a mile and came out at the base of Hyde Park, a few blocks shy of Prince Albert Hall. He ran uphill toward the high street, dashed through traffic and bolted into the park, sped past the huge golden tribute to Prince Albert, a tribute surrounded by lights and sculptures. Those bright lights kept me from losing him. He kept running, never slowing down. I was running behind him. I chased him through the darkness and light, ran another good mile across the park to the Bayswater Road and came out by the Corus Park Hotel. He went to his right, bolted across the streets and through traffic, headed by the Swan restaurant, another intersection, looked back, saw I was still there, then bolted inside the Lancaster Gate tube.

He had me by thirty seconds.

I chased him into the tube station, slapped my Oyster card on the sensor, and waited for the gate to open. People were at the elevator, but I heard his feet racing down winding stairs that went into the bowels of the earth. I went that way as fast as I could. I was halfway down the two-hundred-step descent when I heard a train stopping down below. I stumbled, got my balance, raced around a few people, and tried to catch him. I was catching up, had made it down the stairs and was racing through the final tunnel that led to the trains, but he had me by a good twenty seconds. Just enough time for him to jump on the Central Line before the doors closed.

He looked back at me.

Scowling as the train pulled away.

He didn't look fifty anymore. He looked like he could pass for thirty.

The next train was in two minutes. But he could've gotten off the Central Line tube anywhere from the next stop at

Marble Arch or where the train ended an hour away at Epping.

I was drenched, winded.

He hadn't broken a sweat.

I had chased him over three miles and he hadn't broken a sweat.

Twenty-five

out of control

Eight stops later he exited the Central Line at Bank, nose aching.

He exited the tube at one of the busiest stations in Central London, got off looking to see if Gideon was following him. The man with the broken nose was shaken. He was sweating. Running like that had aggravated his nasal fracture. Pain was rising and spreading across his face. Felt like blood was dripping from his nose. The bruising around his eyes felt magnified, his eyes again feeling swollen. He slowed down. He could run over twenty-six miles, wanted to do a one-hundred-mile run at some point, but with the hard time breathing, running in a suit and shoes and having to inhale through his mouth on a cold and damp night, he was momentarily spent.

He'd run away from Gideon expecting the man to give up chasing him in less than a quarter mile. No one chased for much longer than one lap. Gideon had kept up. That surprised and . . . frightened him. Gideon was a killer too, after all. Then he expected to hear a gunshot ring out. His contact told him that Gideon had picked up a SIG. And with that contract out, the man knew his days were numbered. Gideon had run like a monster that had been set on fire.

A monster he could've put to sleep. If only he had been prepared.

He didn't have his Eagle with him. He could've completed the transaction in that shit-smelling alley in Soho. But the money wasn't in place. The goddamn money wasn't in place.

If he did the job before he was paid, then he wouldn't get paid for the job.

Business. Just business.

He had decided to follow Gideon. See where he was hiding out. But that went wrong.

Now the enemy knew he was out there. The enemy was aware.

That changed everything.

He felt like he had been hunted. Nobody hunts the hunter.

He touched his face, didn't see blood, but it ached again, still felt he looked like some sort of sweaty, grotesque monster that had risen from the pits of hell. In a dark Italian suit.

Every man on the tube had on a dark suit. Every other man was running for the tube as if his life depended on it. But he was the only one with his face bandaged up.

That fucker in Jacksonville had hit him with something made of lead. He wanted to kill that fucker all over again.

He ran over to the Monument side of the tube. Took the District Line to Tower Hill. Came out and walked up the stairs, both his feet and muscles aching. His anger never-ending. One hundred and fifty meters later he was coming up on Novotel. Across the narrow street women were putting flowers on the curb and in the doorway at 1 Pepys. Mourners had been doing that all day. Like the dead WAG was their replacement for the late Princess Diana.

Touching his nose, he passed by the teary-eyed mourners. That fucking fracture. He knew he needed rhinoplasty. That was cool. He was going to start a new life. With a new nose.

He changed his bandages. Took aspirin. Wondered how much a good nose job cost.

Then he looked at the package again. Stared in amazement. Gideon was doing well for himself. Nothing like reading about some else's success to magnify your own failures.

He'd do much better than that. He was confident. Once the soon-to-be-ex was gone.

He showered. He wasn't tired anymore. His feet no longer ached.

He owned too much rage to rest. Gnashing his teeth. His father would be disappointed.

Then he put on his custom-made holster. His suit coat.

He picked up the Desert Eagle. Made sure it was loaded.

He put the Desert Eagle inside the holster. The Eagle was in its nest.

He took the earplugs out of the package, dropped them in his pocket.

No need going deaf. No workers' comp in this line of work. No 401(k)either.

All cash-and-carry.

Prepared, he left Novotel, again passing by all the flowers and mourners.

His night wasn't over. The hunter still had to hunt.

Tonight somebody was going to die.

And he would die a good death.

Twenty-six

night of the hunter

I took the Central Line, looking for that broken-nose bastard at every stop.

I'd see that motherfucker again. I knew that. Just had to see him before he saw me.

I saw men in suits.

Men in dark suits.

Men dressed like preachers.

"The wrong you're doing . . . stop doing evil while you can. Stop because one day somebody will come for you. One day what you do to other people, that will be done to you."

That voice from the past came and haunted me, whispers from a shallow grave.

It felt like a knife being stabbed inside my wounded spirits.

Those words didn't come from a television show.

It was the voice of the minister I had killed a long time ago.

I'd never forgotten what he'd said as he begged for his life.

That I would have my day.

That day had come.

Someone had come for me.

Seemed like every man on the train wore a dark suit.

Pallbearers dressed in the color of death.

Every man wore the hue of mourning.

European men. Nigerian men. Russians. Swedish. Old men. Young men.

A killer owned no particular type of face.

And not all killers were men. There were a lot of Black Widows in the world.

In some cases women were the best. They were the last to be suspected.

Ten minutes later I was hurrying by that golden image of Freddie Mercury, making that night-chilled jog past all the people who were partying hard in Soho, Chinatown, and Leicester Square. Rain started to fall as I made it to the Odeon in Bloomsbury, came down with a steady rhythm as I hunched my shoulders and rushed by the red phone booths that served as warm places for picture-perfect whores to post their cards and advertise their well-traveled wares.

No one was behind me.

What was in front of me would be a bigger surprise.

Myhotel was buzzing long after the midnight hour.

The bar that was off to the right side, called Mybar, was packed, all the tables were taken and the drinks were plenty from wall to wall, Europeans at tables, legs crossed, smoking hand-rolled cigarettes and listening to jazz, saw all of that before I sliced through the cold and made it across the damp street.

When I shook the chill off my bones, pulled open the glass doors, and stepped inside the lobby, I stopped moving. Stopped because I was surprised to see her, of all people, sitting on the leather sofa. I thought our last good-bye was the last time I'd ever see her face again. She shifted, coughed, turned, and I saw a frown so deep she was damn near unrecognizable. She was waiting in the small lobby, alone, arms folded.

Her face was painted with ten shades of anger.

I wanted to keep going, but I paused in front of her.

I'd been chased.

Now she was here.

As if it were all part of a bigger plan.

She looked up, her expression changed, moved from being murderous to unsure.

My expression owned no trust.

She wiped tears from her eyes and sighed, that expression now sheer embarrassment.

I squatted, put my hand on her chin, wanted to look in her face, look for trouble.

She whispered, "Surprise."

"What are you doing sitting out here in the cold, Lola Mack?"

"This is a nice hotel. That sushi bar is off the chains. Cool the way the sushi is on the conveyor-belt thing and rotates around the bar and you grab what you want, huh? I ain't ever seen anything like that before in my life. Food passes by and people grab what they want to eat."

"Lola. Focus. Look at me. Thought you were with your boyfriend?"

"I'm . . . I was . . ." Her stomach growled and she moved with the pain. She wiped the tears from her eyes, pulled herself together, said, "Looking for Mrs. Jones. I'm looking for Mrs. Jones."

I licked my lips, tried to recall Mrs. Jones's flavor. It was gone. "Mrs. Jones isn't here."

"Damn. Where is she?"

"She didn't . . . she moved on. Got a room somewhere else, I guess. Have no idea."

"Didn't know what to do."

"What's going on?"

"Now I'm the one crying, huh? Damn shame. I'm crying like Mrs. Jones was crying."

"What happened?"

Her bottom lip trembled. She took a hard breath. "I didn't have anywhere to go."

Again I asked, "What happened with your boyfriend?"

"That jerk." That murderous look reappeared in her eyes. "Son of a bitch."

"What happened?"

"Son of a bitch said he missed me . . . said he loved me . . . wished I was here . . . and . . . I mean . . . I spent my last dime . . . got on a plane . . . gave up auditions . . . came over here . . . the lies . . . he's been lying to me for God knows how long . . . *Rent* closed down months ago . . . he's been here . . . because . . . because . . . he met somebody while he was touring . . . and . . . and he stayed here . . . he lied to me and stayed here . . . said he met somebody . . . shit happens he said . . . that's it . . . shit happens . . . and he shrugged . . . told his ass he better talk to me . . . tell me something . . . said he was working on the show and met somebody . . . and they'd been traveling together for months . . . they'd been doing it for months . . . now . . . he said he's in love . . . been shacking up with somebody . . . in love and shacking up. And I'm his damn girlfriend. I mean, how messed up is that? I know we haven't seen each other, but I didn't know it was like that. I mean, we've been having phone sex and text sex and . . . and I spent a lot of money at Victoria's Secret too . . . another reason my charge card is over the limit . . . this is so fucked up. I came here to be with him and—"

"Lola."

"I'm rambling."

"Yes. You are rambling."

"I got my butt played. This is so humiliating."

I looked at her two overpacked suitcases, at her stuffed backpack.

She carried too much shit to be in this business. We traveled light.

Again I thought about the man I had chased.

It bothered me that he had appeared as soon as I left my mother.

Made me wonder if my mother had sent him after me.

Confused and anxious, I looked around.

Nobody inside the lobby seemed to be concerned with me.

The left side housed the sushi bar. It was packed too.

No one over there was concerned with me either.

I asked Lola, "How long have you been sitting here in the cold?"

"Forever. Was too tired to leave. And the tubes shut down, so that means my travel card has expired. Got frustrated." Her voice cracked as tears fell. "Didn't have anywhere to go."

"So you're telling me you're stranded."

"Yeah. Broke and stranded and stuck with all this damn luggage."

"Where have you been since you got to London?"

She shrugged. "Walking around like a damn homeless fool from America."

"You walked around dragging two hundred pounds of luggage?"

"Call me Erykah Badu because I'm a damn bag lady."

First I rubbed my temples.

Then I thought about Mrs. Jones, leaving this warm hotel, almost being run down in front of the hotel, standing in her anger and sorrow, cold rain falling on her hot skin, her hair wild as her dress fluttered, carrying no luggage but dragging all of her invisible anguish behind her.

Lola nodded. "I don't have any money. Told you, maxed out my charge card flying my butt over here. Stupid, huh? Love makes you do stupid shit. And I spent the few dollars . . . I mean pounds . . . spent every pence of that funny-looking money I borrowed from you. The travel card, it sure came in handy. Well, I rode the train . . . thinking . . . got off one train . . . got on another . . . did that for hours . . . like a damn homeless person . . . tried to figure out what I could do . . . don't know nobody."

"Slow down. Catch your breath. Breathe. Talk to me. When is your return flight?"

"Uh . . . bought a one-way ticket. All I could afford. I figured I'd crash with my boo . . . with that son of a bitch I thought was my boo . . . figured I would be with him and not need anything . . . we used to be like that . . . now I don't have a ticket back. I know, I know. Stupid is as stupid does."

She wiped her eyes a thousand times. That murderous glare came and went.

She said, "He said he's in love with somebody else. *In love.* Asked him how in the hell could he be in love with somebody else and he said some stupid shit, said love had its own laws."

Not knowing what to say, I said nothing. Part of my mind still back on Berwick.

She said, "First I get thrown on the back of the plane, now this shit. I *hate* London."

Drama had built a nest on my doorstep. I had enough going on. I didn't want Lola to be here, but I couldn't kick her out in the cold. I rubbed my eyes, my own tiredness swooping in on me.

Her eyes were on the sushi bar. Anguish was in her face as she watched people eat.

I asked, "Have you eaten?"

"I was in Pizza Hut and these tourists left some of their pizza and I grabbed it before it was tossed. And they left some soda too. Did you know Pizza Hut had apple soda? The apple soda was off the chains. Ever tried it? Apple soda. Pizza Hut carries it over here. Cool, huh?"

"You ate somebody's leftovers?"

Tears fell from her eyes. "I know. That's fucked up, huh?"

My eyes searched the darkness. I was an open target. Needed to get out of this lobby.

I went to the front desk, tried to get a room for Lola. Something away from me, on a different floor. They told me the hotel was booked solid. I looked out at the cold rain. Not the best kind of weather for Lola to go out and hunt for a hotel. Not this time of night. Not with all of her backpacks and luggage. And I didn't want to go back out into Bloomsbury, not since I'd had that footrace, not with somebody hot on my trail. I told myself that I was safe here. If he knew I was here, he wouldn't have needed to follow me. I went back to the front door. Looked out. Dark clouds. Freezing air. Rain.

Then I went back to Lola.

Didn't have a lot of options at this point.

I said, "Why don't you come up to my room and get comfortable."

"No, that's okay."

"You don't really have a choice."

She hesitated. "I don't want to be an inconvenience."

Her stomach growled.

I said, "Hungry, huh?"

"Little bit. Yeah. I'm starving right about now."

"Let's get your two tons of luggage situated and get you some real food."

"For real?"

"Let's kill the fatted calf and get you situated."

"I need a bath."

"Come on up."

"You sure?"

"Your stomach is growling so loud it sounds like two bears fighting."

"Had that slice of cold pizza around noon."

"Thirteen hours ago."

"I'm used to eating three squares. I'm getting missed-meal cramps."

"How does room service sound? You like sushi? Could have them bring up some sushi."

"Hell yeah, I *love* sushi. But I'll be happy with McDonald's."

I smiled at her. "You didn't come all the way to London to eat clown food, did you?"

"You sure about sushi? It costs a grip. And with the exchange rate, it'll be a *super*grip."

"If you want a bottle of wine, order that too."

"Sushi and a bottle of wine?"

"Take a long bath. Eat. Drink. Be a queen for a while."

"Thank you, thank you, *thank* you. I want to jump up and down and *scream*."

"Please don't."

Again she cried, a different kind of tears. "I can't pay you back, not right now."

"Don't worry about it."

"I mean . . . I will, I promise." She wiped her eyes. "I'm not a freeloader, I promise I'm not."

"Just don't talk me to death, okay?"

She laughed.

We dragged all of her luggage toward the lift. Then I felt uneasy. Lola had shown up here right after I'd been chased.

Maybe Lola getting placed next to me on the plane wasn't a coincidence.

Maybe when I hooked up with Mrs. Jones it threw off her plan.

Right now it was all about having my enemies closer.

While we waited for the lift, the receptionist called me back to the front desk.

She handed me a FedEx box. The sender's name was written in bold letters. **Scaramouche.** No return address. My eyes went toward the darkness out on Bayley Street, to a group of drunken people coming inside. She wasn't there. But she was there at the same time.

Arizona had delivered information for the other jobs. I went back to the bar, looked around, but didn't see her. She would only be seen when she wanted to be seen, I knew that.

There was no note to say it, but I understood. Arizona was saying she was sorry for acting like a square, for the things she said, we could still be associates, we could still do business. She had work for me. And there was money to be made.

Lola held the lift door open for me. I struggled, crammed all of her luggage inside the small vertical carriage.

She wiped her teary eyes. "You look like somebody just killed your favorite cat."

I wanted to say I'd accepted a contract and killed a friend.

And I'd found the source of my pain and anger on Berwick Street. That soon I'd go back to Berwick. Might go back to Soho in the middle of the night.

And I would leave Berwick Street with blood on my hands.

But I pushed my lips up into a strained smile and sighed. "I don't like cats."

She laughed like she really wanted to start crying again. "Me either."

FedEx underneath my arm, I got on the lift, two hundred pounds of luggage separating us.

She took her tears to one side of the small vertical carriage, I took to the other.

Lola was nervous.

"Gideon . . . found out a lot about London today. Being homeless gives you time to read. Lot of black people over here. Some areas are like Compton and Detroit and Oakland. Found out that most people thought black people were new to England. But black people have been here more than fifteen minutes. People think we just got over here like in the forties, came here to play jazz and run away from wars. But blacks have been here forever. Have fought in every war with Britain. Romans brought black warriors with them to Britain. And black people still don't own shit."

I said, "Three."

"Huh?"

"Push the button for three. I'm on the third floor."

"Oh. I'm sorry. Guess I was rambling."

"I guess."

"Sorry. I'll stop. At least I'll try to."

When the elevator door closed, Arizona's scent became stronger. I inhaled, the vague scent of cloves and expensive perfume, her body gone but her essence remaining in the dank air.

Cloves.

The scent of a love gone by.

Like her man Scamz used to smoke.

Like she now smoked.

Arizona had been here. She'd been inside this elevator.

I expected to see her waiting outside my door when the elevator opened.

I looked for my golden-skinned Cylon. Looked for the grifter who had chosen to employ fear to gain respect.

And, like a Cylon, I wanted to destroy my creator.

We were both Cylons.

The third-floor hallway still smelled of cloves.

I looked up and down the hallway. No one was there.

She'd been here moments ago.

I didn't trust Arizona.

Women and treachery. Deceit and murder had been a part of my life.

My eyes went to Lola.

I didn't know what her angle was. Didn't know what her game was.

She didn't say anything, just kept her eyes down while we dragged her luggage down the slender hallway.

I opened the door, let Lola inside my room. I left both of her bags at the foot of the bed. She shifted, took off her backpack, put that load down in front of the desk.

She took her coat off, looked around. "This is a nice room."

"Thanks."

"I mean this is a really nice room."

"Order some food.

"Thanks, Gideon. I really mean it."

I repeated myself, maybe sounded a little irritated, told her, "Order some food."

She wiped her eyes with the back of her hands, got on the phone, called room service.

Shrimp tempura roll. Spicy tuna roll. Rainbow roll. Tuna tataki. Spicy squid roll. Softshell crab roll. Island roll. Tobiko with quail egg. She ordered a bottle of shirakawago sansannigori, a bamboo leaf sake. The way she ordered, she had to be starving.

Still I kept thinking about having my enemies closer.

I watched Lola, no trust in my eyes, wondering what game she was playing.

I stared at her and kept hearing whispers from a shallow grave haunting me.

It was the voice that had once belonged to a reverend in Detroit.

"The wrong you're doing . . . stop doing evil while you can. Stop because one day somebody will come for you. One day what you do to other people, that will be done to you."

Twenty-seven

wetwork

He was still swimming in anger, the undertow pulling him under.

He'd find Gideon.

Tonight.

As soon as he was done with this little matter.

He'd been sidetracked.

Sam had called.

Another target had been located. The money was in place.

The man with the broken nose went for the bird in the hand.

He had taken his unbridled rage outside the city to north London, was in Bruce Grove. Again he was in a footrace. He had found his contract, the Jamaican with the gambling debt.

The Jamaican was fleeing. That was expected. His profile had said he was a runner.

The man with the broken nose chased the Jamaican the way Gideon had chased him.

He chased him through urban areas that looked like Houston's Fifth Ward, New Orleans's Fourth Ward, South Central, East Oakland, Harlem, and Blackhaven in Memphis combined.

He convinced himself that he had tested Gideon. Wanted to see how strong Gideon was.

Told himself that fear didn't make him run; it was only a test.

Fear was there. Fear was part of the business. Fear kept a man alert.

But fear wasn't why he had run.

He'd run three sub-six-minute miles. In a suit and shoes. Gideon had almost caught him. Not many men could run three sub-six miles fully dressed. Wearing street shoes.

His father would've chastised him, shouted at him. If he had still been around. His father had been the ultimate sprinter in his youth and then a marathon man in his later years.

He used to hear his father talk to his friends about doing big jobs in other states, the sound of death in his voice. All the men wore suits. They always wore suits. And they all carried big guns. When the men left, his father would loosen his tie then come and play with him and his siblings.

His father would leave at night. Not come home for days at a time.

No one ever questioned what he did or asked where he was.

He ran because his father loved to run. He had admired his father.

Even though he never went to visit his old man after they came and took him away.

His brothers and sisters didn't go visit their old man either.

But his mother did. His mother went to see his father once a month.

Conjugal.

It had been that way for the last twenty years.

His old man didn't want to look at his kids through Plexiglas. Not then, not now. He said he didn't want them to see the man he'd became as he rotted in a four-by-five cement room.

His father had never run from anyone. Not even the police when they came to get him.

The house had been surrounded.

His old man finished his coffee.

Kissed his kids

Kissed their mother.

Then undressed.

Went outside naked, smoking a Lucky Strike cigarette. "You sons of bitches looking for me?"

Guns aimed at him, he kept on smoking his cigarette.

His old man had balls.

But unlike his fearless father, the man with the broken nose regretted that he had run from Gideon. Gideon had chased him the way Pacino had chased De Niro in the movie *Heat*.

This time he was Pacino, not De Niro.

He chased the Jamaican by homeless who slept in the doorways of businesses.

Chasing the Jamaican wasn't a test. Unlike Gideon, this contract had been paid for.

And the Jamaican knew it was his night to die.

The man with the broken nose wondered how it felt when you had been dealt a hand made of aces and eights.

He chased his prey.

The Jamaican's back-length locks were flying like a cape as he sprinted by the row of eateries on the strip by Loks 4 Life, raced downhill by Chicken Express and Regency Car Park, stumbling through Bruce Grove, waving for the night buses to stop, but the buses didn't slow down. He ran toward Seven Sisters, toward his flat, ran toward his weapons and friends.

Just like the package said he would do.

He chased the Jamaican another mile. A fast mile. The Jamaican looked back.

The Jamaican was tired.

The man with the broken nose was right behind him.

He wanted the Jamaican terrified.

He wanted him to die a thousand deaths before he caught him.

So he slowed down.

Let the Jamaican run his best run.

They were running against the wind.

Running against the rain.

Another mile went by, this one not as fast as the one before.

No longer a challenge.

He was tired of chasing. The chasing had been fun, but he had things to do tonight.

Still running, he took the Eagle out of its nest.

A piece of hot lead tore through the Jamaican's right leg as he stumbled by the Seven Sisters tube. The Jamaican fell, got back up limping, left a trail of blood marking his final steps.

Not many people were out, not like in Soho and Oxford Circus in Central London. It was cold. The tubes had closed. And it was an area where muggings at gunpoint had shot up in numbers. And it was raining. Few residents heard the screaming Jamaican, few had seen him hobbling down the high road, blood running out of him like rainwater, praying for mercy and strength.

The man with the broken nose took easy steps and caught the Jamaican.

Like a blubbering five-year-old child, the Jamaican cried and begged for mercy.

The man with the broken nose looked down on his prey.

But he saw Gideon. All he could think about was Gideon.

A double-decker bus was speeding down the high road toward Bruce Grove.

He knew that what the bus driver and his passengers on the 279 saw would have them in need of therapy the rest of their lives. He threw the Jamaican headfirst into its path.

Nobody had seen his face.

They'd only seen the horror in the eyes of a bloody Jamaican.

He could do better than Gideon had done in Tampa.

He could do much better.

———

Desert Eagle in hand, the man with the broken nose jogged into the darkness.

He didn't jog far. He didn't hide. He took out his earplugs and slowed to a stroll.

Nobody would see anything.

Nobody would hear anything.

Everyone would be too afraid that trouble would come looking for them.

He headed down Holloway Road toward Holloway Station.

When he was near, he found a black cab.

He got in, headed back toward Central London.

Infuriated.

He'd find Gideon. He'd make Gideon run. Like the Jamaican.

His cellular rang. It was his family phone. He didn't answer.

His family had called minutes ago. When he was creeping up on the Jamaican. That ringing phone had alerted the Jamaican. That ringing had been the bell at the start their race.

He touched his nose. It ached. Damn it ached.

He was dropped off on Charing Cross and Shaftesbury.

Leicester Square was to his left.

Bloomsbury was to his right.

Gideon wasn't far.

He felt it.

He looked to his left. Pondered Leicester Square.

Then changed his mind, looked toward his right. He took steps toward Bloomsbury.

He paused. Darker clouds were in that direction. The weather horrendous.

He headed straight, went down Shaftesbury toward Piccadilly Circus, passed Chinatown, then slowed and looked to his right, took his search back toward the red lights in Soho.

The whore.

Maybe the whore Gideon had visited was his favorite whore.

Maybe she knew things that would help him end this transaction.

Men always said secret things to whores.

He had had therapeutic conversations with a few working women over the years.

Men always revealed secrets to whores.

Streets were damp. A few puddles. The rain had stopped. But it was still cold.

His nose still ached.

He touched his bandages, walked through the piss-and-shit stench, again passing by the children, young boys and girls kicking a shit-smelling soccer ball down narrow Berwick Street. He went to the door that Gideon had entered. Looked up and saw pretty feet at the top of the stairs.

Her friendly voice came down and greeted him, "Full service or blow job?"

He took the stairs, the weight of the Desert Eagle hardly noticeable.

He stopped when he was face-to-face with Gideon's whore.

She'd talk.

He'd beat the whore and make her talk.

Twenty-eight

shadow of doubt

Close to an hour later.

Lola had unpacked a few things, was on the other side of the frosted bathroom door.

She was crying and running her bathwater.

Or crying and plotting. I wasn't sure what she was doing. I was waiting to find out.

I sat on the far side of the bed, on the edge, my eye on the bathroom door, my mind on the man I had chased. And Arizona. The FedEx box was in front of me. Still unopened.

My gun was on the floor, at my feet. Just in case.

The room smelled like jasmine, Lola's scent, the aroma of purity and deception.

Empty sushi plates were on a tray we'd left on the floor near the door. I had a small glass of sake on the nightstand, and Lola had taken the rest of the bottle into the bathroom with her.

The fish smell might permeate the room, so I got up long enough to leave the tray in the hallway. Then I called room service to come get the tray before the hall smelled like sushi. I stumbled over a suitcase. The room had become an obstacle course. Lola's luggage and backpack took up most of the space.

Almost two in the morning. Nine P.M. on the East Coast. Six on the West Coast.

The television was on the news. First the never-ending talk about the WAG.

I wasn't interested.

Then news about Sledgehammer's death in Trinidad came on.

It confirmed what Arizona had told me a few hours ago.

That bothered me.

It scared me.

Not much had scared me over the years.

But this had me opening and closing my hands.

I clenched my teeth.

That report was followed by news about the demise of the Big Bad Wolf of rap.

The blood that had been shed in Tampa unnerved me as well.

I turned the television off. Was only so much of that shit I could take.

I opened the FedEx box. Saw pictures of two people. One of an overweight man. A local. This contract came in from Texas. Had nothing to do with Arizona. The other contract was Amsterdam. Those images kept my eye. Several pictures of a beautiful young woman.

Her name was Sierra.

Sierra was Arizona's younger sister.

My mouth dropped open.

Arizona had sent me a package on her little sister.

The package said Sierra was living and working out of Holland.

The men who came to cripple and rape Arizona were from Holland.

I tried to remember what Sergeant had said.

It wasn't too hard to connect the dots.

Arizona's sister was in bed with Sergeant as well.

Both were in on the FEMA scam. Shit went bad. Arizona

wanted her cut. Sergeant refused. Sierra had supplied the brawn to damage Arizona and take her out of the business.

Sierra had sent men to do major damage to Arizona.

Un-fucking-believable.

Sierra was working in Holland.

I stared in her eyes like I was staring inside another ancient memory.

She looked like the girl I had visited. The girl from window 693.

I put her picture down.

This shit was too deep.

A new SIM card was inside the box. I put my SIM card inside my mobile, turned it on. One number already programmed into the memory. Programmed without a name. Arizona's contact number.

After the shit we just went through, she had the nerve to drop this shit off at my hotel.

I pulled up her number, had my finger over the SEND key.

Arizona knew this would fuck me up.

That's why she didn't tell me. She sent me a fucking package.

I put the mobile away. Sipped my sake. Took a deep breath.

Again I stared at the picture of Arizona's younger sister.

Sierra was the spitting image of her older sister, only slightly darker, her body a bit fuller.

Arizona wanted her younger sister dead.

Still found it hard to believe Sierra had supplied the men who came after Arizona.

I wanted to chastise them both. But that would make me hypocritical.

I wanted Thelma to be in the same state.

I whispered, "The pot calls the kettle black."

My mind shifted.

Went to a dark place.

Thought about Thelma.

Thought about my mother.

I rubbed my eyes, rubbed away all memories.

I went to the window and looked out, opened and closed my hand.

I heard Lola in the bathroom. Still singing.

I grimaced out toward Berwick Street. A son should never hit his mother.

But I had.

We had done all of the things a mother and son shouldn't do.

Felt like I was about to have a panic attack. I sat down again. Sipped more sake. Stress had me feeling like I was about to have a stroke.

Rubbed my eyes. Eyes were on fire. Was tired in more ways than one.

My dark thoughts stayed there with my mother.

Couldn't remember the number of times she was locked up.

In those days, when she was taken away, whether we were in Chicago, Memphis, or Stillwater, I'd sit at home, would stay in our apartment for days, until she was free, cooking for myself, not answering the phone, going to school, doing homework, being as normal as I could, hoping she would come back. There was always food there. Enough for me to get by for days. Once she was incarcerated for a month. I was fourteen years old then. A grown man.

She walked in the door a month later, came in as if she had been gone fifteen minutes.

Miniskirt. High-heel shoes. She was amazing. She had pictures of Dorothy Dandridge, Sophia Loren, Audrey Hepburn, Tina Turner, Marilyn Monroe, Lauren Bacall, Lana Turner, and Eartha Kitt Scotch-taped all over our small apartment. Even with the wigs, shoes, and clothes she had, she was none of those women, yet she was all of those women at once.

My mother said, "I have something I need you to take care of for me."

I looked at her. No hello. No talk about missing me. She was so expressionless.

My mother slid me a picture of a man. A knife was next to the picture.

She said, "This john beat one of my friends."

She dropped pictures on the table. Red-haired woman. Face bloodied. Eyes swollen. Teeth knocked out. She looked horrible. The hazards of her chosen occupation.

"She fought him good. Did her best. But she's a tiny little woman. He beat her bad. You can see how he busted her face up. Bastard dropped his wallet when he ran out of the motel."

I pushed the pictures back to her.

Pushed the pictures away like I was rejecting the lifestyle she offered.

She reached inside her purse, put a stack of wrinkled money on the table.

I counted the small bills. Five hundred dollars.

She said, "We have to eat. You have to eat. We have to pay rent."

I went back to my book, to the complicated equations I was trying to comprehend.

She whispered, "Please?"

I ignored her.

My mother put her arms around me, rubbed her hands up and down my body.

She grabbed between my legs, rubbed my groin. I didn't stop her. Hoped she would quit. That excited me. I pretended nothing she did fazed me. She ran fingers over me, touched me and rubbed me in places, held me in ways a mother should never handle her son.

"You're getting to be a big boy. A real big boy."

I jerked away from her.

She laughed. It was her real laugh. She'd changed. Become a sadistic soul at heart.

I was embarrassed. Her whore's touch had stirred me. The stimulation showed.

She asked, "When was the last time you had some pussy?"

"When was the last time you sold some?"

"I'm more worried about the next time. Last time pays no bills."

"Trying to study."

"Son, I met this young girl. Twenty. From Hollywood. Long black hair. I can get her to give you some pussy. She's a good friend. Showed her your picture. She thinks you're cute."

"Is she a whore?"

"All women are whores. Just some have the sense to get paid."

That had become the language of our household.

Years of living on the run had hardened us.

After that back-and-forth with my mother, I went to the kitchen, poured a glass of water, wanted to get away from her. I liked it when she was gone. Liked it when she was in jail.

Mother followed me. "Ever had your little man sucked?"

"Stop it. Will you stop it?"

"She'll suck your dick for you if I tell her to."

She made a peanut butter and jelly sandwich. Left the bread open on the counter. I went behind her, cleaned up her crumbs. Had to before the roaches came out to feast.

"She's from Antigua. Trifling husband walked out, left her with all the bills. Good thing God gave her a pussy for bartering, else she'd starve to death, her and her five-year-old son."

My mother tapped the table. Five hundred dollars and a man's information stared at me.

I said, "I can't. It makes me sick. I get sick. I want to throw up."

"When I first started, every time a john left, I would get nauseated. Pretend you're somebody else. I do that and it helps. Let it be somebody else, another part of you that's doing the stuff you don't like doing. When I'm at work entertaining those men, when they have their hands on me, it's not me they're touching. Not me at all."

I went back and looked at the money on the table.

She said, "We have to eat. We have bills. We need the money."

We headed for the car. I had the knife in my hand.

Later on I'd find out that the lady who hired me had given my mother $1,500. My mother had asked for two thousand, but that fifteen was all the woman could afford. People would pay her as much as five thousand and I'd never see more than five hundred.

Inside every whore there lived a pimp who was trying to get out.

My mind was on fire, each thought like gasoline being thrown on flames.

I wanted to be alone right now. Needed to be alone so I could think.

Needed to sip on sake and do some reevaluation.

I looked at the luggage in the room. Two hundred pounds of somebody else's problems.

Too late for that. Too late to be alone.

Lola's suitcases and backpack were in front of me.

One was open. One wasn't. One was turned upside down, harder to get to.

I crept to the one that was right side up and open, most of its contents already taken out. What was packed wasn't folded, just tossed in, like she had left home in a hurry.

Lola was not a neat freak, not at all. She had already turned my room into a pigpen.

With easy movement, I looked through her things, felt around for anything suspicious. Lola had been gone for hours. She could've picked up anything since she made it to London. I searched. She had more lingerie than any one woman should be allowed to own, enough sexy gear to let me know that she had planned to spend a lot of bedroom time with her boyfriend. Lots of shoes. Dresses. Jeans. Workout clothes. Two new vibrators, one black and the other pink, both about five inches long. I moved all of that stuff aside and found what I was looking for. First, inside her wallet, was a picture of her and her boyfriend. Then, next to the DVD, I found an old theatrical playbill from *Rent* stuffed inside her backpack. It was a program from when he was touring with the production back in the States. I was searching for information on the man who had shattered her heart. And I wanted to make sure she wasn't part of something larger.

Outside of having two vibrators and a clit stimulator, nothing looked suspicious.

No weapons. No multiple passports.

No reason to take her down and leave her rotting in a mews out in horse-and-grass.

I put everything back the way I found it.

The vibrators. Two of them. Those were her weapons. Unless she was planning to torture me West Hollywood style, what she was carrying was harmless.

Two colorful vibrators.

I chuckled.

I wondered if she took both of her vibrators at the same time.

I gathered up everything I had taken from the FedEx box, then went to the room safe. Each room had one hidden away from plain sight. I read the instructions and reprogrammed the safe with a new pass code, then tucked everything from the FedEx box inside, locked it away.

Lola was singing another song, something about going out tonight. Sounded like she was howling part of the song. She was all into the tune. That almost made me laugh.

Then I was glad Lola was here. It was awkward, but it was nice chilling with a square.

Sergeant had said men like us shouldn't become personal with the women in our business.

I'd never forget that.

I'd put myself in the middle of shit between Arizona and her sibling, a problem that involved Sergeant. Had to be bad if her sister had sent men to do things worse than death.

I regretted that contract on Sergeant. Wished I'd taken his offer before he sipped his Jack. Needed to put up two shots of Jack and drink one, then apologize and pour one on the ground. Sergeant was right. I should take his advice, retire to a tropical island, find a pretty woman, maybe have some babies, get out of this business before it killed me. It had killed him. Just like it had killed a lot of us. Scamz had been gunned down in a pool hall. Sledge had been blown up in a van. I couldn't count or remember the number of people who had been assassinated in between.

I'd been followed like it was the prelude to my demise.

I sipped more sake. Looked at the clock.

Almost two thirty. Barely dinnertime back in the States.

I lay across the sofa, television on, BBC news showing another terrorist bombing that had blown up red buses and part of the tube system. It was like the universe was sending me a message. Now I was nervous. Imagined getting blown into a thousand little pieces.

I closed my eyes.

Focused on my breathing.

Relaxed.

Let the sake take me into a peaceful darkness.

Then came the dream. I knew the dream would come again, like it did on the plane.

I was back in Tampa.

Bodies all around me.

The stench of Chinese food making me want to puke.

Twenty-nine

we who are about to die

Two days after meeting with Sledgehammer.

Portable GPS at my side. Destinations programmed into memory.

Not too far from Tampa International Airport, down in the stadium area, a block or so from the Yankees spring-training camp, driving in the shadows of their International Plaza. Nervous, I followed the trail of tattoo, pawn, and brake shops that shot down Dale Mabry, saw Asian massage parlors, the type that had discreet business signs and darkened windows.

Had to check out the lay of the land, plan an emergency escape route, if needed.

I didn't have to import weapons. Weapons were everywhere. All I had to do was find a hardware store. And finding pepper spray or Mace was easy. Within an hour I had hit four stores and had everything I needed. I found my way back to Dale Mabry Highway, headed toward the stadium, spied the area, and parked in a lot next to Mons Venus, Tampa's most famous spot for pole swingers. This lot was where Big Bad and his crew always parked.

This was where they would die.

I was tempted to lounge inside Mons Venus. Twenty to thirty

for a lap dance and I could touch the women anywhere except on the cookie. Thirty bucks to get dry-humped by one of the most beautiful women in the world. Paying thirty for that with no upsale wasn't too bad.

I didn't go inside.

I waited.

One hour turned into two. Two turned into three. Three became four.

Just when I was about to call it a bust, a stretch SUV pulled up in the dark parking lot, music blasting, wheels spinning. The Big Bad Wolf had arrived. My heart sped up. Hands went clammy. I took a deep breath. Focused. I got out of my ride and headed toward the parking lot.

Their music was loud enough to muffle a nuclear explosion.

They were too busy getting high to notice a shadow coming their way. As they unloaded, one man in thick jeans, a short leather jacket, and boots, he saw me first. They were an army dressed in oversize gear. I eased part of the way out of the shadows.

The one that had seen me barked, "What the fuck you want?"

"An autograph. I'm a big fan."

Then another. "We ain't doing no motherfuckin' autographs."

Both sported bulletproof vests.

Big Bad Wolf got out of the SUV.

Big guy. Saggy jeans. Long blond hair in dreadlocks. Tattoos all over. His teeth reflected, even in the dark. His mouth was decorated with a half million worth of platinum with white gold–plated, diamond-encrusted crowns, the 18-karat kind.

I held up what was in my gloved left hand.

I said, "Chinese food. You said to bring you some Chinese food, right?"

He knew.

Right then, he knew that Death was here.

I had marked that spot. Where I stood, my weapon was on

the ground. I grabbed what I had hidden and ran at them. Three of them charged at me. They were bad as hell, until they saw what was in my hands. A sledgehammer. I was holding what people used to knock down buildings. It was too late for them to stop their charge. I swung hard, connected in the chest of one of the attackers, saw pain and surprise light up his eyes as he fell on his friend. The second one was hit between his eyes before he could get back to his feet.

Then a third one met the same fate, the sledgehammer taking him down.

The third one was dressed better, wore a suit.

This was what I had become. I was so far from being seven years old and riding down the streets of Charlotte admiring the big houses. So far from being the little boy who wanted to go to Six Flags. For money, this was all about collecting money, all about trying to be somebody.

Two more of Big Bad's crew got it bad. Those men were dead before they understood what was going on.

Faces smashed so bad it would take two seasons of *Nip/Tuck* to fix what was left. And even if it was put back the way it was ten minutes ago, their brains were swollen beyond repair.

Big Bad Wolf ran like he was Little Red Riding Hood.

I pulled a knife from its sheath at my waist, threw the knife hard and fast. Not my best throw, but it was good enough. It hit his calf hard and deep. He went down, his face sliding across the asphalt. He grabbed his wound, looked up, and saw me holding a sledgehammer high over my head. His lips moved; the music was so loud nothing could be heard.

He was terrified. He was sorry for the shit he had said. He didn't want to die.

Nobody wanted to die.

The sledgehammer came down hard.

His face was smashed in. Just like my client wanted. Killed him with a sledgehammer.

That feeling of nausea swept through me, slowed me down.

Left me vulnerable.

Then I was hit hard.

Two more of the terrified hood rats pulled it together, attacked me at the same time. They were late getting out of the SUV. They came after me. Assaulted me the same way their music was attacking my ears. The first one hit me like he was a professional boxer. He was fast, but he was high on chronic, still managed to hit me with too many hard blows to count. Don't know. Was numb after the first blow clipped my eye, was going down after the second blow hit my mouth. I was dazed. Another blow hit my face and I went down like Sonny Liston.

The weapon was far away from me.

Death was standing in the shadows, smiling, not picky about who he claimed.

His drunken homeboy kicked me until I grabbed his foot, grappled with him while his buddy threw blow after blow at my head and back. I didn't let go. I held on to that foot, made my way up his leg, yanked his oversize jeans until they fell and tangled at his feet, put my weight into him, made him stumble, got some room, and yanked his weight from up under him.

Death applauded.

Floundering, spinning, struggling to get his balance, he hit the ground quick and hard.

His hard-hitting buddy kicked me and I stumbled over him.

They were shouting, screaming. But the music in the SUV drowned out all of their calls.

I tackled the one who hit like a boxer, lifted him up the same way a minister in Detroit had done me on the night he died, on the icy night we fought to the death. I growled like an animal, lifted him up, and crashed him into the pavement, drove him into the concrete as hard as I could.

That hurt him. That shit hurt me too. Knocked the wind out of me as well.

Death was laughing.

Had to get up. Had to get the fuck out of here.

But the first one I had dropped pulled his pants back up, wobbled to his feet before I did.

The second one struggled, got help from his friend, made it to his feet before I did too.

I heard debris on the filthy asphalt crunching as they stumbled toward me.

Death hovered over me with its sardonic smile.

From the ground, I looked up at both of them. They were breathing hard. They were in pain. I was breathing hard.

Bloody mouth, eye swollen, fists hurting, neon lights, vision blurry, this was my death.

Saw both of them standing over me. Screaming at each other. The one I had tackled pointed at the SUV. His homeboy stumbled back inside the SUV and came back with a gun.

By then the one I had tackled was holding my sledgehammer.

Death started doing cartwheels and back flips.

I hadn't killed the one person I promised myself I would kill.

I hadn't killed Thelma.

The one I had tackled was panting, cursing me, struggling to raise the sledgehammer while his wounded buddy kept his gun trained on me. I was on my knees, trying to get up, head tilted toward my executioners.

The pepper spray on my belt. That's what I was going for.

I sprayed at the eyes of the one with the sledgehammer, then rolled to my left.

He screamed and swung the sledgehammer, hit the ground where I used to be.

I kept rolling.

He swung hard, like Thor swinging his mighty Mjolnir, the hammer that destroyed all it touched. But he was hurting bad and the sledgehammer was heavy. He didn't have the muscles or concentration to use it like I had. He was freaking out. He was terrified. Death was on the ground, those cold spirits rising though him. The one with the sledgehammer kept swinging. His friend ducked, but he ducked in the wrong direction. He ducked in the direction of the swinging sledgehammer. He was hit in the center of his forehead. Instant death.

The gun fell to the ground. I went after the gun.

Panic had the best of the last one. He kept swinging the sledgehammer and hit the SUV.

Winded, he stopped. First he screamed. Then he was crying. Like a child. He was breaking down.

Then the gun I had in my hand, I pulled the trigger, put hot lead in his belly.

He grabbed his wound, let the sledgehammer drop, stumbled, fell against the SUV.

Another bullet in his gut made him slump a little more, but he wrestled with gravity and refused to fall to the ground.

I limped across the pavement, picked the sledgehammer up. Now it weighed a ton. With the butt of the hammer I knocked him down, then stood over him. He begged. Winded, wounded, sweating, in pain once again, I grunted as I raised the sledgehammer high, like a kid at the circus pretending to be the strong man, closed my eyes, grunted again as I brought the hammer down hard into the center of his chest. His insides crunched with internal injuries.

With the exception of my heavy breathing and bad music, the alley became soundless.

My vision blurred. I staggered. Went down on one knee, then the nausea hit me again. I fought it, didn't lose my insides. Held my DNA inside. The trembles. I pushed it all back.

I blinked away my agony and saw that I was surrounded.

Dead, their bodies broken and twisted like rag dolls, sprawled on uneven asphalt.

The parking lot had become a graveyard waiting on tombstones.

Death grabbed the collars of the expired, dragged their broken bodies into the shadows.

As Death vanished into the night, the chill that had me changed to numbness.

My emotions were gone. I'd detached. Like my mother had taught me.

I staggered to the Chinese food, took it, and stood over Big Bad.

I poured lo mein all over his shattered face.

I looked over, saw one of them moving his leg. The one who was dressed like a businessman was still groaning. He was still breathing.

Nausea rose, gave me a new battle. If I threw up, my DNA would be all over the concrete. That queasiness and my pains stopped me from going to finish him off.

The man I'd been paid to kill was gone.

My job was over.

Seven out of eight were dead.

I couldn't kill anymore. Not that night.

Empty Chinese food container in one hand, gun tucked in my pants, sledgehammer in the other, I limped away, that stench in my nostrils, knowing I'd never eat Chinese food again.

There was a crash.

I jerked awake, reaching for the gun I had hidden on the floor.

Lola was in the room.

I saw her coming toward me. Her hair was in a ponytail. No makeup on her face.

She gave me that Hollywood smile.

"Lola?"

"Didn't mean to wake you."

"You okay?"

She grunted.

She had on blue sweatpants, gray sweatshirt. Old Navy sweats.

Lola was sneaking up on me. Something heavy was dragging at her side.

I thought it was her luggage.

I saw that her suitcases had been moved.

The second suitcase, the one that had been left upside down, it was wide open.

And was empty.

A suitcase that had weighed over one hundred pounds was empty.

I asked, "What are you doing?"

"Are you afraid?"

"Just sleepy."

"I think you're afraid."

"What do you mean? Afraid of what?"

Then I saw what she had at her side.

It was a sledgehammer.

She said, "The Big Bad Wolf."

Fear magnified.

"I think you're afraid of the Big Bad Wolf."

She grunted and raised the weapon high over her head.

Lola became a silhouette standing over me with a sledgehammer in her hands.

She growled, "Who's afraid of the Big Bad Wolf?"

Lola brought the sledgehammer down.

She brought the hammer down hard.

Thirty

beauty betrayed

The sledgehammer crashed into the sofa where my head had been.

The hammer was too heavy for her.

I had the gun, had it off pause and ready to go.

I didn't want to shoot her.

But I would.

Gun aimed at her, I made it to the television, grunted out my fear, pointed the gun at her.

She held the sledgehammer high again.

I snapped, *"Back the fuck down, Lola."*

Lola grimaced, raised the sledgehammer high, came running at me.

I pulled the trigger.

Pst. Pst. Pst. Pst.

Shot her over and over, the silencer making the bullets exit like a coarse whisper.

Blood stained her sweats as she stumbled backward.

Lola dropped the sledgehammer, it fell across the nightstand, destroyed a lamp.

The light from the lamp blinking on and off, fizzing out, Lola crumpled into her death.

I stood there, teeth tight, focused, gun trained on her.

That lamp kept fizzing in and out.

Shadow and light.

Shadow and light.

Chest rising and falling, I waited.

Caught my breath, looked at the damage she had caused.

Looked at what I had done.

I cursed a thousand times.

Then I eased the gun down, leaned against the dresser, neck sweating like rain.

Lola was dead.

Her body riddled with bullets.

Blood was everywhere.

That light refusing to die, fizzing in and out, from shadow to light.

The noise from that sledgehammer had to wake up everybody in the hotel.

Out toward Centre Point, I saw lights coming on in every flat in Bloomsbury.

If anyone was in their window, they could've seen what just went down.

Soon there would be sirens.

Soon the place would be surrounded.

Had to get the fuck out of here.

Had to wipe the room down and get the fuck out of here.

Lola Mack was dead.

I'd been set up. She'd been sent by my enemy.

Then.

Noise came from behind me.

The sound of the broken lamp crumpling, being pushed to the side.

Lola wasn't on the floor.

She was already on her feet.

That light still going from light to dark.

Bullet holes in her sweatshirt showed me that she had been wearing a bulletproof vest.

She had the sledgehammer back in her hands.

Again she took the sledgehammer, grunted, and raised it high.

She handled the weight from her weapon much better this time.

Her control was much better.

Because she handled it with rage.

Rage had given her a new level of strength and a new speed.

Again she came at me.

She came at me fast.

She came at me hard.

She came at me with that sledgehammer raised high.

Gun raised, I aimed at her again.

Head shot this time.

Fuck her face being so damn pretty.

It was time for a bona fide kill shot.

I pulled the trigger.

Click.

The gun was empty.

Lola was on me.

That sledgehammer was up high, at its peak, about to come down with deadly force.

It came down toward my head.

I threw my hands up in vain.

This was my death.

This was my Tampa.

I jumped awake.

Still on the sofa.

Heart beating inside my ears.

I fumbled through my panic, grabbed the gun from the floor.

Felt its weight in my hand.

No dream this time.

No goddamn dream this time.

Gun in hand, I panted, pointed left, pointed right.

Was suffocating. Room was so hot I was suffocating.

Lola wasn't there.

Nothing was there.

Nothing was in front of me but fear and shadows.

I stood up, gun still going left to right, then right to left.

No broken lamps.

No Lola.

No sledgehammer.

I looked in her suitcases again.

Saw nothing in either.

Just clothes.

And vibrators.

The second suitcase.

I went to it.

Eased it over.

Opened it.

A hundred pairs of shoes. And clothes. That's all. A lot of damn shoes and more clothes.

I closed her suitcase.

Turned it back over.

I swallowed. Pulled it together.

Then I sat back down on the sofa.

There was another crash.

I jumped, again the gun aimed at the bathroom door.

The noise had come from inside the bathroom.

I listened.

Lola had dropped something. She was still messing around in the bathroom.

Gun in my lap, I rubbed the nightmare out of my eyes, took a deep breath, shook off the anxiety the best I could, then looked at the clock. Almost two hours of nightmares had passed.

I had slipped.

Sweetness and humidity flowed from the bathroom, blended with the room's warm air.

Lola was humming. Singing some song with the words 525,600 in the lyrics.

I waited for her to step out of the bathroom wearing sweats, big socks, a baggy T-shirt, maybe her hair in a ponytail, have on the terry-cloth robe that the hotel supplied in each suite.

Like in my dream.

The gun remained ready to handle whatever problem that femme fatale brought.

Finger on trigger, just in case that nightmare was a storm warning.

Just in case this moment was a déjà vu.

The bathroom door opened, that bathroom light disrupting the room's darkness, and she stood at the sink brushing her hair, her body draped in a red satin number that ran out of material right below the curve of her backside. Her breasts gave a wonderful shape to that shiny material.

Nothing like my dream.

Just like that I was staring at her. Fucking mesmerized.

She picked up her glass, took in the last swallow, mumbled something that had *son of a bitch* in it at least ten times, then brushed her hair over and over. I tried to not watch her and failed miserably. Never expected her to look like that.

I put the gun back in its hiding place.

Stared at Lola.

Her hair was down, hanging beyond her shoulders, cascading down her back.

Had no idea her hair was that long.

Satin flowed over the curves of her tight frame.

Her nipples were pushing their way through that smooth material.

I swallowed.

She moved and one of her straps slipped, showed most of her right breast.

Foolish thoughts came and went.

Lola tiptoed out of the bathroom.

Her arms were toned, legs toned, stomach flat and tight. A Hollywood body. The kind that hit the gym two, maybe three times a day. The kind that lived on tofu and salads.

Lola glanced at me. Her eyes told me that she was surprised I was awake.

She went back to the bathroom, took the robe off the hook, eased it on.

Lola said, "I'll grab a pillow and sleep on the sofa. Cool?"

"Take the bed."

"I can't do that."

"Take the bed."

She was tipsy. Her words slurred. "I can't put you out of your bed."

"Take the bed."

"Thanks. Bathroom's all yours."

I grabbed a few things, managed to slide my gun inside a towel when she wasn't looking, and headed for the bathroom, closed the door, turned on the shower. Her smell was in here. She had finished the sake, the empty bottle left on the counter.

Maybe this wasn't a good idea, now for another reason.

Gun on the counter, I stood there for a minute.

Shaking that nightmare away.

"One day what you do to other people, that will be done to you."

I shoved that ghost out of my mind, showered, and pulled on a pair of sweats.

When I came back out, Lola was under the covers, the white robe off to the side, but not out of her reach. The furry cover that had been on top of the white comforter, some brown leopard-print thing that would make the people at PETA have a heart attack, was off to the side. I adjusted the temperature in the room, took it down a few centigrades, and crashed on the sofa.

The gun was slipped under a pillow on the sofa. Still within reach.

Minutes went by. Besides the mild sounds brought on by the winds, no noises came from outside the double-pane windows. London was quiescent. Or in bed with their lovers.

I sat up for a minute, readjusted the covers.

She whispered, "Gideon."

"Thought you were sleeping."

"Just, you know, being quiet."

"Why you being so quiet?"

"Because you told me to shut up."

"No, I didn't."

"You said for me to be quiet. Said don't talk you to death."

"Oh."

"So I've been . . . I'm being quiet."

"You okay?"

"No."

"What's wrong?"

"Gideon, it's a king-size bed. I feel bad with you on that hard sofa."

"I'm cool."

"We can share the bed."

"You sure?"

"It's a big bed. We're adults. We can put pillows between us or something."

I moved to the bed, got under the covers, but kept to the far side of the bed, stayed within arm's reach of my gun. I couldn't count the number of nights I'd slept that way, gun within reach.

Lola moved around a lot. Couldn't get comfortable. I was fidgety too.

Lola whispered, "Gideon."

"Yeah."

"Think I drank too much sake."

"You gonna throw up?"

"No."

"What's the problem?"

"Something else."

"What?"

"My mind is messed up. Son of a bitch is in bed with somebody else right now."

She wept a little.

Lola said, "That's all I keep thinking about."

"You want to talk about it?"

"I feel so alone right now. I feel so unhappy."

"Anything I can do?"

"Gideon?"

"Whassup?"

"I can't sleep. And I have all of this energy. Want a massage?"

"You don't have to."

"I really need to do something."

"You've been up for hours. Aren't you tired?"

"Exhausted, but not tired. Need to . . . use this anxiety . . . this energy."

"Okay."

Lola got up, moved to her things, opened her bag, took out lotions and oils, took out the things she had planned on surprising her lover with, took out tools from her trade.

Lola paused, thinking. "Look in my eyes, Gideon."

I did.

She whispered, "Breathe with me."

I did.

Lola put her hands on my face. I felt a surge. Her touch was electrical. Sent energy through my body. Fear abandoned me. We sat there gazing into each other's eyes, our breathing finally becoming synchronized, the palms of her hands caressing my face.

I touched her cheeks in return.

She shook her head, did that in a polite way, and moved my hand away.

I understood. She was serious about her work, even when she was tipsy.

She asked, "How did you hurt your face?"

"Fight."

"Figured that much."

Unnerved. I waited for her to pry, ask me more questions.

Lola whispered, "Relax."

I did my best.

She said, "You have a lot of tension and hostility in your body."

"You can tell by looking in my eyes?"

"You have a lot of yin fighting with yang."

"Doesn't everybody?"

"Not like you. Never seen so much light and so much darkness at the same time."

I thought I had scared her. She didn't pull away. We gazed, kept breathing together.

She whispered, "Lie down. Facedown."

"Okay."

"Take your clothes off first. If you're comfortable. Or I can massage you through your clothes if you want, but it would be a lot better, if you know. Only if you're comfortable."

I stripped down to my birthday suit.

I closed my eyes and Lola fell quiet, rested her hands on my upper body, then moved her healing to my lower back, warmed oils in her hands and worked on me, that relaxing massage flowing from my back to my legs, her touch easing down to my feet. Her hands never left my body, always maintained contact, took her time, her movements both rhythmic and sensitive, long, gliding strokes that led to deeper ones. She used her body weight more than arm strength for the deep strokes, and during gliding strokes, since she didn't have her professional table, she made do with the bed I was on, adjusted her technique and remained fluid.

I was floating away and groaning like Mrs. Jones had groaned on the flight to London.

Felt it was a warm summer day and I was resting underneath Carolina blue skies.

I relaxed, released my paranoia, and enjoyed her touch on my skin.

She whispered, "Turn over."

My erection betrayed me. My penis betrayed me. Lola didn't say anything. Didn't react. Her touch didn't stop, just moved to my chest, arms, and hands, glided down to my legs.

Her hands brushed my hard-on, took a slow journey toward my legs. Her tender touch made me want to explode. After she finished my legs and feet, her hands teased across my skin, glided back up, and brushed my genitals again. Then her hands touched my inner thighs, her touch staying near my hard-on, near that erection, her hands moving toward that stiffness.

I opened my eyes. Looked at her as she stroked me.

She blushed.

I blushed too.

She whispered, "Somebody is as tense as I am."

"Yeah."

She hesitated, tendered her tone. "You have a girlfriend?"

"Nope. No girlfriend."

Her voice tendered. "I don't have a man."

"I guess we don't have anybody."

"Guess not." Lola paused, tendered her voice even more. "I can try erotic if you like."

"Thought this was erotic."

"I mean . . . you know . . . happy ending. If you want me to, I can try."

"Don't want to do anything that would make you uncomfortable."

"I'm very comfortable with you. Very."

"I'm putting you up . . . you don't have to . . ."

"I want to. I like you. I'm feeling you. And I want to. That okay?"

"Sure."

"Sure you don't have a girlfriend?"

"I'm sure."

"Don't want to disrespect anybody, you know."

"Nobody to disrespect."

With her warm hands, she cradled my genitals, held on to my erection, her touch sending a new surge, her eyes asking me if that was okay. I nodded. She massaged me right there, focused on my genitals, every now and then her fingers and hands making sweeps up and down my body, her touch moving that sensation all over me, balancing it out.

She did different massage strokes that felt so damn good, firm and consistent stroking, alternating between those strokes. Lola had my penis resting on my belly, had cupped my balls with one hand, the heel of the palm of the other hand gliding up and down the underside of the penis, doing that from root to tip. Then she brought one hand down, stroked my penis from top to the bottom, and when it hit the bottom, she released it. Insanity rose. Again she changed, took my penis in her hand and held it for a moment, held it with gentleness, and gave it a quick up-and-down stroke. She did that for a while, then changed to slow up-and-down strokes, then changed, gave two quick up-and-down strokes. Caressed. Then gave three quick strokes.

I was in Fiji. The sunrise was in a thousand colors. A happy ending was on the horizon.

But Lola slowed down when my moans got too deep, when I moved against her motions.

She whispered, "Relax."

I focused on my breathing, calmed down.

I gazed at her. She stopped stroking me, but didn't let my penis go.

Lola got on top of me, hovered over me, slight contact, took her straps away, let her breasts hang, then moved her breasts across my skin, tickled her breasts from my face down to my erection, kept my genitals ablaze with desire, came back up again, eased back down.

She sat on the bed next to me. Lola's leg touched mine and I almost came. Her skin was hot. She brushed her leg against mine and she released a soft moan. I moved closer to her. Her breathing halted, then she swallowed. I put my hand on her shoulder, my fingers moving across that red satin until I felt her flesh. She made another sound, this one getting caught in her throat. Our legs rubbed, skin moved back and forth across skin. Her hand came up, touched my bare chest. She moved closer to me. I brought my hand up, touched her breasts. God, have mercy. They were full, soft, nipples erect. I moved closer to her, pulled her toward me.

I needed her. Needed to let her help me forget about a lot of things.

My mouth went to her neck, eased to her right breast, licked, sucked, then licked and sucked, then my tongue went to her left breast, licked and sucked. Again she moaned. My tongue traced up to her lips. I kissed her. Her kiss was intense, sucked my tongue to the point of pain, then she eased up. She held on to me. Her nails dug into my skin.

My hand went down to her waist, underneath her satin.

She moaned good and long. Moaned like she needed this too.

Two fingers slid inside her while my thumb rested on her swollen clit. Her legs tensed, her breathing did the same. She held me tighter. I found the right rhythm, the right pressure, and Lola moved against my hand. I kissed her, used my trigger finger, gave her a slow clit massage; finger-fucked her until my hand became sweetened with her juices. Her nostrils flared and she pushed her hips into my hand, her moans deepened as her nails dug deeper into my skin. My mouth moved back to her breasts and I sucked and bit her nipples, finger-fucked her while her jaw clenched and she sank deeper and deeper into that well of pleasure. She jerked, made sounds that told me she was on fire. I sucked her breasts as she trembled.

Sleeping with Strangers   303

She moaned like she was singing the sweetest song.

Lola turned her body.

I shifted, got on top of her, did a slow grind, kissed her for a while.

"Gideon?"

"Yeah."

"If you want to . . . you know . . . we can . . . you know."

"If I want to what, we can what?"

"Don't make me say it."

I kissed her again, sucked her tongue, did the same with her full lips.

I said, "Say it."

"You want me to say it?"

"Say it."

"Damn you. You know you ain't right."

"Say it."

"You excite me."

"Do I?"

"I'm wet right now. Looking at you, I'm wet. Touching you made me wet."

"Are you?"

"Touch me. Feel me."

I touched her again. I felt what was damp and on fire.

She kissed me.

Her voice became a sweet song. "I have a dozen condoms."

We kissed and moved against each other, my hardness rubbing her softness.

"Get the condom," I told her as we kissed. "Let me massage you for a while."

"Let's trade happy ending for happy ending."

My heart beat fast, this time for a different reason.

The heat I felt was a welcome heat.

I had a feeling that Lola was dangerous, but in a different way.

I put a finger back inside her.

She moaned. "Sake has me feeling right."

Lola moved against my hand.

This was the real deal.

Right then I knew I didn't need to worry about that gun any-more.

Not right now.

I kept my hand on what might have been her true weapon, on the heat between her legs.

Thirty-one

warm place to hide

Lola reached underneath her pillow.

With nervous breath and a smooth motion, I stopped her hand.

My smile masked my lingering suspicion. "What are you hiding?"

"Okay, now I'm really embarrassed."

I moved my hand away.

She pulled out a condom.

Lola surrendered a shy smile.

I helped her out of her red satin. I kissed her breasts, licked her skin, laid her back, moved her knees apart, and went down on her. Held her ass, put my tongue between her legs.

Hands on my head, Lola shifted her hips toward my face, released a slow, long moan.

Lola struggled to open the condom, gave up, handed it to me, and sat back with her hands in her hair, waited while I ripped open the package and struggled to roll it on. She scooted toward the head of the bed, knees together. I moved toward her and she got on her back, her legs easing apart, and I crawled between her warm thighs, found my position between the gates to a new paradise. I kissed her again. Her hand found its way back to my penis. She checked to make sure I was wrapped up tight, then she kissed me and guided me. I moved toward her, grazed the edges, made her moan.

Then I sank inside her.

Lord, have mercy.

She held her breath for a moment, her nostrils flared, her back arched, her legs tightened, and she let out a slow, saccharine-filled sigh. My moan was abrupt, guttural.

I was on top of her, looking down on her, her hair framing her beautiful face.

Lola was beautiful, not cute. Cute was temporary. Beautiful was timeless.

She closed her eyes, frowned while I stirred her. A sensual frown.

My hands went in her hair, pulled her face to mine. She gave me her tongue.

"You can pull my hair if you want to. It's real. No tracks."

"Breasts real?"

"All me, baby."

"All you?"

"All me."

"No weave?"

"Hair. Ass. Breasts. Fingernails. Everything on me is real."

Deep. I sank deep. Came out and sank deep again. Each kiss more intense than the last, each kiss twice as desperate, each moan louder, each stroke devastating, more fulfilling.

I pulled her hair while I kissed. Pulled her mane and stroked her good.

Her frown deepened, became the most beautiful ugly face I'd ever seen.

Her knees came up, she locked her legs around my back, held on to me as I pumped, as I searched for the rhythm she wanted. I moved her legs, had her on her side while I was on my knees, stroking her, making her gasp and throw her head back. Then, as the rain began to fall outside the window, as the winds kicked in, I was behind her, my hands cupping her breasts while I kissed and nibbled her damp skin, my own sweat dripping from my face, adding to hers.

Lola didn't talk while she fucked, just gave it as good as she got, moved like an ambitious woman who was still trying to learn how to get it right, and held me as we made our way around the bed, everything so fluid, changing positions more than a few times, ending up with her on top of me, rising and falling, eyes still tight, face cringing with pain and pleasure, then when she was about to come, she moved up and down, made skin slap skin so hard, did that like the devil inside her had been released, gasped and moaned a lot. The second time her legs wobbled, she made sounds like she was drowning. I was behind her, that prickly hot rush in my thighs, legs braced, buttocks tight, my world a wonderful blur, had Lola's face deep in the pillow, pounding and long-stroking my way toward my own nirvana. My jaw clenched with determination. Again, her nostrils flared. She made curt sounds like *mmm* and *ahhh* and came violently, collapsed on the bed and came gripping the sheets. I didn't stop. She had an exceptional way of rolling her hips, responded to what she was feeling, and moved in subtle ways I'd never seen a woman move before.

I gave her two happy endings, the second being more intense, more joyous than the first.

Then I was making the ugly face, straining, pumping hard, her hands pulling me into her, encouraging me to reach satisfaction. My happy ending came with power. God, it came hard.

Anxiety and frustration and fear poured out of me.

While I came I thought about her.

Thought about the first time in New York.

Thought about the last time in Chapel Hill.

I looked down, expected to see Arizona.

In those final moments, that was who I had imagined was beneath me.

Reality brought a different face into focus.

I rested on top of Lola, dizzy, catching my breath, the room now feeling too damn hot.

She panted like she was woozy as well, ran her nails over my skin. "Was that okay?"

I swallowed, my brain still buzzing. "Brilliant. It was great."

"I can do better . . . just . . . you know . . . jet lag . . . been up for over twenty-four hours . . . tired."

"How was it for you?"

"Better than sake. Good Lord that was better than sake."

I rolled off her. She slid from under me at the same time, turned over on her back.

"Thanks, Gideon. Damn, I needed that."

"I could tell."

"If you . . . you know . . . want to . . . again . . . you can."

"What are you trying to say?"

"Well, I do have eleven condoms left."

"We'll have to do something about that."

Lola blushed, the combination of sex and sake tightening her light brown eyes.

We kicked the covers away from us, were silent for a moment, listening to the rain.

My mind was on Berwick Street. My headache and anger trying to come back.

I went to the wall and turned the heat off. Then I flushed the condom and used the bathroom. When I went back to the bed, Lola was on her back, staring at the ceiling, her postcoital bliss a different kind of frown. Looked like she was dealing with her own headache.

I got back in the bed, became irritated by silence, asked Lola if she was okay.

She rolled over toward me. Whispered, "Sure you want me to start talking?"

"I'll cut you off if you start rambling."

"That's mean."

"Talk. I'll take my chances."

"I've been saving myself and being loyal to that son of a bitch . . . he's over here shagging and shacking . . . has his bitch living with him . . . should've known . . . things had gotten strange between us anyway." She cleared her throat. Even now her voice was soft, pleasant, no hint of pain, but the angst was there, just well disguised. "I think I was used to not seeing him. Sex wasn't popping no more. He never did it twice. One nut, he was done. Hated that. Last time I saw him he was tossing my salad and I was looking up at the ceiling wondering when he started doing that. I mean, was I supposed to like that? I had to focus on the ceiling so I wouldn't poot in his mouth. That's what that made me feel like doing, pooting. I hoped that he didn't think I was going to toss his salad in appreciation of him tossing my salad. I don't even like salads."

"Lola."

"Rambling. Sorry."

"No, you're on my arm. Need to shift."

"Oh. My bad."

Lola sat up, took a deep breath, rose to her feet, and staggered toward the bathroom. She stopped at the bathroom door, ran her hand over her hair like she was still dizzy.

She said, "I had wanted to meet the cast from *Rent* while I was here. Thought that *maybe*, you know, *maybe* I could get an audition for Mimi's part, would consider coming on as a swing, as long as I got to stay here in London and work and spend some time with my . . . with that son of a bitch . . . make it work . . . and now, guess that ain't gonna happen."

Her breasts were so damn nice. Stood high and full, nipples dark and large.

"Son of a bitch. I ever see that son of a bitch again . . . and I'm the motherfucker who encouraged him to audition for *Rent*. I'm the one who bought him a plane ticket to fly to New York and audition. I helped him with his vocals. Too bad my family ain't over here. They would handle this. I should look in the phone book and see if I can find any McVeighs."

I watched how her small waist curved down into her strong backside, watched her firmness. She sat on the toilet, took a long-overdue piss. When she was done, she turned on the water and washed her hands, caught a glimpse of her first grabbing a towel, then saw her washing between her legs. She came back with towels, cleaned me, then tossed the towels.

Lola cuddled up next to me, her soft and firm leg moving against mine, her sake-scented breath on my skin, her hand on my chest. She held me like we had been lovers for a lifetime.

I held her breast. Squeezed it, touched the nipple.

In return she held my penis. That remined me of Arizona. She had held my penis after sex. Maybe that was what women did. Lola stroked my penis for a while. Then she stopped. She shifted around a lot. Sighed a lot shook her head a lot. Made her foot bounce a lot.

Lola said, "What am I going to do? I'm stuck over here without a dime to my name."

"I'll get you back to America."

"Will you? Just get me to any part of North America: New York, Miami, Boston. Wait . . . not Boston. Son of a bitch is from Boston. Anywhere else is cool. Alaska. Canada. I don't care. Just get me back over the damn Atlantic and I'll figure out something once I get there."

"Lola, relax. I'll fly you back home."

"I'll pay you back, I promise. I'm not a freeloader."

My hand moved over her body, and she touched my hand, eased it back down between her legs. My trigger finger found her spot, massaged her until she moaned and came again.

"God, you are so good with that finger."

"Like the way I massage?"

"Hell yeah. Want me to get another condom?"

"In the morning. Will that be okay?"

"Condoms on the dresser. Just tap me on my shoulder. Or flip me over."

"Really?"

"Actually, it's been seven months. I'm angry and tired and horny as shit. And since I'm a free agent, this is my coochie, so, hey, you want to get up in my loving, get up in my loving."

"Eleven condoms left."

"Hey, you gave me the money to buy 'em. Feel free to use 'em all."

"You game?"

"Right now I'm game like a motherfucker."

She held me the way I had held Arizona that first time we had been together.

We kissed again.

Whores didn't kiss. Whores didn't cuddle. Whores never stayed the night.

Lola wasn't a whore.

For a moment I felt uncomfortable, wanted her gone. Not gone, just wasn't used to women staying after the deed was done. Either they left or they were paid and vacated.

Squares hung around. Squares wanted to cuddle. Squares wanted breakfast.

Squares had a heart. Right now I needed to be with somebody who had a heart.

Even if that meant that in the end, squares became too emotional.

When it came to the heart, squares were deadly and dangerous in their own way.

I'd become too emotional with Arizona. I'd become dangerous to her.

Always a vicious fucking cycle. The one you wanted always wanted something else.

"Son of a bitch. After all I did for him. He lived with me, I cooked for him, did everything."

"Would you be sad if something bad happened to him?"

"*Hell no.*"

She had said that without hesitation, her angst-ridden voice laced with pure venom.

My anger rose up and I almost offered to ease her pain. Almost. Caught myself.

Guess I'd heard that angered and vindictive tone so many times.

Lola whispered, "Good night."

"You can sleep now?"

"I think so. For a while."

She stopped shifting, breathing slowed, sleep imprisoned her before ten minutes had passed. I looked at her for a few moments, gazed at the condoms, her electric touch still sending sensual currents through my body, and despite only being tired, my nature wanted to rise. Arizona never offered herself to me like this, not without reluctance. Lola. Damn. I wanted to lose myself inside her again, get inside her womb, try to find my own release and move toward peace.

I wondered, if to her, I was the whore. A slut. If I was my mother's child.

You're a whore like your mother.

My thoughts stayed on my mother. Saw her bright red lipstick. Felt her hands on me.

While the stranger in my bed slept, I moved the gun from its hiding place to the backpack, then I stood in the window. The rain came down hard on London's dark side, the wind howled like a beast in chains, screamed like it was warning people that this was the land of butchers and train robbers, where they used to have public hangings at Old Bailey, where Braveheart was tortured, where the KGB dumped bodies in the Thames, where women were executed within the confines of the Tower of London.

With all the lights off I was looking down, searching for Jack the Ripper, making sure no one was watching or waiting, the man with the broken nose no longer an immediate concern of mine, Arizona's anger and recent threat now being more urgent. Arizona had sent a package, but that didn't mean anything. In this world people sent you roses before they put you in the ground.

Like I had shared a drink with Sergeant before I sent him to an early grave.

I remained in the window, naked, the room dark, staring out toward Centre Point.

Arizona's insults had fucked me up beyond repair. Beyond forgiveness.

Then I smelled her on my skin. My mother. I inhaled the stench of my mother.

From time to time I caught her scent deep in my skin. That whore reek was there. The horrible smell of a woman who didn't bath between johns, only rinsed between her legs, her own cheap perfume and salty sweat mixed with the stink of cologne and musty odor of many men.

Like your mother.

My mother, my enemy.

I looked toward Berwick Street, no more than ten minutes away.

Wondered if the woman who had birthed me was on her back or her knees.

Over the years, wherever we lived, I had watched the men come and go.

I felt her heat where I shouldn't feel her heat, her red lipstick stains where they shouldn't have been. Then, once again, I saw Thelma on the ground, beaten and laid out like a rag doll.

Anger rose up inside me, mixed with all the other bad feelings I was having.

Then Lola groaned, turned over.

She was probably the nicest girl I'd ever met.

I was the last kind of man she needed to be laid up with.

But I was afraid of her.

She'd looked in my eyes and recognized my inner struggle.

That struggle had me awake now.

I had to move on.

I'd leave London in the morning. Would leave now but Lola

was here. I'd have to wait until morning, get her packed, get her to Gatwick, put her on a plane, get Lola back home.

I'd part ways with Lola, put these memories behind me, move on with my life.

Leave the past behind.

I sat on the sofa. Watched Lola sleep. A square. For once I was in bed with a real nice girl. Lola shifted and I moved back to the bed, got under the covers, my skin next to hers. She moved closer to me, her breasts on my skin, her hand holding me close. Moments like this made the square that lived inside me want to try that love thing. But I wasn't a square. I'd killed too many people to ever be forgiven. And one day, just as I'd gone after so many, someone would come for me. This was my world. Yeah, I should've gotten Lola her own room. I knew that. If I had to walk from Bloomsbury to Mansion House, I should've checked every hotel until I found a vacancy.

Eyes trained like a sentry, staring out at the darkness and the rain, I fell asleep.

It was a deep, peaceful sleep, the kind that didn't torture me with bad dreams.

But as soon as peace covered me and warmed my body, Lola nudged me.

I jerked awake. Her sweet face was close to mine.

I said, "Want me to get a condom?"

In a shaky voice she whispered, "Somebody's at the door."

That woke me up. I sat up, heard nothing. I asked, "You sure?"

"They've been moving around out there for a while. At least five minutes. I looked out the peephole, didn't see anybody. But I can hear them out there."

I pulled the covers back, eased my feet down on the thin carpet.

Lola moved to the edge of the bed, her breasts a beautiful silhouette in the darkness.

Sledge had been blown up in Trinidad.

I had been followed by the man with the broken nose.

"The wrong you're doing . . . that will be done to you."

I stood up and listened. Heard movement outside my door.

She whispered, "You expecting company?"

I put my finger to my lips, shook my head, had to figure out how to handle this.

I whispered, "Go inside the bathroom. And close the door."

Now Lola owned fear.

Lola did what I asked, grabbed the white robe and hurried to the bathroom.

I rushed to the backpack, grabbed my loaded nine, silencer on, crept to the peephole.

It was Death's peak business hours.

And Death had a business that was open 24/7.

I spied out the peephole.

A new kind of fear gripped me, its sharp claws running deep.

It was worse than anything I imagined.

I'd fought in Chinatown. Been stalked. After that I'd killed in Lakenheath. Was stalked again in Soho. Was slaughtered in my dreams. And I hadn't been in London twenty-four hours.

The night wasn't over.

Trouble had found me.

And the bad part was this was only beginning.

I knew how to end trouble before it started.

I raised my gun to the peephole.

This motherfucker had balls.

Don't miss

Waking with Enemies

Coming from Dutton in August 2007

Acknowledgments

Before we get started . . .

If you're holding *Sleeping with Strangers*, its sequel, *Waking with Enemies* drops four months later and the story picks up where *SWS* leaves off and moves on, full speed ahead.

Sleeping with Strangers is due out in April 2007.

Waking with Enemies will hit the bookstores in August 2007.

If you're holding *Waking with Enemies*, make sure you read *Sleeping with Strangers* first.

Well, this is the back of the book, so I guess it's kinda late to say that, huh?

Duh.

Oh well.

☺

I started playing *What if?* and working on *Sleeping with Strangers* and *Waking with Enemies* back in March 2006, tried to come up with a story line. Initially I wanted to create a dark narrative, maybe come up with an antihero who had his or her adventure play out while driving across the States, some sort of

West-Coast-to-East-Coast voyage, his or her motivation (or motivations) yet to be determined, but I didn't come up with a decent way to keep that interesting for me.

No story came to mind. Not at that moment.

The well was dry.

Then I changed gears, decided to try and find a way to include most of the cities I hit on tour, London included, in one story. That meant I had to write and tour all at once. Had to take notes while people were keeping me busy. Trust me, that wasn't easy. Any writer will tell you, writing on tour, being creative while dealing with jet lag, no real sleep, and trying to be productive while sitting at the airport—it just ain't happening. But I gave it a shot. A lot of spots I went to on tour I was barely there a day, some places only a few hours, and didn't see much outside of an airport, one or two bookstores and a hotel that I couldn't tell you how to get to if my life depended on it. All I knew was that I needed a good character. An antihero who traveled a lot.

And I wanted it to be noir. And sexy. And a challenge. Didn't want to recycle plots.

Enter Gideon.

I was in my office writing one day and when I turned around, there he was.

Gun in one hand and a knife in the other, the guy scared me at first. Could tell he was troubled. Thought he had come for me. But he said he just wanted to be in the book. Said he had a lot of personal shit he needed to work through and maybe being in a book would help.

I said cool. Told him he had a part. He left. Then I upgraded my security system.

If you believe that I have a freeway I want to sell you out in Los Angeles.

Gideon started off being a serial killer. I played the *What if?* game and wrote scenes with him, well, at work. Tijuana.

Jacksonville. Detroit. Brazil. Some, if not all, of those original scenes made the final cut. Somewhere along the way, my man Gideon evolved into being a contract killer. When I'd flown to the UK (much love to Bill, Claire, and the rest of the staff at Turnaround Publishing) to promote *Genevieve*, I had moved on, started writing the scenes that included the supporting cast. Eventually the man with the broken nose showed up and asked me if I needed somebody like him to be in this one. I tried to say no but he pulled the Eagle out of its nest and that convinced me. Truth be told, I liked the crazy bastard. Great character. Every novel needs a supporting cast, and since this tale involved killers and grifters, for the most part, it gave me a chance to reach back into the Dickey Universe, tap on a few doors, and ask Arizona, one of my favorite characters, if she wanted to be in this one. She asked me if she would get a hot sex scene. I said no. She slammed the door in my face. I knocked again. She wouldn't answer. Then I yelled that I would put her in a damn steamy scene. She said she wanted *two*. Damn women. Anyway, I told her I would promise her one, and I'd do my best on a second one. Then she demanded to be more than a grifter, wanted to carry weapons and kick some ass. I told her that grifters didn't carry. She didn't give a shit. I think she had seen one too many Angelina Jolie movies. Anyway, my agent called her fictional agent and we got it worked out. She lit up her Djarum, grabbed her boots, and came along for the ride. Despite being so demanding, she's good people. If you like those kind of people. The Queen of the grifters. I have no idea why I like her, but I do. She's evolved since she first drove onto the pages of *Thieves' Paradise*, become a little more intense since *Drive Me Crazy*, now she's operating on an international level.

Anyway, once my plane landed in London, so did the rest of the story.

I have to thank my UK peeps for helping a brother out

while he was over there locked up in hotels and flats, writing from sunup to sundown, taking a nap, then back in front of the laptop until sunup again. My UK peeps were great, showed me around London on buses and tubes, drove me around in clown cars that had steering wheels on the wrong side of the dashboard.

They were there for me whether it was sweltering, raining, or bloody cold.

Kayode Disu, thanks for collecting me at Gatwick, making sure I was okay, getting me to Paris and back in a day, and getting me and my luggage back to Gatwick every time I came over.

My homie Monique Pendleton out at www.myspace.com/soulful_women, I think you've read every version of Gideon, saw changes in plots and subplots, well over a thousand pages, that's my estimate, and I thank you for that. And thanks for making sure the book kept that Brit flavor.

Inca Nixon, my girl Sam from the Islands, Tosh from wherever, thanks for coming down from horse-and-grass to hang out and show me around. See y'all at TGIF in Piccadilly soon!

To my military peeps stationed at Lakenheath and Mildenhall, be safe and see you soon. Neo Gwafila-Bulayani, thanks for Botswana and looking over the details of Tebby.

My boys at Progressive Entertainment (www.myspace.com/UKFridays) thanks for the birthday celebration. I'll see you guys at the Motion Bar soon. Save me a spot!

To my UK publisher, Bill, Claire, and the entire staff at Turnaround, thanks for everything. The events were fantastic and I look forward to returning in February 2007.

If you peeps find me a place to live, I'll become a UK citizen and rent an accent so fast . . . you have no idea. We just have to come up with something better than beans and toast.

☺

Everything I got right, I thank my friends.

Until I can find a scapegoat, I'll take the blame for all I got wrong.

Time to thank the rest of my crew. The ones on this side of the pond.

John Paine, thanks for the input and the notes. Writing is all about rewriting.

DeMarMc, thanks for reading this one over and over and over and . . .

Lon in IAH, once again, thanks for the information early on. It made a big difference.

Christine Pattyn, thanks for Motown! Hope to make it to your club one day!

Lolita Files! You're the best! Thanks for being you!

Hazel Verzola in Montreal, thanks for the Tagalog!

Thanks to my agent, Sara Camilli. How many books before I get to book number 100?

To my wonderful editor, Julie Doughty, much love. You rock!

Brian Tart, thanks for believing in this double-sized project. I hope it has wings and flies.

To Lisa Johnson, Beth Parker, and all the people in publicity, thanks for everything.

And a special thanks to you. You, the person holding this book.

You didn't think I'd skip you, did you?

O faithful reader, thanks for coming back.

And if you're a new reader, thanks for coming on board.

I hope you enjoy this journey across the pond.

And if you're across the pond, I hope you find this tale enjoyable.

In case I forgot anyone, which wasn't intentional, here's your chance to shine.

I wanna thank _____ for _____ because without your help I'd be _____ at a _____ with _____ and wishing I was _____ in _____.
You're the best of the best!

Make sure you check out www.ericjeromedickey.com.
Or stop by www.myspace.com/ericjeromedickey.

Holla!

EJD
12/18/06
Latitude 33.76N and Longitude -84.4W
5:34 A.M.

About the Author

Originally from Memphis, Tennessee, Eric Jerome Dickey is the author of fourteen novels, including the bestsellers *Chasing Destiny*, *Genevieve*, *Drive Me Crazy*, *Naughty or Nice*, *The Other Woman*, and *Thieves' Paradise*. Dickey writes full time and in 2006 developed a six-issue miniseries of comic books for Marvel Enterprises featuring Storm (X-Men) and the Black Panther. He lives on the road and rests in Southern California.